ANYONE CAN KILL

PAUL FERGUSON

2QT Publishing

First Edition published 2025 by

2QT Publishing

Cover image: © iStock by Getty Images. Credit: satajean

Printed in UK by IngramSpark

A CIP catalogue record for this book is available from the British Library

ISBN 978-1-9193271-1-2

Also published by Paul Ferguson

A Father's Duty

Retired bomb-disposal expert Steve Foley faces his toughest mission when his son, "Crazy" Eddie, takes a dangerous job as a bodyguard in Afghanistan. Something about the offer—and the man behind it, Malik—doesn't feel right. When Eddie's dream job turns into a nightmare, Steve must risk everything to save him. A Father's Duty is a gritty thriller of kidnapping, terrorism, and family loyalty—exploring what binds families together and what can tear them apart.

Killing the Dead

A story of a writer looking to make it in Hollywood. A series of rejections and ridicule from the industry he loves forces him down a road he never intended to go. Alone and desperate for recognition, he decides to bring his script to life and take it to the streets of LA. Within days, his chilling deeds spread fear and panic in the city. California was no stranger to serial killers, but this one was different.

1

June 2014, Mosul, Iraq

The hands behind Arlo's cracked watch face rotated slowly, eventually coming to rest at 6.59am. A tap of the right index finger on the glass couldn't kickstart the $10 Seiko he'd purchased in the bazaar two streets away. 'Really?' he muttered, resignation in his voice.

It had been a long hard night and he was struggling to keep his eyes open; it didn't help that there wasn't a cloud in the sky and the temperature had already reached 30°C. The forecast was for the day to get much hotter. Shards of burning sunlight broke through holes in the raggedy tarpaulin that stretched precariously high above the narrow street. There wasn't a lot of cover for those working and dying below.

Arlo wiped the sweat from his forehead then shielded his eyes as he looked at the latest bullet-ridden body that had been carried into his makeshift hospital. He knew instantly that the man was dead but he still checked his pulse and listened intently to his chest with his stethoscope. Even if the dead man's wife and children hadn't been standing beside his lifeless frame, it was the right thing to do.

Nearby, a narrow dusty corridor leading to a gutted storefront that had once been a proud local bakery was strewn with wounded men. An eight-year-old boy was wailing at the top of his voice. It was carnage. A sea of bandaged bodies, some with missing limbs lay scattered across the floor. An emaciated black-and-white mongrel puppy sniffed and licked its way from open sore to open sore before being kicked onto the street by a passing soldier.

Just another bloody day at the office.

In the distance gunfire and sporadic explosions rocked the perimeter of the small northern Iraqi town. A black cloud of smoke blocked out the sun's rays, providing a temporary yet much-needed respite. Then the ground around him trembled and cracks appeared on the wall on the adjacent building, and alarm bells started ringing inside Arlo's head.

He turned and spotted Jennifer walking quickly along the street. Dressed in pale-blue scrubs with her hair neatly tucked beneath a dark-green scarf, she looked happy and composed. 'Where are you going?' he shouted.

She smiled and made a rolling gesture with the palm of her hand over her stomach then adjusted the shoulder strap on her medical bag, blew him a kiss and quickly disappeared around the corner. Arlo opened his mouth to speak but it was too late. She was gone.

I pity the child born into this shit show, he mused as another wounded fighter arrived. This one was lucky: he was alive. A bullet had entered through his mouth and somehow found its way out through his cheek.

Sami, a local man who'd been helping Dr Arlo and Nurse Jennifer since their arrival two months earlier, escorted the injured soldier to a table made from four wooden pallets stacked on top of each other.

Arlo reached for a syringe in his bag. 'The sound of gunfire seems to be getting closer,' he said. Sami didn't respond. 'Is the Iraqi army holding? Have reinforcements arrived?'

Still no comment from Sami.

Arlo worked his magic on the soldier's mouth and face, applied a covering then directed him to an unoccupied space on the floor. The man hunched down and Arlo moved towards him but Sami intervened. 'Come,' he muttered abruptly.

'Hang on a second.'

'No time,' Sami snapped. Without warning, his huge, callused hand grabbed Arlo by the arm.

'What the—?' gasped Arlo.

'Someone needs your help. Now.'

That was all Arlo needed to hear. Clutching his bag, he followed the big man along a narrow passage, made a sharp left turn then climbed a short flight of stone steps to the market area of Mosul.

The Iraqi army might have been fighting a fierce battle with ISIS on the edge of town but the locals were still going about their business, although at a much faster pace. The souk was packed, the road obstructed by traders, shoppers and those delivering goods in vans and horse-drawn carts.

Sami barged forward and Arlo tucked in behind him. Bodies were coming at them from all directions but any comparison he might have made to last-minute Christmas shopping in London's Oxford Street disappeared when he saw the fear in the eyes of those near to him.

Finally they reached the last of the tented stalls and their pace quickened. Just as they were about to cross the main street, a massive explosion brought concrete debris and slivers of glass raining down on them.

With his face firmly planted in the dirt, Arlo's world suddenly turned dark and silent. After what seemed like an eternity, he lifted his chin just high enough to spit out whatever was clogging his mouth and slowly wiggled his fingers and toes. He gave a sigh of relief: he could feel them all.

Gradually he raised himself until he was sitting back on his heels and wiped the dust from his eyes on his shirt sleeve. Screams and cries for help told him that his ears were now functioning normally.

It was chaos. For the past two months he had been on the periphery of a war but now he was in the middle of it.

Sami reached out and helped him to his feet. There was no time for Arlo to thank him; Sami was already moving his huge frame towards a small restaurant further down the road. The shutters were down and the outside tables stacked neatly against the wall. It was clear the establishment was closed but Sami was on a mission.

His powerful left shoulder smashed easily through the locked front door, and the chairs and flimsy tables inside were helpless against his enormous legs as he crashed his way to the rear of the premises. The restaurant was empty except for the owner, an elderly man who was casually sipping tea at a table in the corner. Arlo looked at him and made a gesture of help, but the old man smiled and waved him away.

Sami turned to Arlo. 'Put this over your head,' he said, offering up his keffiyeh. He moved to the rear door and surveyed the street then forced a smile. 'Stay with me and try to look like an Arab.'

Once on the pavement, they threaded their way through the throngs of people to an empty apartment building on the far side of the square. After climbing three flights of stairs, they arrived at a roof-top terrace. A battle-scarred four-foot-high concrete wall surrounded the abandoned, dust-covered ground.

Arlo rotated 360 degrees. 'So, where's the patient?'

'I'm sorry,' Sami said. 'I lied. I had to. If you'd stayed at the hospital, you would have been killed.'

'But surely the Iraqi army and all the volunteers…'

Sami shook his head before Arlo could finish.

At that moment the sound of gunfire and approaching vehicles drew both men to the wall. A man dressed in black was standing on the back of a pickup truck shouting instructions in Arabic through a megaphone. Arlo looked at Sami for an explanation.

'He's saying that ISIS are here, put down your weapons and identify the infidels.'

After a short pause Arlo turned and moved back towards the stairs. Sami reached out and held him back. 'Where you going?'

'To get Jen.'

'You can't! You'll be killed! Besides, you don't even know where she is.'

Arlo reached for his phone and tapped her contact. When the ringing stopped he said cautiously, 'Hello.' There was no response. He tried again. 'Jen?'

'Good morning, Arlo.' The man who spoke had an English accent.

'Who are you? Where's Jen?'

'You can call me Spider. I'm afraid Jen is dead – I shot her after she stuck a syringe into the face of one of our brave fighters. It's a pity. She could have lived a long and contented life as one of my wives.'

'I don't believe you!' Arlo cried. A moment later his phone made a pinging sound. He opened the attachment. 'You bastard!' he screamed as tears started tears rolling down his cheeks. 'I'll get you for this.'

'It's more likely that I'll get you. The city is surrounded and we're going from house to house. Give up now and I will make your death a quick one.'

Covering his face with both hands, Arlo fell to his knees. His phone tumbled to the ground. Sami picked it up, listened for a moment then shut it off. 'You must hide,' he ordered.

Arlo remained on his knees. 'She didn't want to come here. I talked her into it. I killed her,' he said softly

Sporadic gunfire and screams drew their attention to the square below. Peering through the cracks in the wall, they saw a human chain walking with heads bowed and hands on the shoulders of the person in front. Balaclava-wearing guards were directing them to the fountain.

Arlo retrieved his phone and started filming as a man appeared, naked above the waist, carrying a chainsaw. A large tattoo of a spider covered his left shoulder.

A couple of tugs on the cord started the sinister cutting machine. Although he kept on filming, Arlo couldn't bear to watch what was about to happen. 'Oh, my God,' he murmured. 'What kind of people are they?'

'Come on, it's time to hide.'

'Where?'

Sami pointed to a rusty water tank on the left side of the terrace.

'Seriously?' asked Arlo. Sami nodded and handed him his bag.

Reluctantly, Arlo moved towards the tank. He pulled out a plastic bag and wrapped it around his phone then sealed the opening with two pieces of tape.

'Put a scalpel in your pocket,' Sami told him. 'You may

need to defend yourself or…'

'Or what?'

'Or you may want to take your own life.'

Arlo studied his friend's face before asking, 'And what about you?'

'I'll be fine. Just keep your head down. I'm going to put some broken glass on the stairs. If you hear a crunch, you'll know someone's coming. If you hear a tap on the tank, you'll know it's me.'

As Sami disappeared, Arlo tossed his bag into the tank. He climbed onto the wall, reached up to the lip with both hands, pulled his six-foot frame over the edge and slid head first into the water. It was warm, dark, with a pungent stale odour. There was a taste of rusty pipes that reminded him of the pump on his parent's farm in Kent. He'd hated having to drink the water there.

Once he was upright, he floated to the surface. Although the water line was about a foot from the top of the tank, he still wondered what he would do if someone came. How would he stay underwater?

After taking a breath, he dropped to the bottom, which he estimated to be seven or eight feet down. He felt around until he grasped his bag on the floor of the tank, but it wasn't heavy enough to keep him down and once again he floated to the surface.

A second attempt proved more successful. A row of rivets stretched down the side of the tank and one near the bottom protruded enough for him to grasp it with his fingers. If he had to, he could sit under the surface of the water and not worry about being seen. One question remained unanswered: how long would he be able to hold his breath?

He rose to the surface and took another deep breath before positioning himself cross-legged on the bottom of the tank After counting to twenty-eight he started to panic – it felt like his lungs were about to explode.

Within seconds his head was out of the water and he was gasping for air. *I'm in trouble*, he thought, as he bobbed up and down.

Down in the square, the roar of the chainsaw suddenly stopped. *That can only mean one of two things – they've either run out of petrol or they've run out of...* Arlo shook his head and hurriedly erased the thought from his mind.

For the first time since ISIS had invaded, Mosul was quiet. There was still occasional gunfire and the sound of loud male voices, but the buzz and bustle had faded. Life had literally been sucked out of the city.

It was now mid-afternoon; the temperature was pushing forty and the sun was beating down on his head. Arlo's arms and legs grew more and more tired from treading water. Reluctantly – and infrequently – he clung on to the top lip of the tank to gather his strength. Short periods on the bottom of the tank helped increase his lung capacity as well as providing a respite for his limbs.

Following a forty-five second stint on the floor, he returned gently to the surface. A moment later he heard broken glass crunching under foot. He waited, his heart pounding. He knew he could stay where he was without being seen if the person who was approaching stayed on the terrace, but what if they climbed onto the wall to get to get a better look at the surrounding rooftops? He couldn't take the chance.

At the last moment, when the footsteps were loudest, he took a deep breath, slipped beneath the surface and grasped the rivet. He started counting slowly as he stared up at the blue sky. At twenty-five there was no sign of anyone above him; at thirty-five, still nothing.

Where the hell is he?

Fifty seconds elapsed and Arlo's lungs began to hurt; at sixty, it felt like his chest was about to explode. Hesitantly, he headed upwards but before his head emerged from the water he removed the scalpel from his pocket and gripped it in his right hand. He didn't know what to expect but whatever it was, he was ready.

After leaving Arlo in the tank, Sami sneaked out of the rear door of the apartment building. The street was empty now except for a couple of stray dogs ripping apart a trash bin. To reach his mother's house he crept through back lanes, a vacant industrial site, along a huge drainage ditch and across the floor of a disused electrical power station. Mosul was where he'd been born and where he'd lived every day of his thirty-two years. He knew his way around.

Once he was home, he greeted his elderly mother with a gentle hug. She looked fragile and pale, and her attempt to squeeze his huge frame proved futile; there was no strength left in her wizened arms.

When she asked him if he'd had a good day he lied, just as he always did. He drove a truck and volunteered at Arlo's hospital, and that was all she knew because that was all he wanted her to know. There was no point in talking about the chaos and bloodshed in the city because she wouldn't understand; dementia had crept in and there was no way back.

Wrapping his arm around her waist, he helped her to the kitchen where he made tea. Sami talked about his father, who had been taken by Saddam Hussein and never seen again, then he mentioned his brother, her eldest son, who had suffered the same fate. Still there was an emptiness in her eyes; she appeared lost and confused.

Finally she yawned and he placed his arm around her again and helped her walk to the bedroom. Sitting on the edge of the bed, he gently stroked her cheek. 'Mother, I'm going away. I want you to know that I love you very much. Some day we will all be together in a better place. Sleep well, my dear.'

His mother smiled and closed her eyes.

Sami wiped a tear from his eye. He held her hand for a while until she fell asleep, then carefully placed a cushion over her face. There was no struggle. It was almost as if she had been waiting for this moment.

When Arlo poked his nose through the surface of the water he thought the coast was clear, but when he turned his head to the right he saw two bloodied hands with bruised knuckles gripping the edge of the tank.

Going back to the bottom was not an option. There was no time. Slicing the intruder's fingers with his scalpel was tempting but would only make the situation worse – the last thing he wanted was a wounded man screaming for help.

He waited, and while he did he took several deep breaths. A slight groan came from the other side of the tank as the man hoisted himself onto his chest and leaned over the water. For a moment they were face to face, eye to eye.

The man froze, caught off guard; this heavily trained ISIS killing machine was at a disadvantage. Without hesitating, Arlo reached up, grabbed him by the straps of his backpack and pulled him headfirst into the water. Down they plunged until Arlo felt the man's head hit the steel bottom. Still, he kicked and violently swung his arms as he tried desperately to get upright.

It was clear to Arlo that his opponent was no fan of water and within seconds he was struggling for air and fighting to get to the top. Arlo held him down, but the man was strong, pushed him away and headed to the surface.

With one hand, Arlo latched on to his trousers and pulled him back to the bottom of the tank. They'd been under water for about forty seconds and Arlo was fine, but the bearded fighter was wearing boots, backpack and an ammunition laden vest and he was in a bad way. His energy was draining and his strength was fading.

In a last attempt to free himself, the stranger pulled out a knife and thrust it towards Arlo, striking his shoulder with barely enough force to pierce the skin. A second attempt fell short of its target and the man's arm eventually floated harmlessly to his side as the knife disappeared into the depths.

Although Arlo's lungs were on fire, he remained under water with his arms around the terrorist for another twenty seconds.

Finally the sun touched his face and air drifted through his body, but the sound of crunching glass sent him scurrying to the bottom of the tank once more. It was too soon and too fast, and water flooded into his mouth.

Exhausted and gagging, he'd had enough. *This is it*, he thought. Holding his scalpel in his right hand, he bent his knees and pushed off the floor with both legs.

The journey to the surface seemed to take for ever. Every part of his body was either aching or numb and he wanted to throw up.

He pushed his head out of the water, eyes wide open and right hand ready to strike. For a moment there was silence. Arlo struggled to hold his breath as his eyes followed the edge of the tank. He felt like he was dying but he knew he had to keep quiet.

A tapping noise on the tank drew his attention to his right. *Could it be?* A second tap-tap-tap gave him the confidence to peer over the side. 'Sami,' he spluttered as he clung to the edge.

Sami looked confused as he lifted an ISIS flag and a Kalashnikov off the ground.

Arlo eventually gathered enough strength to tell him what had happened. 'It looks like he was here to fly the flag but decided to have a drink of water first.'

Sami lowered the weapon into the tank but held on to the flag. 'Do you have a watch?' he asked.

Arlo looked at his Seiko. The hands were still stuck on 6.59. He shook his head.

Sami unfastened his own watch and handed it over. 'I have a plan,' he whispered. 'Listen carefully – your life will depend on getting it right.'

As he talked, Arlo closed his eyes and visualised the movements. 'Will it work?' he asked.

Sami shrugged, tucked the flag behind the water tank and walked away.

※ ※ ※

The day was drawing to a close but the nightmare continued. Although power in the city had been completely knocked out, a huge bonfire next to the fountain provided enough light for the bloodthirsty to carry on enjoying the show. It was curtains up again as the roar of the chainsaw shattered the uneasy calm in the square below. A bizarre mixture of screams and cheers collided as they bounced off the surrounding stone walls and buildings. If a picture of hell on earth was painted on canvas, this would be it.

A chill ran through Arlo's body. He wasn't a religious man, but he prayed, prayed hard for his girlfriend Jen and the poor souls on the street. There was some consolation that she'd been killed instantly and hadn't had to endure this horror and suffering. But repeatedly saying 'sorry' did nothing to ease his pain or guilt.

It was now 10.30pm; Arlo had been awake for more than twenty-four hours and in the water for just under fourteen. His limbs ached, his skin was wrinkled. Fatigue and light headedness, a sign of dehydration, were playing havoc with his mind. Tiny sips of water from the tank didn't stay down long enough to stop his head from spinning.

With the dead terrorist propped in a sitting position on the floor of the tank, Arlo was able to rest by standing on the man's shoulders and keeping his head above water. It was a precarious situation, to say the least, and from time to time the torso flopped forward forcing Arlo to tread water once again.

At exactly ten minutes to eleven, Arlo climbed out of the tank. His legs wobbled as he placed his feet on the ground and he reached for the tank wall to help him balance. He was not in a good state.

A few deep breaths and some gentle stretches helped him regain a little self-control, and a few steps in a circle reassured him he could still walk. He took a moment to wring out the keffiyeh before he wrapped it around his head, then unfolded the ISIS flag and held it aloft. After a quick mental run-through of the path ahead and a check to see that he still had his scalpel, he was ready.

Under cover of darkness, he crept along the roof, climbed over the wall and lowered himself on to the terrace next door. *One down.* Without warning, the familiar sound of indiscriminate rapid fire from an automatic weapon forced him to hit the ground. Bullets ricocheted off the wall behind him.

The blasts lasted just a few seconds, but Arlo knew that time was short and he had to keep moving. Back on his feet, he tiptoed across the concrete floor and approached another wall – only this was about two feet higher than the previous one. With the flag tucked under his shirt and both arms extended, he reached up and grabbed the top of the barrier, but he didn't have the strength to pull himself off the ground.

'Bloody hell,' he murmured.

He glanced swiftly over his shoulder and saw a plastic chair lying upside down in a corner of the terrace. When he put it in position, it tipped over. Angry that he hadn't noticed a leg was missing, he gritted his teeth and whispered, 'Breathe.'

A moment of calm followed. He leaned the chair against the wall, placed his foot on the side of it with the legs still intact and raised himself high enough to clamber to the next terrace.

Two down. Now turn right.

Easier said than done. As he took his first steps Arlo collided with huge, knee-high chunks of concrete that lacerated his shins. Unable to see the way ahead, he went down on all fours and crawled like a toddler until he heard male voices ahead.

He waited, his pulse quickening, then inch by inch he moved to a shattered skylight. Peering over the edge, he saw two ISIS soldiers smoking a shisha pipe on the candle-lit floor below.

If only I had that rifle. Thankfully, that moment of madness disappeared as quickly as it arrived.

Still on his hands and knees, he crawled silently around the opening but came to an abrupt halt again when his hands slid onto a blanket of broken glass. With no time to remove the tiny slivers from his fingers, he wrapped the flag around his hands and crept at snail's pace to the edge of the building where the wall had been destroyed.

The drop to the next level was about twelve feet and he had no idea if anyone was in the house below, so a soft landing was vital. He took off his shoes and tucked them under his shirt, then clung to a ledge by his fingertips as he lowered himself down the side of the building. Pieces of glass burrowed more deeply beneath his skin.

He was now about four feet from the roof and time was running out. Holding his breath, he released his grasp and fell. A quick glance around confirmed he was alone.

He put on his shoes before stooping almost double and hurrying along the edge of the roof. When an elderly man down on the street suddenly yelled at him, Arlo's response

was immediate: he turned his head away and raised the ISIS
flag. It worked a treat, just like Sami had said it would, and
the man vanished.

Arlo walked along the roof until he was positioned above
a water tanker on the street below. He surveyed the area;
when he was confident it was clear, he jumped onto the top
of the vehicle, his knees buckling as he smashed onto the steel
surface.

Limping slightly, he moved along the rusty shell of the tank,
lowered himself through an opening and shut the hatch door.
Immediately the truck's engine fired up and all six wheels
moved forward. For the second time in a matter of minutes,
Arlo was submerged in water.

Sami moved through the gears with ease. His twenty-five-
year-old battered and bruised water tanker, with more than
100,000 kms on the odometer, ran as if it had been built
yesterday. Hardly a day went by when he didn't tinker with
the motor or some other moving part. It was his statement:
behind the wheel of this beast, he enjoyed a feeling of
prominence in the community. *Look at me, look what I have
achieved.* His truck was his wife, his children, the place where
he felt most alive.

Mosul had fallen and was relatively calm, but still very
dangerous. ISIS soldiers were standing on most corners and
there were a lot of roadblocks. Rumours had spread that
each soldier was a law unto himself; there was no referral to
a higher authority. Life was cheap. If your face didn't fit, you
were dead.

20

To get to Route 2 North, Sami chose the long way around the city avoiding the centre, the university and the airport where most of the fighters had congregated. It was a good time to escape because small pockets of resistance were keeping ISIS occupied. A water tanker flying an ISIS flag was of little interest to them.

Ibrahim Khalil, the border crossing into Turkey, was about three hours away. It was a long time for Arlo to be in the water but Sami knew there was no alternative. A prayer for his passenger was all he could offer right now. Arlo was on his own.

Floating in a pitch-black water tank moving at 50kmh was like being inside a washing machine. Arlo bounced from side to side when Sami negotiated corners, was suddenly flushed to the back of the truck on inclines and jettisoned forward when the nose of the vehicle pointed down. With about a foot of airspace above the water line, he didn't just worry about drowning: he wondered if there would be enough air to last the journey.

After roughly ten minutes of being thrashed about, Arlo swept headfirst into a series of metal rungs attached to the front of the tank. Examining then by touch revealed a ladder. Of course. If there was a hatch door, there must be a way to reach it.

With his limbs wrapped around rungs at different levels, Arlo breathed a sigh of relief. For the first time in hours, he could keep his head above water without having to move his arms and legs. He even managed to remove the glass slivers embedded in his fingers.

Then, just as he was starting to feel comfortable, the truck went into a descent that seemed to last forever. His airspace was gone and his lungs were being tested once again. Desperation set in as thousands of litres of water pinned him against the front wall.

Weak and disorientated, Arlo released his grip on the ladder and began swimming upwards, only to find he had travelled just a few feet to the roof of the tank. Disappointed to still be under water, he tracked the line of the roof and eventually reached a large pocket of air at the rear of the truck. He spluttered loudly then took several deep breaths.

He rubbed his eyes and combed back his hair with his fingers. For a moment he was safe, but he knew it wouldn't last. It was time to brace himself and get ready for the levelling off.

And so, it went on.

Every pothole and tilt of the truck gave Arlo a water slap. Flat roads appeared to be scarce in this part of Iraq, but although he was tired of being hit by tiny waves, he was grateful that Sami's truck kept going. The longer the wheels turned, the further they moved away from Mosul.

Although there was no concept of time in the tank, Arlo estimated they had been travelling about an hour, maybe more, when the truck came to a complete stop. With his ear pressed against the metal casing, he listened to the conversation outside The language made no sense but the male voices didn't sound aggressive. Was it an ISIS roadblock or just a friendly chat between locals?

A period of silence left him confused; why weren't they moving? An answer came sooner than he'd anticipated, and the sound of boots thumping on the roof above him sent a chill through his damp and withered body.

A deep breath, a quick dive and within seconds he was hovering close to the bottom at the back of the tank, his right hand locked onto his scalpel. The hatch creaked open and a beam of light floated over the surface. Arlo waited and prayed the man didn't want to get wet.

His prayers were answered; after a cursory check, the hatch was slammed shut and Sami's engine roared. Arlo floated to the surface – but at that moment the hatch reopened. With no time to take a proper breath, he sank like a stone.

This time there was no light, just a long teasing pause; it was like the man knew Arlo was there and wanted to see how long he could hold his breath. It was a game. Who would blink first? Then without explanation, the hatch shut and he heard footsteps climbing off the truck.

Once Sami started to roll forward again, Arlo shot to the surface, opened his mouth, filled his lungs and thanked God for fresh air.

Fatigue, hunger and dehydration were making it difficult for him to retain a firm grip on the ladder. He felt dizzy and he started to vomit. Fearful that he might pass out and drown, he looped his belt through one of the upper rungs then tied it back around his waist. He laughed as he imagined himself hanging like the head of a deer on a wall in a hunting lodge. He also worried about what impact an extended descent would have on him. Tethered to the ladder, would he survive?

It was just after 3am when Sami tucked the ISIS flag under his seat, crossed the Khabur River and entered the Ibrahim Khalil border crossing. The approach road was noisy and chaotic with a long line of drivers in cars, trucks and tractors waiting to be processed by a solitary customs officer who looked tired and fed up. A second officer was keeping a careful eye on things through an opening in a guard station made from piles of sandbags. Two snipers occupied positions on the top of buildings to the right and left of the road.

Sami had thought hard about what he would tell the officer, but he still hadn't made up his mind. Was he there to see a dying relative in Silopi Hospital, or was he carrying water to a site just over the border? Both explanations were unconvincing and he knew it.

As his vehicle moved closer to the barrier he started to sweat. Panic was setting in. If he was turned back, what then? Sami glanced at his ragged backpack containing his life's savings tucked in behind the passenger seat. It was a terrible idea, yet it might be his best chance of getting across the border.

He inched up to the barricade and stopped. The officer circled his truck and glanced briefly underneath the rear section before stepping on the running board and placing his head through the open window. He examined the cab, looked square into Sami's eyes, grunted then gave a thumbs-up to the officer in the bunker.

Arlo had no idea where he was or why the truck had stopped. Preparing for the worst, he unbuckled his belt and released it from the ladder then took a couple of deep breaths as he listened for sounds that might provide a clue as to what was happening. If the hatch opened, he would dive – he had to for Sami's sake – but he didn't know if he had the strength to come back up again.

The wait almost killed him but finally Sami's engine turned over and a slight vibration ran the length of the truck. Arlo forced a half-smile as water splashed gently against his face. They were moving again.

Silopi was a 16.1km drive from the border and Sami covered the distance in just under thirty minutes. As he approached the city limits, he turned to the right and eased his truck into an out-of-the-way layby. As soon as the handbrake was locked into position, he hurried to open the hatch, lowered head inside the tank and looked around. There was no sign of the doctor.

'Doctor Arlo! Doctor Arlo!' he screamed, but there was no response.

Without hesitating, he lowered himself into the water and swam towards the rear of the tank. Something brushed against his leg. He turned and saw Arlo with his scalpel raised, about to strike.

He reached up and deflected the blow. 'You're safe,' he shouted. 'We made it – we're in Turkey.'

A moment later Arlo was flat on his back on the grass, staring at the stars. 'Thank you,' he murmured as his eyes closed. 'Is it okay if I rest here for a few minutes?'

It was four hours later when he awoke.

It was a short drive to the Habur Hotel on the east side of Silopi. The family-run, no-questions-asked refuge was well known to those who wanted to keep their business to themselves.

Arlo checked in using the name of his old roommate at medical school in England, Peter Stanforth. Payment had to be made in advance in cash, but there was no need to show your passport.

Around the corner was a market where he bought some clothes. It was cheap and cheerful stuff but he didn't care; it just felt good to be dry again.

The café across the road didn't look like much but it served food and that was all he wanted.

The two men found a table and ordered. 'You saved my life. Thank you,' Arlo said.

'And you saved many lives in Mosul, so thank you,' Sami replied.

'Are you going back? What about your mother?'

Sami lowered his head, avoiding Arlo's eyes. 'She's not with us anymore.'

'That was sudden. What happened?'

His friend kept his eyes on his plate. 'Let's talk about you. What are you going to do?'

Sami's body language spoke volumes. Arlo had a gut feeling but he kept it to himself. 'I'm going back to England, but first I need to call Jen's parents.' This time it was Arlo who stared down at his food. The two men ate in silence and didn't speak again until they were standing outside the hotel.

'I'll never forget you,' Arlo said.

Sami gave him a wide smile, reached into his pocket and handed him the scalpel. 'Hang on to this. You never know when you might need it.'

❋ ❋ ❋

The phone call to Jen's parents was hard. When they got over their initial shock and stopped crying, the blame game started and the questions were endless and painful.

'Why did you force our daughter to go to Iraq? Why didn't you protect her? How could you leave her?'

Arlo tried to respond but they didn't want to listen and took turns assaulting him with words like 'coward' and 'murderer'. When the vitriol ceased, the call ended.

He wasn't sure what he'd expected them to say but he'd certainly not anticipated such a cruel reaction. He had dedicated his life to saving lives but he'd been responsible for two deaths in twenty-four hours. He'd made mistakes and would have to live with them; turning the clock back was not an option.

It was midnight. In the morning Arlo planned to book a flight from Sirnak Airport to London via Istanbul; in the meantime, he was still feeling lightheaded and tired, and he needed to get to bed.

His head had barely touched the pillow when someone pounded on his door. Within seconds Arlo was face to face with three burly men, two of whom were carrying handguns and wore face coverings. 'You the doctor?' asked the man without a weapon or mask. Arlo remained silent. 'Come with us.'

'Who are you?'

'Emir. Now come.'

Arlo tried to close the door but was easily pushed aside.

'Now,' Emir insisted.

'And if I refuse?'

Both armed men pointed their weapons and Arlo immediately raised his hands in surrender. Shaking, he quickly dressed, grabbed his phone and was led to an old rust ridden van parked in front of the hotel. Despair swept over him as he tumbled on to the cold steel corrugated flooring. Once inside the vehicle, the light went out and a hood was placed over his head.

'Is this necessary?' he asked. A long period of silence followed before the hood was finally removed. 'Thank you.'

The next forty-five minutes were spent travelling off-road at high speed. The van wasn't built for this type of terrain but Emir obviously thought differently and pushed it to the limit. At times it felt like they were rolling downhill in a barrel. With nothing to hold on to, Arlo bounced up and down and side to side, much to the amusement of the men next to him.

Despite his discomfort, there was more he wanted to know but all attempts to strike up a dialogue failed and his questions went unanswered. His mind was working overtime. Were they ISIS, police, was Spider behind this? Were they taking him back to Mosul? Were they going to kill him?

When the van eventually stopped and the back door opened, Emir smiled. 'Welcome to Iraq.'

Arlo's heart sank. *This is it*. But just as he began preparing for the worst, Emir brightened his day. 'You looked worried,' he said. 'Don't be, we're the good guys. We're not ISIS or Al Qaeda – we just need your help.'

That was something – but he still didn't know who they were or whose side they were on. Once again, he tried to engage Emir in conversation, to try and build some connection between them. 'How did you know I was a doctor?'

'The owner of the hotel saw your shirt – you know, the one

doctors wear.'

Arlo managed a smile. 'You speak English very well. Where did you learn it?'

'I lived in London for many years,' Emir replied.

'Will you ever go back?' Arlo's comment made the other two men snigger. 'What's so funny?' he asked.

'I was deported for overstaying my visit so I can't go back.'

A five-minute walk took them to an encampment nestled amid a cluster of huge boulders. Several well-armed men and women sat around a fire while others lay fast asleep nearby. Emir pointed to a man wrapped in a blanket.

Arlo kneeled beside him and gently removed the bloodstained cover to assess the damage. 'I don't have anything to…' Before he could finish, Emir handed him a bag packed with medical supplies. 'You have a bag, so where's the doctor?'

'You're looking at him,' Emir replied, nodding at the wounded man.

'What happened?' Arlo asked.

Emir spat before he grunted, 'IED.'

Working by flashlight, Arlo spent the remainder of the evening removing shards of metal from the left side of his patient's body. None of the injuries were life threatening, just painful and debilitating. By first light more than thirty metallic fragments lay scattered on a blood-stained cloth on the ground. 'He's a lucky man,' said Arlo. 'He'll be fine.'

'Unfortunately his brother wasn't so lucky,' Emir responded. 'He took the full force of the blast.'

Washing the blood from his hands, Arlo asked, 'What next?'

'You're a good man. We would like you to stay and help us.'

'Do I have a choice?'

'Of course. We are not kidnappers.'

Arlo raised his eyebrows. This time it was Emir who lifted his arms as if to surrender. 'I apologise,' he said, 'but it was necessary.'

The two men exchanged a few pleasantries but Arlo made his intentions clear: he wanted to go home. Emir scribbled his number on a piece of paper and laughed as he handed it over. 'Just in case you want someone killed.'

'Funny you should say that.' Arlo passed his phone to Emir. 'The Englishman with the spider tattoo murdered my girlfriend.'

Emir studied the screen. 'Who is the woman in the background? She's not an Arab.'

Arlo shook his head. 'I've no idea.'

'They are most likely together,' Emir said. 'Forward the picture to my phone and I'll see what I can do. Now, let's get you on that plane.'

2

Berkshire, Southern England – present day

Steve Foley and his son Eddie pulled up outside the local radio station, their black van emblazoned with the On Guard Security logo. Steve backed into a parking bay while Eddie stared glum-faced out of the window. 'How many more of these interviews do we have to do?' he asked. 'We've had three months of the same old questions, same old answers.'

'Well, if you hadn't got yourself wrapped up in a suicide vest, we wouldn't be doing any interviews at all,' his dad replied. 'Besides, saving your ass was good for business – we now have more clients than we can handle.'

Eddie snarled, 'It may have helped the business but I lost a brother and a friend.'

'It wasn't my fault!' Steve protested.

'I know, but you're talking like it was a good thing.'

As they pushed open the heavy glass door and entered the foyer, Steve turned to his son and whispered, 'Remember…'

Eddie raised his hand. 'I've got it, Dad. Don't tell them anything they don't need to know.'

They said nothing more until they reached the desk where a smartly dressed young lady pointed them in the direction of the producer's office.

Suddenly Eddie threw up his arms and shook his head.

'Sorry – I can't do this anymore, I'll wait for you in the van.'

Eddie was sitting in the passenger seat of the van, radio on. News, weather and a traffic update then the smooth-voiced host introduced Steve as the retired bomb-disposal officer who'd disarmed an explosive device attached to his son. Eddie grimaced; it was all so familiar.

When Steve explained to the DJ that his son had been kidnapped and tortured because of a mistake, Eddie mouthed his father's every word. And when his father was asked why defusing this bomb was different from those in a war zone, he quoted mockingly, '"This one was personal."'

He turned off the radio.

Twenty minutes later Steve returned to the van looking solemn. 'You were right, son. I'm done with this crap. No more interviews.'

'Really?'

'I've never discussed my life in the army, so why am I telling the world what I do as a civilian?'

'Money? Fame?' Eddie's tone was almost teasing.

Steve nodded reluctantly before switching on the ignition and pulling out of the parking bay. 'Did I tell you that Lager has decided to stay with us?' he asked.

'I didn't know he was thinking about leaving.'

'He changed his mind. Good news, huh?'

'So, let me get this straight.' Eddie's tone was snippy. 'Lager leaves the army to become a cop then leaves the force to become a security guard. What's his next career move? A lollipop man?'

Steve chuckled. 'He's a good man. He risked his life for you.'

'I know, but I still get the feeling he doesn't like me. Everything he does is to please you.'

'He's military. He needs to know you have his back. That was something he didn't feel he was getting with the police.' Steve paused and then added, 'And as you know, there was a time when you weren't very reliable.'

Eddie hung his head. 'I'm working on it,' he muttered.

A call on Steve's phone ended their conversation. Malik's name appeared on the screen. 'I wonder what he wants?'

'I bet it won't be good news.'

Steve pressed the hands-free button. 'Hello, Malik.'

'Mr Foley. I thought you should know that my son Qasim left our home here in Peshawar just before I returned from England three months ago.'

Eddie and his father exchanged curious glances.

'I know he travelled to Afghanistan,' Malik added.

Steve whispered out of the side of his mouth, 'Wait for it.'

'I think he's been training with a terrorist group there.'

'That's – unfortunate,' Steve offered. 'But why are you telling me?'

A long pause followed before Malik said, 'I found a letter he wrote blaming you and Eddie for the deaths of his sisters.'

Steve shook his head. 'That's not entirely true. Does he know that Rana and Benazir were terrorists?'

Malik ignored his comment. 'I think he's coming to England to kill you and your son.'

How was Steve supposed to react to that? He did his best to keep his tone casual. 'Thanks for the heads up.'

'One more thing,' added Malik.

'What's that?'

'He's not a strong or courageous boy, so when he comes I'm confident he won't be alone.' Malik ended the call.

Steve and his son sat for a moment in the van outside their house. Eddie's right leg had started to shake. 'This is serious,' he said. 'Who knows how many of those bastards could be coming for us.'

Steve placed his head on the headrest and closed his eyes. 'I feel sorry for Malik,' he said softly. 'It can't be easy being the father of two – possibly three – terrorists. It must have been hard for him to make that call and to choose us over his son.'

'I'm not sure I could do that, no matter what my kid had done,' Eddie said.

'Let's hope you never have to make that decision.'

'When Qasim stayed at our house, he was a pussy, afraid of his own shadow. Could he become a terrorist in just three months?'

'Any asshole can strap a bomb to their body,' Steve snapped. 'There's not a lot of training needed for that.'

'So, what do we do?' Eddie demanded.

'We get him before he gets us.'

3

The automatic doors leading to the Bramley Park A&E swung open releasing a sanitised odour. Arlo inhaled and smiled; for some it was a smell that instilled fear but for him it was comforting. It signalled hope.

A large waiting room stretched ahead of him, packed as it was every morning at this time. Patients nursing hangovers sat coyly gazing at their self-inflicted wounds, while some of those with more genuine reasons to be hurting were being excessively vocal.

As he approached the reception desk a choreographed, 'Good morning, Dr Arlo,' drowned out the whimpers and moans.

'Good morning, ladies,' he replied, trying his best to make eye contact with each member of staff on the early shift.

He collected a clipboard from the counter 'What's on the menu today?' After studying the list of sick and wounded, he moved towards Consultation Room 3. Pulling back the curtain, he saw a young girl with blonde curly hair. Her left arm was in a makeshift sling. 'Hello,' he said. 'And what's your name?'

'My name is Jennifer,' she said. 'But my friends call me Jen.'

Arlo shuddered and a chill shot through his body. Distracted, he mumbled something unintelligible while resting his hand on the end of the bed. For a moment he was back in Mosul with Jennifer, the love of his life.

Nurse Lorraine's gentle hand brushing against his elbow quickly refocused his mind. 'That's a lovely name,' said Arlo. 'Now let's have a look at that arm.'

Four hours later Arlo was sitting alone in the hospital canteen. Oblivious to the chatter from staff around him, he stared into an empty coffee cup. A sandwich on a plate next to the cup remained untouched.

'Penny for your thoughts,' Lorraine said as she pulled up a chair.

Arlo half-smiled and said nothing. He knew she wasn't there to discuss the weather; she and Arlo had been friends and work colleagues long before he went to Mosul with Jen, and she could read him like a book.

'I know it's none of my business,' Lorraine continued, 'but you really must move on. It's been years. Stop punishing yourself.' Another moment of silence followed. 'You can't undo what's been done,' she added.

'I know,' Arlo said. 'I'll stop when I get closure.'

'And when will that be?'

'When I see him dead,' he snapped.

'Arlo, he could be dead already or working in a bank in New York. You don't know anything about him except that he has a spider tattoo on his shoulder.'

'I know what he looks like, what he sounds like, and I know he's coming for me.'

'How do you know that?'

Arlo managed a wry smile. 'Because I've been texting him for some time now.'

'Bloody hell! You've been communicating with a terrorist?'

He grimaced then quickly looked around the canteen before placing his finger over his lips. 'I figured if I can't go to him then I'll try to convince him to come to me.'

Lorraine shook her head in disbelief as he continued, 'I said I had a video of him killing people and, if he wants it, to come and get it.'

She sat with her mouth wide open as Arlo stood up and walked towards A&E. Within seconds she was by his side. 'But he could be here now, waiting outside!'

'I have someone in Turkey feeding me information. Our terrorist left Mosul before it was retaken in 2017 then travelled to Baghouz in Syria. He fled two years later for Afghanistan or Pakistan.'

'So he could be anywhere now?' Lorraine said. 'He could be here.'

Arlo nodded and reached for his clipboard but she was standing in the way. 'Have you got a death wish?' she sniped.

There was no response and none expected.

※ ※ ※

Eight hours later, Arlo left a supermarket with a ready meal tucked under his arm. His marathon shift at the hospital was finally over and it was time to go home. Exhausted, and still reeling from Lorraine's 'death wish' accusation, he walked towards his car.

Twenty metres away there was a man dressed in black wearing a baseball hat and sunglasses. Arlo froze and his mind went into overdrive. *It's dark, what the hell is he doing wearing sunglasses and why is he leaning on my car?*

Backing slowly, he moved behind a parked 4x4 where he stayed out of sight until a woman approached the man, handed him a white cane and guided him across the car park.

Feeling foolish, Arlo cursed himself quietly then pretended to inspect the rear tyre of the 4x4 as a woman pushing a shopping cart strolled past him. As soon as she was gone, he ran to his car and threw himself onto the driver's seat, locked the doors and reached beneath his seat to touch the scalpel.

A sudden knock on the window made him jump. Without thinking, his hand moved again towards the razor-sharp implement.

'You dropped this,' shouted a middle-aged man holding up the ready meal.

Arlo thanked him, opened the window to accept the package then closed it again.

For a moment he sat with his head resting on the steering wheel. 'What have I done?' he murmured.

❄ ❄ ❄

Steve's black On Guard Security van rolled slowly up to the flattened wooden fence surrounding the disused paint factory. Derelict for three years, the building had become a hot spot for raves and drug parties. His job was to make sure that no one died there, but with such easy access keeping people out was an impossible task.

Loud chatter and giggling drew his attention to the third floor; it was a familiar situation.

Steve approached from the southern entrance while Eddie came in from the north. Avoiding particles of broken glass and discarded syringes, they moved quietly to the top floor where two teenage boys and a girl were painting on one of the walls of a narrow hallway.

When Steve cleared his throat, they turned in his direction. 'Cops,' blurted the pink-haired girl.

One of the boys rotated slightly as if to run but reconsidered when he saw Eddie's muscular frame only a few feet away.

'Sorry, mister,' the girl said. 'We didn't think it would matter because it's such a shit place.'

Steve silently agreed: it was a shit place and painting the wall wasn't a problem. The building was marked for redevelopment so a bit of colour wouldn't change anything. What concerned Steve was the content of the graffiti.

'Move away from the wall,' he ordered as he scanned the area. Gradually the youngsters shuffled across to the other side of the hall. After taking a moment to digest what was written, he read out loud: '"Friends first, family next, then you, Steve. Are you ready?"'

He moved closer to the girl who was still holding a paintbrush. 'What's this all about?'

'We don't know. Some guy gave us the gear and a tenner each.'

'What did he look like?' Eddie asked.

'He was black, skinny. Kinda tall.'

'How old?' snapped Steve.

'Seventeen, eighteen?'

'Did he have a chipped front tooth?'

Eddie looked curiously at his father as the girl nodded.

'Anything else?' Steve probed.

'Nothing, except this paper telling us what to write,' the girl said. 'We were supposed to put a Q at the bottom, like it is here,' she added, pointing to the paper.

Steve studied the child-like scribble. 'Bloody Qasim,' he muttered.

A dismissive wave of his hand sent the three troublemakers scurrying down the hall.

'I'll bet the kid who broke into our house put them up to this,' Eddie said.

'You mean the one you tossed out of the upstairs window?' There was mischief in Steve's voice.

His son looked uncomfortable then mumbled, 'I don't do that anymore.'

'I know, I'm just taking the piss. Anyway, you're right. He's the bugger who spied on us before Qasim came into our lives.'

Eddie thought for a moment. 'How did he know we'd be in this building? We only signed the contract three days ago.'

'Because he's watching us.' As Steve finished speaking, footsteps echoed off the concrete stairway. He signalled to Eddie to slip into a side room while he stood in the hallway, truncheon drawn.

'Hey Steve, Eddie you up here?' Lager shouted as he rounded the corner.

Eddie re-appeared and Steve relaxed. 'Yeah, down the hall,' he called.

As Lager strutted confidently towards them, he caught sight of the writing on the wall. He read it once, then read it again. 'What's this?'

'Qasim is back, or on his way,' Steve told him. 'The skinny black kid who broke into our house arranged this colourful message.'

Lager looked at Eddie. 'Is that the same kid you tossed—?'

Looking fed up, Eddie interrupted with a grunt and a nod of the head.

'So it looks like I'm top of the list,' Lager joked. 'I'm flattered.'

'I think we should take this seriously,' Steve cautioned.

'Why? Qasim is hardly a hit man.'

'I spoke to Malik. He told me his son spent time in Afghanistan. He thinks he's been at a terrorist training camp and is coming to England.'

'So?'

'When he comes,' Steve said, 'he won't be coming alone.'

'Do we get the police involved?' Lager asked.

'And tell them what? That Qasim wants to kill us because we blew up his sister.'

As they left the building and crossed the car park, the three men looked formidable. Steve and Lager, ex-military, were confident, toned, heads shaved; Eddie may have been a wannabee marine, but he was fit and cocky and he definitely looked the part. Who in their right mind would want to take them on?

Eddie, who had been silent until now, spoke. 'Malik called to say his son was coming to kill us and now the same message is written on a wall. What's with the warnings? Do they want to kill us or just scare us?'

'A bit of both,' said Steve dryly. 'Intimidation is their strategy. They hope we'll panic, but we won't. We'll stick to the plan.'

Lager and Eddie exchanged glances.

'What's the plan, Dad?'

'Not sure,' Steve responded, 'But I'll think of something.'

4

It was just after 3am when Arlo woke to the sound of a text pinging in his ear. He sat up, turned on the bedside lamp and reached for his mobile. At first he hesitated, reluctant to see what was in front of him but eventually lowered his eyes and saw it was from Emir. He started to read.

Hi, it's me. Arlo smiled: that was how Emir started all his messages. *I have good news. Spider is dead, killed while trying to cross into Pakistan from Afghanistan. ISIS is finished. My work here is done. Soon I will be coming to England for a holiday. Can you let me know where you are so we can have a beer to celebrate? Emir*

Arlo jumped out of bed, fist pumped the air and shouted, 'Thank you, God.' He took a deep breath as a massive weight fell from his shoulders.

Wide awake and beaming from ear to ear, he put on his dressing gown and marched into the kitchen to make coffee. Humming an unrecognisable tune, he settled at the table and started to reply to Emir's text with words like 'fantastic', 'brilliant' and 'unbelievable', together with a few thank-yous. Without thinking about it, he shared the information about where he worked and lived.

Suddenly distracted by the sound of a car alarm nearby, Arlo went into the living room and peered through a crack in the curtains. An upstairs light came on in the house across the street and a moment later a man opened the front door, pointed his fob at the offending vehicle and the noise stopped.

Closing the curtains tightly, Arlo returned to the kitchen but stopped before he stepped on to the polished parquet flooring. Something was bothering him: something wasn't right.

The more he thought about it, the more annoyed he became that he couldn't put his finger on it. Finally he sat back down at the table. 'Retrace your steps,' he whispered to himself as if to prevent someone from hearing.

Slowly scrolling back through Emir's text, he read and re-read every sentence, analysed every word. There it was, in plain sight: *Soon I will be coming to England for a holiday.*

Arlo's mind flashed back to when Emir had told him he'd been deported from England and could never return. 'Son of a bitch,' he shouted, slamming his fist on the table. 'You bastard! Leave me alone.'

He sat with his head in his hands, knowing that the text could only mean one thing: Emir was dead and Spider had his phone.

Immediately he was beset by guilt and fear. Once again he'd been responsible for the death of someone he knew.

Had he done the right thing by trying to get Spider to come to England? And if Spider came, could he kill him? And if he could find the courage, how would he do it? He'd thought about none of this when he'd impulsively contacted Spider. Anger and revenge had influenced his decision, not common sense.

Arlo moved quickly to the rear of the house to check the back-door locks, then ran to the front door and went through the same routine. Satisfied that the house was secure, he returned to the text he'd been writing before the alarm had sounded. He deleted all the details about where he lived and worked and concocted a story about how he'd been offered a job in America and was heading to New York in the morning. He wished Emir well in whatever he did and signed off.

As he put the phone in his dressing-gown pocket, there was a moment of absolute stillness in the room. His heart was no longer beating like a drum, he was no longer twitching at every sound. He had dodged a bullet.

For the first time since he'd seen the text, Arlo relaxed. Conscious that he needed more sleep, he went back to bed, turned off the light and closed his eyes. Breathing deeply – in for five, out for seven – he tried to shut out the world, and for a few precious moments it worked. But deep down he knew better; deep down he knew that a man like Spider, who had stayed alive in a war zone for more than six years, wasn't stupid.

A second ping that seemed louder and more aggressive than the first announced the arrival of a new text. Arlo rolled over and picked up the phone again from the bedside table. For a moment he thought about tossing it against the wall, but a third ping a few seconds later appeared to take on command-like qualities and he obediently read the message.

Hi, it's me (smiley emoji).

Arlo snarled, 'Asshole,' then continued reading.

How did you know it was me? What did I say that gave it away? I like the NY thing, very inventive – but your friend Lorraine told me all I need to know. Oh, you forgot! I still have lovely Jennifer's mobile and it's full of numbers and photos. Remember, tough guy, you could have walked away. See you soon. Spider.

Rage flowed through every vein in Arlo's body as his thumbs went immediately to the keypad. He pressed hard on 'F' and

'U' and 'C' before stopping. What was the point?

Breakfast was an unusually sombre affair. Eddie hid his face in his phone and Steve couldn't stop thinking about the words on the wall. He wasn't worried about himself but Qasim targeting his friends and family was a real concern. 'You know,' he said finally, 'he seemed like such a nice kid.'

'Who?' Eddie asked, looking up.

'Qasim.'

'Really? He pretended to like Tim to stay at our house to get intel on me, and now he's threatening our friends and family. And don't forget that when I was getting the crap beaten out of me, he came along and gobbed on my head.'

'I guess if you put it that way he's not very nice.' Steve smiled. 'But the question is, is he a killer?'

'For Christ's sake, Dad, what's got into you? Anyone can kill – you taught me that. Remember those lovely shopkeepers in Iraq who had tripwires stretched across the doorway? And what about those sweet children with grenades tucked inside their teddy bears?'

Steve acknowledged his son's words with a reluctant nod.

Eddie continued his rant. 'And Qasim's sister Benazir may have been just a college student, but she was a heartbeat away from blowing up half of London. And what about his big sister, Rana? She was a bloody primary-school teacher while moonlighting for Al-Qaeda! I'm sorry, but the whole family is in it up to their necks, and that goes for the father too.'

'Eddie, he kidnapped and tortured you to get revenge for those who hurt Rana.'

Eddie stood up, left the table and headed for the hallway. His father stayed right behind him. 'Son, I'd have done the same thing if anyone hurt my family.'

'But first you'd have made sure the guy you were about to punish was guilty,' Eddie retorted.

The conversation ended abruptly when Eddie grabbed his keys and went out of the front door, pushing past Lager, who was standing on the porch.

'Come in,' Steve told his friend.

'What's got into him?' Lager asked. 'He didn't even say hello.'

'Am I getting soft?' Steve asked, ignoring his question.

'No, you're tough but fair, just like you were in the military.'

'Sometimes I wish I was still in uniform. Coffee?'

In the kitchen, their only topic of conversation was Qasim's threat. 'I don't have a number for Victoria,' Steve said. 'She's not on Facebook and her old email isn't working. I guess if I can't get hold of her, there's not much chance Qasim will find her.'

'Even if you did reach her, what would you say? Lager asked. '"Hide, leave the country, someone's going to kill you"?'

Steve thought for a moment. 'I guess I could bring her here until this blows over.' He saw Lager's wince. 'I know, bad idea. An ex-wife with a baby she had with someone else – Eddie would go ballistic.'

'What about you? Would you go ballistic?' Lager demanded.

An uneasy smile crossed Steve's face as he carried on making the coffee.

Slivers of early-morning sunshine tumbled through the partially open blind and splayed across Arlo's bathroom wall. Instantly his mind raced back to the makeshift hospital in Mosul where the shredded tarpaulin had let in more of the sun's rays than it had kept out. Yet another trigger. Yet another reminder of the death and despair he had witnessed daily.

Handfuls of cold water splashed over his face gradually brought him back to 7am on a Monday morning in September. The room was still, but his reflection in the mirror was screaming at him. Bloodshot eyes, pale skin and a scattering of pimples on his forehead would have indicated to any other doctor that all was not well.

Arlo took a slice of pizza out of the fridge, carried it into the living room and peered cautiously through a gap in the curtains. There wasn't a soul in sight. Grabbing his keys and bag, he rushed to the front door, locked up and hurried down the street to his car. Once he was in the driver's seat, he put the pizza on the dashboard, locked the doors and glanced over his shoulder to check out the back seat.

He continued to scan the area as he put the key in the ignition. Finally, he lowered his gaze to focus on the steering block, then moved slightly to the left so he could see beneath the dash. The sea of wires shooting off in all directions told him nothing.

'To hell with it,' he mumbled. He sat upright, closed his eyes, held his breath and turned the key. The car engine roared into life.

Fifteen minutes later he was walking through the door to A&E and making a beeline for Lorraine.

※ ※ ※

Sitting cross-legged beside his brother's grave, Eddie picked up a blade of grass and stuck it between his teeth.

'Hey, Tim, it's me. You probably won't believe me but I miss you, little brother. I'm sorry if I took the piss sometimes, but that's what big brothers do. The house is so quiet without you – I hate it. Dad's good but he's working too hard. The business has grown a lot since he saved my ass. I'm still on the payroll and so is Lager, Dad's cop friend. Haven't seen Mom since your funeral. Did you know she had a baby? Don't know who the father is, but I bet he loves reggae.'

He chuckled. 'Sorry about that. I'm trying to be more PC but it's not working. By the way, your pretend friend Qasim has reared his ugly head. He's threatening to kill us. I hope he tries so I can make him suffer for jerking you around. Gotta go now but I'll be back. Sleep well.'

'We have to talk.' Arlo's tone was heated as he marched into Consultation Room 4.'

'I'm in the middle of something right now,' Lorraine replied calmly.

'It's important!'

'So is this,' snapped Lorraine, holding up a catheter tube.

A gruff voice from the far end of the table announced he hadn't been able to pee all night and if he didn't get relief soon someone would get hurt – and it wouldn't be the nurse. Arlo backed off and waited in the hall.

Twenty minutes later Lorraine followed him to a vacant office. 'A man called you and asked about me,' Arlo blurted.

'Yes – it was Derek.'

'Derek who?'

'I can't remember, but he said he was your roommate at med school.'

'I don't know anyone called Derek. What did he want?'

Lorraine hesitated; the look on her face spoke volumes. 'Arlo, I'm sorry.'

'What did he want?' repeated Arlo.

'He wanted to know where you work so he could surprise you.'

'Lorraine, I didn't even know you back then! Didn't you think it was strange that he called your number. How did he get it?'

'I'm sorry, I didn't think…'

'That's for damned sure.'

Lorraine's face turned red. 'Well, if you hadn't been so goddamn macho with a terrorist, he wouldn't know you had his photo and he wouldn't be thinking of coming after you to get it!'

Tired and frightened, Arlo leaned against the desk. She was right. What the hell had he been thinking?

'Have you spoken to the police?' she asked.

Arlo nodded. 'They weren't interested.'

'Why not?'

'They said the photo was poor quality, it happened in Iraq and there's no proof he's British. Shall I go on?'

'So, what are you going to do?'

'I don't know.' Arlo sighed. 'I've thought about moving but I'm a doctor, for God's sake. My name is everywhere. It's like I've got a target on my back.' His shoulders slumped forward. Looking pale and dishevelled, he shuffled slowly out of the room and into the hall.

'Go home, lock the door and get some sleep,' Lorraine said. 'You look like shit.'

Eddie sat on the edge of Tim's bed and looked around the room. It was the same as it had been when he was alive; neither he nor his father had the heart to remove or change anything.

The ball, perfectly placed in the closet directly beneath the Reading Football Club jersey, made him smile. Tim had been an ardent supporter of his local team but rubbish when it came to playing the game.

Maybe I should have kicked a ball with him more often, Eddie thought. The bat leaning against the wall was never used for baseball but was one of Tim's many items of protection, though the chance of him hitting someone with it was zero.

There's no way he could have hurt anyone, so where did he get the courage to shoot himself in the head?

Eddie's moment alone with the memories of his brother ended abruptly when his father ran into the house shouting his name. 'Up here,' he yelled. The heavy boots crashing up the stairs sounded threatening. 'What's up?'

'Did you go to the cemetery this morning?'

Eddie nodded.

'Did you see it?'

'See what?'

'Another message, only this time it was painted on Tim's headstone.'

'Son of a bitch.' Eddie scowled. 'What did it say?'

Steve swallowed hard then barked, 'Q's coming.'

'That bloody kid is at it again! He must have followed me to the cemetery and done it after I left. I'll get some turps and clean it off.'

'It's okay. I've done it.' Steve paced the room, mumbling obscenities under his breath. 'That little bugger has crossed the line!'

'I agree, but I don't think threatening him will work. I threw him out of the upstairs window, you smashed his head against the dashboard in your van, and he's still being naughty. Maybe we should just kill him.'

Steve glared down at his son, looking for a sign that Eddie was joking but none was forthcoming. 'I think you need to make another appointment with Dr Mo,' he said.

Eddie lifted himself off the bed and stood toe to toe, eye to eye with his father. His tone was calm and controlled. 'When someone's behaviour hurts this family, nothing a shrink says will change what I do.'

<h1 style="text-align:center">5</h1>

Steve had a plan, a simple one. He and Eddie would go to work in the van as usual and Lager would follow at a safe distance on a motorbike wearing a full-face helmet and black leathers, looking like any other biker. If someone was tailing the van, he'd contact Steve.

Three nights passed without incident but on the fourth, around 10pm, Lager noticed a Mercedes with blackened windows following the van. He made the call.

Steve drove to the end of the street, turned sharp right and then left before pulling into a large gym and swimming-pool complex. Once in the empty car park, he did a U-turn and came face to face with the Mercedes, while Lager stopped a few feet away.

Eddie leapt from the van, ran to the vehicle and tried unsuccessfully to open the door. With a truncheon in his right hand and his arm cocked, he only stopped short of smashing the side window when his father screamed his name.

A moment later Steve's phone rang; the call came from a woman claiming to be inside the Mercedes. She wanted to know if it was safe to open her window. After a short conversation, Steve apologised and she drove away.

'That lady owns a garden centre in Wokingham,' Steve said angrily. 'She followed the van because she wanted to give us her business. Needless to say, that's not going to happen. What the hell were you doing, Eddie?'

Eddie kept his head down. 'I thought—' he mumbled.

Steve jumped in. 'You didn't think. You assumed, and you were wrong.'

As Eddie returned to the van, Lager moved closer to Steve. 'Your son is a loose cannon. One day he's going to drop us all in it.'

'I'll keep an eye on him.'

'Is he still seeing the shrink?'

Steve shook his head. 'Not as often as he should.'

The night shift seemed to drag on forever. They may have been sitting in the van with just inches between them but Steve and his son were miles apart; they hadn't exchanged a word since the incident in the gym car park.

Eddie was staring out of the side window while Steve concentrated on driving to the next job. An early-morning coffee break at the golf course did nothing to improve the atmosphere: Steve stayed behind the wheel while Eddie sat on the grass opposite the first tee and ate a chocolate bar.

When their shift finally ended, Steve dropped his son off in front of the house and carried on driving. There were no goodbyes.

Tired and fed up, Eddie lumbered up the path, took a key out of his pocket and raised his head – then his teeth clenched and his body went rigid. There was a large red inflatable letter 'Q' tied by a long string to the doorknob.

He took a step back, turned, faced the street and opened his mouth to scream but an elderly woman walking her dog interrupted. 'What's the 'Q' for,' she asked. 'Is it your birthday?'

'No,' he snapped. 'I'm celebrating coming out of the closet.'

She looked around as if searching for clarification while Eddie turned and unlocked the door. Once inside the house, he held the Q in place with his left foot and stomped down hard with his right. A loud pop echoed along the hall. Eddie kept stamping, not holding back. 'I'm going to hurt you like you've never been hurt before.'

'Charming,' Steve said as he squeezed past his son. 'I hope that wasn't directed at me?'

Eddie lifted the burst balloon off the floor until it was level with his father's eyes. In response, Steve raised a pint of milk to the same level. 'Let's have a cuppa and talk.'

Arlo spent the day fastening locks to his windows and deadbolts to his doors. He fixed lights attached to a sensor to the side and rear of his property. He tucked a large carving knife behind a hardback medical dictionary in the living room and slid his old school cricket bat under the bed. His scalpel was never far away from his hand.

This is bullshit, he thought as he finally took a moment to relax on the sofa. *I need a gun.*

Two hours later Arlo slipped through an entrance reserved for tradesmen at the back of Bramley Park Hospital. 'Keep him guessing,' he mumbled. 'Keep him guessing.'

Kevin Choo, a nurse in A&E, stopped him in the hall. 'I've been asked to tell you there's a woman waiting for you in reception.'

'She asked for me by name?' Arlo asked.

'Not sure, but it sounded like it. I'm just passing on the message.'

Arlo's mind went blank. The hall might have been filled with staff and patients moving, yet he still felt vulnerable and alone. He moved carefully along the corridor past X-Ray and into the men's washroom.

He was trembling as he stared at the mirror. Lorraine had been right: he really did look terrible. Taking a couple of deep breaths, he stepped back into the hall and finished the two-minute walk to the reception desk. Immediately, another nurse came forward with a reminder that someone was waiting for him beyond the swing doors.

Arlo moved reluctantly out from behind the desk and peered through a glass panel into the waiting room. At least a dozen people were sitting there but none of them resembled Spider. Feeling more confident, he pushed through the doors. Immediately a woman in her thirties approached him. 'Dr Arlo?' she asked, She was wearing sunglasses and a baseball cap.

'Yes.'

'Smile.' She raised her phone and snapped a photo. Before he realised what had happened, she'd disappeared through the automatic doors.

'Damn,' Arlo muttered. 'There goes an up-to-date photo for Spider.'

※ ※ ※

'Are you still seeing Dr Mo?' Steve asked again. Eddie shrugged his shoulders like a sulky child. 'For Christ's sake, son, this is serious. He was helping you, but now you want to hurt people again. What's going on?'

'This kid deserves to be hurt. He's threatening our family.'

'Really? A bit of red paint and a balloon? He's winding us up, that's all.'

Eddie ignored his father's comments, finished his tea and went outside. A moment later he poked his head back inside the door and yelled, 'Hey, Dad, come here and check out another harmless wind-up!'

Steve moved to the front door and glared at his van. 'Son of a bitch,' he snarled while Eddie circled the vehicle.

'Nothing to see here,' he mocked, as his finger followed the outline of a large 'Q'. 'It's just a bit of red paint on the back doors, both side doors and the bonnet.'

Three-and-a-half hours later, Eddie ordered a beer at the Duck and Feathers pub then retreated to a stool at the end of the bar. The eighteenth-century inn, about two miles from his home, had been his regular haunt until he became known as the 'man with a bomb in his mouth' and overnight his life had changed.

He hadn't been able to step outside his front door without someone pointing a finger or making a comment. His face had been in every newspaper and on every TV channel. To make matters worse, the huge gap in his front teeth that had been made to retrieve the bomb's metal plates provided the uncaring with a wealth of sick humour.

Now Eddie kept himself to himself. He didn't socialise. With his smile intact and the media's interest fading, he was moving on. Coming here was a first step.

He quietly sipped his pint and scrolled through his phone while politely acknowledging the odd hello and thumbs-up from those around him. Suddenly his face lit up.

'What's tickling you?' the bartender asked.

Eddie slid his phone across the bar. 'I signed up to one of those dating sites yesterday and this just arrived.'

The bartender eyed the photo. 'She's nice. Attractive, thirty-two and size twelve. Hmmm, quite a catch – but be careful, old friend. I've tried these apps and I can tell you the most common things women lie about are their age and dress size.'

'And what do men lie about?'

The bartender leaned over the bar and smiled. 'Everything.'

Eddie looked shocked. 'Really?'

'Yep. Men lie about their age, height, job, marital status and where they live, so you could be at a disadvantage.' When Eddie looked confused, he went on. 'Your life has been played out in the media for the past three months. You're an open book.'

'Is that a good thing or a bad thing?'

The bartender didn't reply, just shrugged his shoulders and gave a wry smile.

'In for a penny,' Eddie declared.

A swipe of his thumb across the screen and in no time at all he'd arranged to meet the woman for coffee.

Late for his appointment and still fuming at the sight of his beloved van covered in graffiti, Steve raced into the Bramley Park Hospital car park. Unable to find an empty space, he pulled in behind a vehicle in a bay reserved for doctors. Once inside the building, he followed the signs to the human resources department.

Thirty-five minutes later he stepped outside, smiled and

punched the air, but his moment of satisfaction soon ended when he saw a man standing next to his van with his arms folded. 'Oh no,' he mumbled before saying more loudly, 'I'm sorry, I'll get out of your way.'

'Hey.' Arlo unfolded his arms. 'Aren't you that guy who disarmed a bomb in his son's mouth?'

Steve released his grip on his door handle and faced the doctor. There were times when he just wanted to say, 'Go away, leave me alone,' but he never did. Instead, he drew breath and answered as he had done a hundred times before, 'The bomb was in a vest around his body. The contacts were in his mouth.'

'And you took out his front teeth to get at them. Bloody genius.'

'I'm sure the work you do is just as clever.'

'The procedures we perform are often the difference between life and death, but nothing we do will end up killing the surgeon.'

Steve acknowledged the compliment and turned to open his door.

'You got the job?' Arlo asked.

Steve pondered for a moment until he realised Arlo was referring to the security gig at Bramley Park. 'Yes, we start on Monday,' he replied. 'And when I come back, I promise I won't block you in again.'

Two pints of beer and a bag of cheese-and-onion crisps didn't do much to ease the hunger pains in Eddie's stomach. He needed more, and Cleo's burger van situated in a layby a few feet down the road seemed like a good idea.

Before leaving his car to join the small queue, Eddie pulled his phone out of his pocket and glanced at the photo of Rachel, the girl he'd met on the dating app. She still looked good. He chuckled to himself. What could possibly go wrong?

He stepped out into the sunlight and stood behind two men in their mid-twenties. One of them turned, looked at Eddie then whispered to his mate. Eddie knew what was coming; he'd been here before.

'Hey, you're the guy with the bomb in his mouth,' the first man said.

Eddie stared at the ground and didn't reply. 'Are you a terrorist?' the same man asked, before giggling like a schoolboy.

Eddie continued to ignore him, though his right hand tightened into a fist deep inside his jacket pocket.

'Hey, dickhead, answer me,' the man went on. 'Are you one of those rag-head terrorists?'

Eddie had had enough. He pulled his right hand from his pocket, drew his bent arm back, then followed through like a missile with a devastating punch to the man's nose. Blood from his nostrils splattered across his face and upper body as he fell like a stone. His mate quickly backed off with his hands raised.

With no one now in front of him, Eddie moved to the serving hatch. 'Cheeseburger with extra onions, please.'

As he handed his money over to Cleo the guy on the floor screamed, 'You broke my nose, you son of a bitch.'

Eddie turned and glared at him. 'If I was a terrorist,' he said softly, 'your nose would be fine but your head would be on a spike.'

※ ※ ※

Barrow's Electrics in Wokingham was a gold mine for both professional and amateur spooks, although from the outside it looked like any normal run-down repair shop. Forget the TVs, fridges and oscillating desk fans: this 1950s' establishment supplied stuff you couldn't buy on the high street. The owner, PK Barrow, a child of the Cold-War era, sold products from that period: bug detectors, listening and tracking devices and spy cameras were all there, although not in plain sight.

PK, a bullish octogenarian, nodded when Steve entered the dimly lit shop. As he browsed the small aisle that split the room in half, he could feel the old man's eyes tracking his every step. When he removed items from a shelf, examined and then replaced them, he knew the old man was making mental notes.

Finally, a gruff voice full of phlegm, broke the silence. 'You expecting trouble?'

Steve turned but PK didn't wait for him to respond. 'Ain't got any of that IED crap you guys play with over there, but my stuff will give you a jump on those trying to get to you.'

'How did you know?' Steve asked.

'I watch the news, and for a long time you were the news. Follow me.'

Steve walked to the rear of the shop while PK pointed a black fob at the front door; the harsh creak of metal coming together signalled it was now locked. Next, the old man negotiated the six-digit pass code on the security panel that released a solid steel door, behind which was a tiny room stacked floor to ceiling with cardboard boxes.

He retrieved a dusty box, once a home to oranges from Spain, and lowered it onto a table. 'Can I help?' Steve asked.

'Nope.'

'Interesting collection of gear.' Steve picked up a tiny listening device. 'The Stasi, East Germany?'

'Spot on,' PK replied. 'And it still works.'

'Who would use it?'

'I've had a couple of people in business plant these things in their competitor's boardrooms. And yes, they sat outside in parked cars taking notes, just like in the movies. But that's enough nostalgia, the state-of-the-art stuff is over here.'

'Now you're talking,' Steve said.

By the time Eddie arrived home there were two more hits on his dating app. 'Who's a popular boy?' he said smugly as he walked through the front door.

Sitting at the kitchen table, his father greeted his son's remark with a raised eyebrow. Not a word was spoken but Eddie got the message loud and clear and quickly shuffled up to his room. With his shoes off and belt loosened, he threw himself onto his bed and studied the women on his phone.

'Let's see who's first up. Seema Chakrabarti from London. Thanks, but no thanks.' He hurriedly swiped her off the screen. 'Okay, who's behind door number two? It's Carol from Bracknell. Wow – she's close by. That's convenient.'

The sound of footsteps drew his attention. 'Hey, Dad, what's up?'

Steve smiled and gestured for his son to follow him downstairs. When he entered the kitchen, Eddie's eyes lit up: the table in front of him was packed with electronic devices and a very sinister looking piece of gear. 'Is this what I think it is?' he asked, pointing at the device.

His father nodded. 'I've come up with a plan to catch the kid.'

Eddie smiled and sat down at the table.

'I don't think Qasim is in the country yet,' Steve told him. 'I'm sure if he was here, we'd have heard from him. So I'm hoping the kid will keep up his silly antics and become even more daring.'

'He's already tied a balloon to our front door and spray-painted our van,' Eddie retorted. 'That's pretty damn daring. What else can he do to us?'

'I'm going to give him the opportunity to attack our office.'

'But we don't have an office!'

'We will have by the end of the day,' Steve told him. 'Get the keys to the garage.'

Eddie grinned. 'Is this Plan B?'

6

Lorraine grabbed Arlo's arm as he walked from Consultation Room 4. With both hands and a forceful right hip, she steered him into a deserted room. He offered no resistance.

'You look terrible,' she barked, 'and your bedside manner is just as bad. That woman you just treated was in pain and you said nothing to comfort her – you just walked into the room, stuck a needle in her arm and walked out. Sort yourself out. If the police won't help, then maybe you should start packing.'

Slumped against the wall with his head bowed, Arlo remained silent.

'Every time a door slams, you jump,' Lorraine continued. 'People are starting to talk.'

Arlo pushed himself off the wall and walked towards the door. 'I'll take care of it,' he muttered.

'How?' she shouted, but she was too late. He'd already gone.

❊ ❊ ❊

When the On Guard Security van pulled into the industrial estate behind the ice rink, Eddie squirmed in his seat. His eyes scanned the makeshift wooden buildings with their corrugated roofs and the uneven gravel yard dotted with vehicles awaiting repair. He shuddered and his stomach churned as bad memories flooded in.

'Do you know how much I hated this place?' he asked as

he stared at the drab concrete building where he'd worked as a mechanic.

'As a matter of fact, I do,' his father replied. 'You told me every day.' He carried on speaking as Eddie unlocked the door and stepped inside. 'When does the owner this place get out of prison?'

'He's got another four months.'

'Perfect. Hopefully this won't take too long.'

Eddie turned on the lights, released the catch on the up-and-over door and had started lifting it when his father cautioned, 'Hang on, son, we don't want the whole world to see what we're doing.'

He felt his face turning red and looked away, annoyed that his father had needed to remind him of something so basic.

As the door creaked slowly down to the floor, Steve raised a hammer and began breaking up the concrete just inside the entrance. Eventually he'd made a hole a dinner-plate wide and a can of beans deep. Next, he dug a long, narrow channel from the hole to a nearby wall. Eddie felt helpless as his father worked his magic, laying wires in the channel, setting up a camera sight line from a nearby wooden beam and installing a voice activator with speaker.

'If you want something to do,' Steve said, sweat dripping down his face, 'how about cleaning the dirt and grease off the door?'

Reluctantly, Eddie took a rag from the work bench and walked towards the front of the building. 'Any chance you could use a little soap and water?' his dad sniped. 'I want this place to look like a legitimate office.'

Eddie took a deep breath, counted five, then moved slowly to the toilet where there was a blue plastic bucket tucked under the sink. A bar of soap splattered with grease lay smashed into pieces on the floor. He forced a smile as he recalled the day his frustrations had got the better of him and he'd tossed the soap, a wrench and a mug of coffee against the loo wall. Working as a grease monkey had never sat well with him.

Water splashing over the side of the bucket, Eddie went back outside and started cleaning as instructed. A moment later, Lager arrived and unravelled a huge vinyl banner displaying the On Guard logo. *Son of a bitch*, Eddie thought. *Lager knew about this plan before I did.*

This time there was no hesitation, no counting to five. He let his feelings show as his right foot knocked over the bucket and sent the contents tumbling across the floor. An overhand throw propelled the sodden cleaning cloth onto a window where it stayed for a moment before gently sliding to the floor. 'Thanks Dad,' he shouted.

'What's your problem?' Steve demanded.

'What's my problem?' repeated Eddie. 'You – you're my problem. You don't trust me.'

Steve stopped what he was doing and glanced at Lager who was attaching the banner to the metal door.

'See what I mean?' Eddie barked, pointing to Lager. 'Why am I always the last to know? Just in case you've forgotten, my name is also on that killing list.'

He watched as his father shuffled awkwardly. No words were exchanged; no eye contact was made. Eddie shook his head and walked away.

※ ※ ※

The Ugly Mug coffee bar was packed full of yummy

mummies with babies in prams and a couple of men in suits concentrating on their phones. Eddie, looking much smarter than he had done at the garage, pulled around to the rear of the building and crept slowly to a side window that provided a clear view of the interior. His mission was to spot the woman he'd agreed to meet before she spotted him.

He wasn't fully aware of dating-app protocol but he knew that he didn't want to waste his time with someone who he didn't want to spend time with, so he had no qualms about bailing out. A cursory scan drew a blank, but a second more careful look at the faces on the other side of the glass proved successful. Standing at the counter waiting for a coffee was Rachel, the woman on the app.

Not bad. Nice face, hair, lovely smile. Happy that his journey hadn't been a waste of time, Eddie moved to the front of the coffee shop and pushed open the door. Rachel, holding a cup of coffee and a large piece of carrot cake, was moving to a table in the corner. Eddie was right behind her and a heartbeat away from calling her name when he lowered his gaze and stopped abruptly. Bloody hell! She had an arse the size of a two-car garage.

Within seconds he was outside and climbing back into his car. 'That was close,' he sniggered.

Twenty minutes later he received a message from Rachel, short and to the point: *Why?*

Arlo withdrew some cash from his bank account on Friday afternoon, took Saturday off then changed his rota to a Sunday morning shift that started at some ungodly hour. He intentionally arrived before his colleagues to scan the list of patients who'd been admitted the evening before. Saturday night was always busy at A&E; domestic violence, pub brawls and gang-related injuries kept the doctors and nurses on their toes.

Arlo was looking for anyone who had been shot or stabbed and might lead him to someone who would sell him a gun. It was a crazy idea, and he knew it. His job was on the line if word got out – but his life was on the line if things went pear-shaped.

A couple of minutes into his search, he found what he was looking for. Fifteen-year-old Daz had been brought in with a stab wound to his upper left arm. It wasn't life threatening so he was in the queue, accompanied by a police officer. Arlo quickly removed him from the waiting area and sat him in an empty examination room while the officer waited in the hall.

'You're lucky Daz,' he said. 'A couple of stitches and you'll be fine.' There was no response. 'Where did this happen?' The teenager remained silent. 'No problem, I'll get the information from the police officer, and while I'm at it I'll tell him about the drugs in your system.'

'I'm not on drugs,' Daz murmured.

'Eyes are a tell-tale sign of drug use, young man. Sometimes they dilate or pinpoint, become bloodshot or glassy. Yours are dilated. You have cocaine eyes, and I'll prove it if I do a blood test. I'm sure your parents and the police would like to know what you've been up to.'

There was a short pause as the youngster lifted his head.

Arlo continued, 'But if you help me, I'll help you.'

Daz appeared confused but interested.

'I want to buy a handgun,' Arlo whispered, after looking

over his shoulder. 'Can you help?'

The teenager's jaw dropped, then he looked around as if expecting to see a man with a microphone and a camera. 'You messing with me, man?'

Arlo shook his head as he finished stitching the wound. There was another short pause before he said softly, 'I'm serious.'

Daz took out his phone and sent off a text. Less than a minute later, the reply came: the deal was on. He conveyed details of the place, time and price through a combination of whispers and sign language.

Arlo nodded and gave him a thumbs-up as he pulled back the blue privacy curtain. 'He's all yours, officer. I've sewn up his arm and he's free to go.'

'Is he high on something?' asked the officer. 'I noticed he was slurring his words when the paramedics brought him in.'

'Trauma will do that to you,' Arlo replied. 'He's fine.'

❊ ❊ ❊

Steve and Lager finished tidying up outside the garage, washed the front door and positioned the sign. It looked good. Lager collected enough rubbish to fill a black sack while Steve removed several handfuls of weeds that were coming up through the gravel. They didn't touch the interior of the building; it wasn't necessary.

The last thing they had to do before leaving was to adjust the lock on the front door so that it opened without too much fuss. Lager fiddled with it then watched as it flew open after a gentle shove. 'No, too easy,' he said. A couple of turns with his screwdriver was all that was needed to make it tighter and less obvious.

As they walked away, he turned to Steve. 'What could possibly go wrong?' he joked.

On Monday afternoon Eddie was back at the Ugly Mug peering through the side window; this time it was Carol's turn to be placed under the spotlight. With the dating app open and her face staring back at him, he scanned the busy room from the far corners to the queue at the counter, then over to the wooden tables stretching from wall to wall. Nothing.

Just as he was about to return to his car a woman's voice behind him asked, 'Are you Eddie?'

He froze. Damn: this was embarrassing. He turned and muttered something inaudible as his cheeks warmed. He felt like a schoolboy caught playing with himself at the back of the classroom.

'Hi. I'm Carol,' the woman said. Eddie made an awkward nodding gesture. 'I was going to do the same thing,' she added.

'Huh?'

'Look through the window to check you out. I've had a couple of dodgy dates lately, so I'm being more selective.' She laughed and pointed to the front door. 'But you look harmless enough. Coffee?'

Eddie nodded again and followed her into the café. Once again, he found himself checking out a woman's backside – only this time he didn't turn and run. Why would he? She was fit.

As instructed by Daz, Arlo bought a ticket to the Cascade Cinema in Bracknell and sat in the back row, second seat in from the wall on the left side of the auditorium. A foreign film on a Monday afternoon meant only one thing: the place was almost empty.

He looked at the unoccupied seats; these kids were very clever. It was a pity they didn't channel their intelligence into something more constructive.

He fidgeted as he stared at the incessant adverts followed by the trailers, but then his heart rate quickened as the sound of an orchestra poured from hidden speakers and the opening credits flashed across the screen. Any moment now.

Two minutes into the film, he felt a tap on his shoulder.

'Excuse me sir, you're sitting in the wrong seat.'

Arlo turned his head. It was the kid who'd sold him his ticket.

'You're in a premium seat, but you paid for standard.'

'Does it matter where I sit?' Arlo snapped. 'There's only a handful of people in the bloody cinema.'

'There's no need to swear. I'm just doing my job and those are the rules. You'll have to move forward at least four rows.'

Arlo silently counted the rows in the direction of the screen. The second seat in from the wall on the left-hand side was free, but there were other people in the same row. This could be awkward.

Begrudgingly, he stepped into the aisle and moved forward. The kid was still there, po-faced and with both hands on his hips like some cinema Nazi. 'Bloody jobsworth,' Arlo mumbled.

While the characters spoke French, and English subtitles

flew across the bottom of the screen, Arlo stared at the rear of the auditorium. Ten, fifteen then twenty minutes passed before the door opened slightly and a shard of light crept in from the foyer. Within seconds the cinema was again cloaked in darkness.

A figure in black quietly shuffled along the wall and stood behind the seat Arlo had occupied previously. Arlo tried to get his attention by discreetly waving his left hand but there was no response. Frustrated, and not knowing what else to do, he stepped into the aisle and headed towards the back row.

The person in black immediately turned his back and hissed through gritted teeth, 'You idiot, I don't want you to see my face. That's why you were told to sit in the last row.'

Arlo apologised and started to explain but he was interrupted. 'Face the front and give me the money.'

Like a soldier reacting to an officer's command, Arlo obediently rotated 180 degrees then reached into his pocket and pulled out a roll of twenty-pound notes. 'It's all there,' he whispered.

'If it's not, you're dead,' came the muffled reply.

Arlo faced the screen until he heard the door behind him open and then close again. When he turned around, he was alone.

A plastic carrier bag lay at his feet.

7

Sixteen days earlier

When nineteen-year-old Qasim had travelled from Pakistan to the United Kingdom a few months earlier, it was a comfortable and straightforward experience. Accompanying his father in BA's business-class cabin, he had scoffed a three-course meal, watched a movie, napped and sailed unhindered through passport control at London's Heathrow Airport.

That was then, this was now, and things had changed. His sisters Rana and Benazir, both deceased, were known to security services for the roles they'd played while members of Al-Qaeda, so the odds were high that his name was on a border-patrol watchlist somewhere in the world. Luxury travel passing over marble-tiled floors with endless aisles filled with gold-rimmed, tax-free goods was no longer an option.

Qasim wiped the sleep from his eyes and drew a deep breath as he lifted his head to peer out of the side window of a beat-up 1967 VW camper van. It was a few minutes before midnight as the vehicle approached the bright lights of Karachi. He'd been travelling for more than fourteen hours on the back seat of an ageing bone shaker. His young body ached; his stomach rumbled.

'Can we stop for something to eat?' he shouted.

There was no reply, which came as no surprise; the driver hadn't spoken or even turned his head to look at his lone passenger during the entire trip. In this line of business knowing someone's name or seeing their face could be fatal.

The man behind the wheel had been paid by those linked to Rana and Benazir to pick up a package in Chaman, Pakistan and deliver it to a port in Karachi and that's what he was doing. Qasim was that package.

Crossing the Afghan-Pakistan border on foot the night before, the youngster had made his way to a quiet side street on the northern edge of Chaman where the VW camper van was waiting. He'd done exactly as he'd been told. With only enough money to last a few days, he was at the mercy of men who were nameless and faceless.

Karachi was buzzing with activity. Late-night markets and a wedding party parading down a main street forced the driver to take a circuitous route to the harbour. He wasn't alarmed by the detour; he had driven more than 800kms over bad roads littered with potholes, broken-down vehicles and animals of all shapes and sizes, some dead and some alive. Delays and diversions were to be expected.

Eventually, as the smell of the ocean grew stronger, he turned off the vehicle's engine and headlights and slipped the gear stick into neutral.

Surprised by the sudden silence and lack of light on the road ahead, Qasim braced himself. He watched in horror as the camper van careened from smooth tarmac to a rut-ridden dirt road and crossed a disused railway line before coming to an abrupt stop on a desolate, uneven patch of land.

For a moment all was still. Qasim picked up his rucksack and was about to speak when he heard the muffled sound of a vibrating phone coming from the vicinity of the driver's seat. As soon as the call ended, the driver ordered him to open the door and step outside.

At first the boy hesitated and stared blankly out of the window, but a second louder and more aggressive instruction had him grabbing the door handle. Once he was standing outside, the vehicle reversed across the track, negotiated a three-point turn and sped away.

Qasim stood in the darkness, open mouthed and alone.

On his left side, water was crashing against the rocks a few metres from where he was standing; in the distance to his right was the outline of a huge building, possibly a factory. Straight ahead, behind a chain fence topped with barbed wire, was Port Qasim. The teenager forced a smile when he saw his name on a sign dangling from the fence, but he knew this was not a welcome but a warning. At the bottom of the sign was written: *Trespassers will be punished.*

Qasim sat cross-legged on the ground; he didn't know what else to do. The journey to Karachi from Afghanistan had been choreographed by unknown forces who controlled him like a dog on a lead. This was the first time he had been left to his own devices – or so he thought.

Twenty-five minutes after the VW disappeared into the night, he spotted dim headlights and heard the familiar rattle of the van's tinny engine. He watched as it returned to where he was waiting. With the engine still running the driver, wrapped in his keffiyeh, climbed out of the van holding wire cutters. Two minutes later he was back behind the steering wheel having cut a large hole in the fence.

Qasim looked at the double-sided doors of the van as they flew open. 'You must be Qasim, the brave Pakistani warrior who is off to kill a load of people in England,' mocked the heavily bearded Englishman as he stood toe to toe with him.

Qasim took a step back and said nothing.

'Let's start at the beginning,' continued the Englishman as he gave him the once over. 'How will you get to England? Planes, trains or automobiles?' He chuckled. 'And when you get there, how will you execute your victims – especially as the main guy is ex-military and trained in bomb disposal? And finally, if you do pull off this amazing killing spree, how will you escape? Or do you plan to press the red button and seek out your allotted seventy-two virgins in the afterlife?'

Head down and silent, Qasim's only response was to nervously shuffle his feet.

'I thought so,' said the Englishman. 'Well, guess what? It's your lucky day, I'm your guardian angel. Now get your bag and follow me.'

Together they slipped through the opening in the fence and walked slowly and quietly to the water's edge where a small black inflatable rubber dinghy was tied to a rock. Once they were both inside the craft, the man handed Qasim a plastic oar. 'Can you row?'

Qasim shrugged his shoulders.

'Do it like this,' snapped the Englishman.

Qasim copied his movements and they set off along the shoreline. As they approached a large tanker, they could hear voices. The man pressed an index finger to his lips sending out a clear but unwanted message. *What does he think I'm going to do, start singing?* Qasim thought.

Waves continued to push the dinghy towards the hull of a second large vessel. The Englishman used his oar to separate rubber from steel, then both oars gently caressed the water as smoke and a strong smell of diesel fuel carpeted the sea around them.

A further ten minutes of paddling brought them to a wooden fishing boat sandwiched between two much larger vessels with a rope ladder hanging down at the stern. Qasim watched as the Englishman did a double take when he saw the name, *Fish Dady*, on the side of the boat. 'Please tell me this isn't it,' he muttered.

'What?' Qasim asked.

'This sad excuse for a ship is our ride to Djibouti.'

'Where's that?'

The Englishman pointed across the ocean. 'Eighteen hundred bloody nautical miles in that direction.'

Qasim, who was about to climb the ladder, quickly sat down on the edge of the dinghy, his mind suddenly filled with doubt, but with the ocean behind him and the Englishman's formidable stocky frame just inches away, he was stuck. There was no turning back.

An unfamiliar voice from on board shouted for them to hurry and both men clambered on deck. The dinghy drifted into the harbour.

Qasim's first impression was that his self-named 'guardian angel' was right: the boat didn't look seaworthy and was disgustingly filthy. Fish carcases dotted the deck and their pungent smell instantly attacked his nostrils and the back of his throat. He gagged as the captain, a short, overweight, bearded Middle Eastern man in his late fifties, gestured for them to follow him along the deck and down a set of stairs caked in slime. Qasim began to retch but somehow managed to keep it together.

A dimly lit passageway led to a storeroom where two sleeping bags were laid out on the floor. With a finger proudly pointing at his guests' beds for the next few nights, the captain joked in broken English, 'I do turn-down service. You like?'

As soon as they were alone, Qasim and the Englishman started rearranging the room. They removed damaged suitcases, an old fishing net interwoven with rope, a three-legged chair and numerous other pieces of junk that should have been chucked out years ago from the floor and stacked them against the walls so they could reposition the sleeping bags.

Qasim placed his backpack in a corner and sat on the sleeping bag while the Englishman removed his T-shirt and used it to wipe the sweat from his face and upper torso. A sudden chill ran through the teenager's veins; mouth open, he froze. As hard as he tried to be discreet, he couldn't divert his gaze from the tattoo of a large spider on the man's left shoulder.

Drawing his legs to his chest, he rocked back and forth like a frightened child. Eventually after a long period of silence, he plucked up the courage to ask, 'Are you the guy they call Spider?'

The Englishman bent down, withdrew a large knife from his backpack and rested the tip against Qasim's Adam's apple. 'Yes, I'm the guy they call Spider,' he replied calmly. 'And if I hear you say that word again, I'll slit your throat.'

Qasim recoiled. 'S-s-sorry,' he stuttered. 'What should I call you?'

Spider thought for a moment. 'Pierrepoint,' he announced.

'Pierrepoint?'.

'Yes, Pierrepoint, after the Pierrepoint family of executioners Henry, Thomas and Albert. Between them they hung more than eight hundred criminals.'

The boy shook his head as if he'd been asked a question.

The man sitting opposite him was quick to educate his young companion and there was no shortage of name dropping.

'Ruth Ellis, the last woman to be executed in Britain, Lord Haw-Haw the American born traitor who spread propaganda for the Nazis, serial killers and war criminals. The list goes on and on.' There was more than a hint of admiration in his voice.

There were so many things Qasim wanted to know but was afraid to ask. Spider or Pierrepoint, or whatever he called himself, was clearly obsessed with killing people and the last thing he wanted was to be one of those people. He would have to choose his words carefully. A few weeks in an Al-Qaeda training camp might have taught him how to handle an AK-47 but there was so much more to learn if he wanted to survive once he had fired the first shot.

'I'm very fortunate to have you as my "guardian angel"?' he blurted, as if trying to turn the conversation away from death.

'You are.' Spider sounded smug.

'How did that happen?'

'Do you mean why is an ISIS executioner helping some wannabe bin Laden?'

At that moment the boat's engines roared and the hull rocked from side to side. Qasim was tossed within inches of Spider's face but a solid push from the executioner's right forearm sent him crashing to the floor like a fly that had just been swatted by a rolled-up newspaper.

Spider continued, barely missing a beat. 'I have business to do in Bracknell. Someone there has a video of me and has invited me to come and get it.' A menacing smile settled on his face. 'And your Al-Qaeda friends said that you want to kill Steve Foley and his son in Bracknell because they blew up your sister who was about to blow up London.'

Qasim opened his mouth to speak but was immediately silenced by a stern look from the man towering over him.

'As ISIS is no more, I am now a legend for hire. And as you are a complete novice, I am your guardian angel thanks to a mutually satisfactory deal with Al-Qaeda.' Spider paused and then laughed. 'You couldn't make this shit up, could you?'

Qasim stayed silent, his mind spinning in all directions. *Guardian angel. More like an angel of death.*

8

Having just finished a double shift at the hospital, Arlo went home, sat at his desk and turned on his computer. He Googled: *What is the penalty for carrying a gun in the UK?*

Five years. With his chin resting on the palm of his left hand, he wriggled uneasily as he stared at the screen. *And it's a life sentence if you use it to kill someone*, was added to the search engine's reply.

Arlo swallowed hard and opened the bottom drawer of the desk. There it was in plain sight: five years or life.

Steve didn't react to the sound of the mail hitting the wooden floor at the end of the hall. Bills, junk mail and charity begging letters were the norm, so no reason to hurry or interrupt his morning cup of tea. Besides, Eddie was coming down the stairs and about to pass by the postman's contribution to the recycling bin.

'Where's the post?' he asked when his son strolled empty handed into the kitchen. His question went unanswered as Eddie reached for a box of cereal. 'You stepped right over it. Why didn't you pick it up?' insisted Steve.

Eddie sighed loudly then muttered something inaudible.

'Eddie,' Steve snapped.

'What? It's bloody junk.'

Frustrated, Steve threw his arms in the air. A knock at the door temporarily ended the discussion and they lapsed into a childish first-one-to-blink contest. There was another knock but still neither man moved. The stone-faced stares continued until there was a much louder third tap and Steve relented.

'Lager,' he grumbled as he opened the door.

'And it's nice to see you too,' the ex-cop mocked, bending over to pick up the post.

'Sorry. I'm having a bad morning. Coffee?'

By the time they reached the kitchen, Eddie had gone into another room.

'I found your wife's address through a friend who works at DVLA,' Lager said. 'It was easy once she bought a car.'

'Thanks. I'll let Victoria know about Qasim. Maybe she can hide away with one of her many lovers. That should keep the kid from Pakistan busy for a while.'

'Ouch,' Lager retorted. 'So what's the plan?'

'Carry on as normal and wait for our skinny friend to step into the garage. It's just a matter of time. I'm sure he's watching us.'

※ ※ ※

With the revolver nestled in his right hand, Arlo strolled into the hall and positioned himself in front of a full-length mirror. Like a gunslinger in a western movie, he lowered the weapon to his hip, stared into his own eyes and whispered, 'Draw.'

As he raised the gun, he discovered he was no Clint Eastwood. Instead of arriving at a shooting position, the pistol banged against the corner of his phone in his trouser pocket, slipped from his hand and crashed to the floor. Annoyed, he cursed. picked it up, put it back in the drawer and threw himself onto the sofa.

With his head in his hands, he sat gazing at the floor with Lorraine's words echoing around in his head. *'If the police won't help, maybe you should start packing.'*

After a long period of reflection, he suddenly had what he thought was a eureka moment. Returning to Google, he started searching for information about bodyguards. 'Genius,' he said aloud. 'If I can't stop him, I'll hire a man who can.'

The list was long and detailed. Ex-forces personnel, retired police officers, boxers and even a professional Lucha Libre Mexican wrestler offered themselves as experts in close protection. Some had little or no experience while most were very expensive, but a more in-depth search revealed two that fell within his budget.

Feeling elated, Arlo started to relax. Then, just as things looked like they were going his way, he glanced at the brief yet succinct comment written in bold letters lower down the page: *Close-protection officers are not permitted to carry guns or any other weapons, including pepper spray, mace, batons or tasers.*

'What the hell?' he blurted. 'This is crazy. How do you stop a killer like Spider with your bare hands?'

It was a rhetorical question and he knew it. A moment later he collected the gun from the drawer and tucked it inside his belt.

'So,' teased Carol, 'we've moved on from a simple cappuccino the other day to pie and a pint. What's next? Somewhere they have cutlery?'

She was funny, took the piss, and Eddie enjoyed that. She wasn't anything like the local girls he'd been hitting on since his teens; most of them couldn't string more than three words together and didn't try. For them, being in a relationship meant tossing someone off in the cinema.

Carol had class. She was good looking, worldly wise and her dad was in the Scots Guards. What more could a guy want?

'A penny for your thoughts?' she asked.

Eddie had been 'off with the fairies', as his dad used to say. He quickly recovered. 'Just trying to think of somewhere I've been where they use knives and forks.'

When Carol laughed, her eyes lit up.

'Your profile mentions you did some charity work,' added Eddie.

'Yes. I was with a small refugee medical unit in Turkey, then in Iraq.'

'Iraq? Wow, that must have been dangerous. Where were you?'

Carol hesitated then lowered her head. 'It was a very traumatic time. I'd rather not talk about it, if you don't mind.'

'Of course, no problem.'

'What about you?'

'Well, according to the guy behind the bar, I'm an open book,' Eddie retorted.

Carol glanced at the bartender and smiled. 'I did read about you. I couldn't help it – you were everywhere.'

'And yet you still wanted to meet me?'

※ ※ ※

Steve slipped into his On Guard jacket and placed a black baseball cap on his head. With keys in hand, he opened the front door and came face to face with Victoria. Taken by surprise, his greeting was awkward and unwelcoming. 'Bloody hell,' he blurted out.

His ex-wife took a step back. 'Well, that was nice,' she said sarcastically.

Caught like a deer in a car's headlights, he stood open mouthed as he struggled to take in the woman she had become. Short, spikey red hair replaced shoulder-length strands of premature grey. Her makeup was subtle yet flattering, her nails immaculate. Gone were the plain, sometimes drab, high-street clothes.

'Are you going to invite me in?'

Steve stepped aside. 'The house is still half yours.'

As she walked into the kitchen, she immediately made the purpose of her visit clear. She didn't even bother to sit down. 'I want a divorce and half the house.'

'Anything else?'

She gave a slight shake of the head.

'That's fine,' Steve snapped. 'I'll sort it. Give me your number.'

'Are you angry? You must have been expecting this.'

Steve didn't get to answer. The front door swung open and Eddie, fresh from lunch with Carol, bounced in whistling some unrecognisable tune. When he saw his mother in the kitchen he stopped. 'Bloody hell.'

'Like father like son,' she mocked.

'Let me guess,' he sniped. 'You're here to pick up some of your dead son's clothes for your latest illegitimate child.'

'Eddie—' Steve shouted, but his son ignored him.

'Or maybe you finally want to apologise for destroying this family?' Eddie went on.

'That's enough,' Steve growled.

A long silence filled the room until, head bowed, Victoria squeezed past the two men and moved slowly into the hall. As she moved to the front door, Steve called out, 'A guy called Qasim from Pakistan has threatened our family.'

She stopped, facing the door.

'And like it or not,' Steve added, 'you're still part of this family.'

'Is this because of what Eddie did to that girl in Afghanistan?' she asked.

'I didn't do anything,' Eddie protested. 'I was miles away at the time. Haven't you read anything about me during the past three months, or have you been too busy spreading your legs?'

Victoria turned to Steve as if looking for support but he remained silent. 'So why are we being threatened?' she asked.

'Qasim wants revenge for the death of his other sister, Benazir,' Steve told her. 'She was killed when the small plane she was in exploded at Fair Way Airport.'

'What's that got to do with us – or should I say you?'

Steve didn't reply.

'Oh, I get it,' Victoria said. 'The clue is in the word "exploded". My husband is no longer disposing of bombs, he's making them.' She faked a laugh. 'And you say *I* destroyed this family?'

'Benazir was a terrorist who was about to blow up London,' Eddie objected. 'Dad did the right thing.'

Steve felt his wife's wrath as she locked on to his gaze. 'Where were the police and security services? Why do *you* always have to be the hero? Maybe if you'd spent less time saving the world and more time saving our marriage, I wouldn't be asking for a divorce.'

Eddie's face turned red with rage and he looked like he was about to explode, but Steve had heard it all before and he wasn't going down that road again. With a gentle hand, he motioned to Eddie to chill then opened the front door to give Victoria an escape route. Within seconds, all was still.

'Lager got your address from someone at DVLA,' Steve announced as she stepped onto the front porch. 'I'm not sure if Qasim has contacts there but you should move in with a friend until this is over.'

'And when might that be?' she asked.

'I'm working on it.'

'Of course, you are,' Victoria mocked. 'Of course, you are.'

9

Eight days earlier

Sunrise was just moments away. A gentle breeze caressed Qasim's face as he stood with his back to the Gulf of Aden on the starboard side of the boat. Djibouti harbour was slowly appearing over the horizon. The sea was calm. For the first time since leaving Karachi, he wasn't leaning over the side of the boat; his stomach had settled, and his head was no longer spinning.

'One thousand seven hundred and ninety-seven nautical miles in just over eight days,' declared the ship's captain with his eyes on Spider. 'Not bad for a sad excuse for a boat, is it, my friend?'

Qasim chuckled silently to himself. He could see that Spider was not amused but tolerated the skipper's piss-taking because crossing the sea meant avoiding overland treks through countries such as Iran, Iraq, Jordan and Egypt where the death penalty awaited him. The Middle East was not a friend of the ISIS executioner.

'And did you notice that no pirates were chasing us in the Gulf of Aden?' added the skipper.

Qasim swallowed hard as he quickly scanned the horizon.

'I have no money, no one to pay a ransom, and my boat is worth nothing to them,' continued the chubby captain. He forced a sinister grin and raised his arms to make his point.

'But if they'd known I had such valuable cargo on board, they would have been like bees around honey as you English like to say.' He laughed as he manoeuvred the boat to head in a southerly direction.

'Thank you,' said Qasim.

Spider jumped in. 'If you think he did this for nothing, you are stupider than you look.'

Qasim backed off slightly and kept his gaze on the captain. 'Why are we heading south? Aren't we going to the harbour?'

'For Christ sake, you *are* stupider than you look,' Spider shouted. 'What do you think would happen if we tied up front and centre, strolled into the customs house and handed them our passports?'

The boy had run out of space to retreat. Despite the cool movement of air across his face, he felt a sudden warm glow on his cheeks. He was out of his depth and he knew it.

'We are going to Beach of Douda,' the captain announced.

'No way,' Spider protested. 'That's not far from the Somali border.'

'Don't worry. A motorboat will pick you up and take you to Djibouti shore. Everything good.'

Spider wasn't convinced. Qasim watched as the terrorist placed his hand deep inside his backpack, withdrew a handgun, tucked it into his belt and covered it with his T-shirt.

Fifteen minutes later the captain of *Fish Dady* cut the engines and slowly came to rest about three hundred metres off Beach of Douda. A motorboat with one man on board was approaching from the coast. 'Look,' the captain shouted. 'Here comes boat.'

Relief swamped Qasim as the motorboat came closer. He was tired of being seasick, inhaling foul odours, eating strange food and sleeping inches away from a psychopath. *Anything but this*, he thought.

With their lift to the shore so close, he pressed the toggles and tightened the straps on his backpack then placed it over his shoulders. It wasn't long before the man in the small craft pulled up next to *Fish Dady* and shut off the engine. Qasim put both legs over the side and quickly lowered himself on to the motorboat.

'Why did he do that?' Spider shouted as he followed.

'Do what?' Qasim asked.

'The engine. Why shut it off?' Spider stepped within inches of the man holding the throttle and yelled, 'Start the fucking engine.'

The man made a feeble attempt to pull the cord but the engine remained silent. Qasim could see panic in Spider's eyes as the motorboat bobbed helplessly on the water and *Fish Dady* pulled away.

A sudden roar drew all eyes to the south. A speedboat with two massive outboard motors and two men on board was suddenly within spitting distance. The man standing at the rear of the boat was pointing an automatic rifle at them. The second man manoeuvred alongside with both hands on the wheel.

Qasim watched in horror as the men, wearing balaclavas and black T-shirts, screamed in a language he didn't understand.

Instructions from Spider came thick and fast. 'Move to the front, raise your hands, look at them and keep shouting, "Don't shoot, I surrender".'

Shaking uncontrollably, Qasim did as he was told. With his eyes on their assailants, he saw their gaze focus on him and in that instant heard two shots. The armed man instantly fell backwards into the water; the driver lay hunched over the wheel. Except for the roar of the outboard motors, all was now calm.

With his hands still aloft, Qasim turned to face the stern. His eyes widened and he screamed, 'Spider!'

The executioner turned quickly and, without the slightest hesitation, fired a shot into the chest of the man next to him. A large machete fell from his victim's hand as the lifeless body crumpled to its knees.

Spider tipped him over the side, collected the weapon and handed it to Qasim. 'The guy at the wheel is still breathing. Finish him off.'

Like a robot, Qasim stepped onto the attacker's boat and stood in a trance over the wounded driver. 'Do it,' barked Spider, successfully re-starting the motor. 'We haven't got all day.'

Qasim looked up at the sky, raised the machete in his right hand, but froze, once more.

'Those shots I fired will have been heard for miles,' Spider said. 'More pirates will follow. Kill him now.'

Qasim swayed back and forth as if to strike, but his arm remained locked high above his head.

'You have two choices,' Spider continued calmly. 'Either you kill him or I kill you.'

Qasim turned and saw a gun pointing at his head. With gritted teeth and closed eyes, he gave a traumatised scream as the machete dropped like a guillotine onto the back of the wounded man's neck.

Spider was quick to comment. 'You have a lot to learn.'

Splattered in blood and shaking uncontrollably, Qasim returned to the smaller boat while Spider positioned the dead man's arms through the opening in the steering wheel and pointed the bow out to sea. Once back beside Qasim, he slammed down hard on the throttle of the twin-engine craft and watched as it raced into open water. With no time for reflection, the pair headed to the shore.

Blood floated on the surface as Qasim dipped his right hand into the sea. His back was now straight and his head turned in the direction of Djibouti. He didn't look at the man who threatened him until they stepped on to the beach.

'I'm still going to kill you,' Spider said.

'Why?'

'You called me Spider.'

Qasim stopped walking, glared at the back of Spider's head and thought, *Is he serious? I saved his life.*

10

After seven visits to the garage in two days and still no sign of any suspicious activity, Steve was getting frustrated. Where was that bloody kid?

After a cursory check of the door lock, the camera and the interior set up, he returned to his van and flipped down the sun visor. A happy, smiling family photo, attached to the visor with a couple of elastic bands, temporarily lifted his spirits but then a switch in his brain hit fast forward to the present day. Victoria was gone, Tim was dead and Eddie was struggling with his demons and had mentally, if not physically, left the family home.

'I couldn't have scripted this disaster if I tried,' he mumbled.

A gentle tap on the window drew his attention. An old man with a long, unkempt, salt-and-pepper beard dressed in a tattered brown duffel coat was gesturing for Steve to roll down his window. According to Eddie, the guy owned the antique warehouse shack across from the garage and was not only eccentric but a real pain in the arse.

Steve hesitated at first but finally gave in following a second tap. 'Can I help you?'

The old man stuck his head through the opening on the passenger side and a cocktail of stale piss and rancid breath filled the van. Steve rapidly climbed out of his vehicle and continued the conversation across the bonnet. 'Can I help you?' he repeated.

After a couple of false starts, the old man said that someone had broken into his warehouse on at least two occasions. 'Did you tell the police?' Steve asked.

'No point. Nothing was stolen.'

'So how can you be sure someone broke in?'

'Two pieces of furniture were moved and I didn't do it.'

Steve didn't want to hear any more. He went back to the van and switched on the ignition, but before he could reverse the man stuck his head through the window again. 'A small table and chair were put by my window.'

'And?' Steve snapped.

'The window looks over your garage. And I found this thing on the floor under the table.' He was dangling a mobile-phone charging cable from his fingers.

Steve turned off the engine and stepped out of the van to have a look inside the warehouse. Two minutes later he was back behind the wheel. 'Thanks,' he said, 'I'll look into it.'

His pulse was racing. The trap was set and the mouse was about to take the bait. A brief call to Lager covered everything the old man had said. 'I'm sure the kid is watching us,' Steve added before ending the call.

With both hands back on the steering wheel, he realised that once again his son Eddie had not been first on the list to hear the news. It was wrong and he knew it, but still his phone remained deep inside his pocket.

Later that same day, Eddie arrived to inspect the garage. Within seconds the owner of the antique warehouse was heading in his direction, pointing his finger. 'I don't need this,' he moaned before the old man shouted, 'I had a break in.'

'Why would anybody break in your place?' Eddie demanded. 'There's nothing in there worth stealing.'

'Maybe that's what you think, but your boss said he'll look into it.' He repeated word for word what he'd told Steve earlier.

Eddie was furious. He scrolled down to his father's number then stopped as a change of mind took him to Lager's mobile. He made the call.

'Hi, Eddie.'

'Lager, did you hear what happened at the garage?'

'Yes,' the ex-cop replied. 'Got a call from your dad about an hour ago. Good news. Sounds like the kid is watching us and may be ready to make a move.'

Once again Eddie felt left out. Annoyed, he didn't even bother to say goodbye. He'd heard enough.

With his newly purchased leather manbag draped over his shoulder, Arlo drove to an isolated wooded area not far from a military firing range. He hadn't fired a live round before and thought it wise to let off at least one, just in case. Being near the military firing range, where explosions of all kinds were a regular occurrence, provided the perfect cover.

A video on Google had shown him the basics about loading and holding the gun, body and arm positioning and squeezing the trigger, and he'd practised aiming and firing without ammunition in his bedroom with the curtains drawn. Now it was time for the real thing.

He put the manbag on the ground, open just wide enough to remove the weapon. With both hands positioned perfectly, his arms slightly bent and his eye looking along the open sight, he raised his arms until they were parallel to the ground. Slowly he rotated to his right and stopped when a large tree trunk appeared in front of him.

'Spider, this is for Jennifer,' he shouted as he fired into a mound of dirt about twenty feet away.

A deafening bang echoed through the trees, Arlo's body recoiled and the weapon jerked upward. An unplanned second squeeze of the trigger sent him leaning back on his heels with his eyes looking skyward. Off balance and disorientated he loosened his grip, dropped the gun and tumbled to the ground.

'Good God,' he gasped, both arms shaking. 'What am I thinking?'

※ ※ ※

Back at her flat, Victoria studied the soiled white envelope that had come through the letter box. There was no stamp, no address, just her name on the front, and she didn't recognise the handwriting. With the envelope tucked under her jumper, she swiftly moved along the hall past the kitchen where Jermaine was warming up a baby bottle.

Once in the bathroom, she locked the door, opened the sealed flap and withdrew a photo of two women. At first she was puzzled – but it all became clear when she turned over the photo and read the note written on the back in a childish scribble.

My sisters Rana and Benazir are dead. Your family killed them so your family must also die. Q

Her initial reaction was to curse Steve and Eddie but then fear quickly took over.

She thought twice about telling the father of her child in the kitchen. He'd ditched her soon after the baby was born then showed up the other day begging forgiveness. She didn't love or trust him, but she hated being alone.

There was no alternative; she needed to confide in someone. With the photo in her hand and tears in her eyes, she hurried to Jermaine's side. There was so much to tell him yet she had difficulty finding the words and putting them in the correct order. Finally, she took a deep breath, sat at the kitchen table and started to speak.

'Jermaine, we need to get out of this place now or I'm dead.'

Startled, Jermaine sat open mouthed and listened as he fed the baby. Most of what she told him he'd read in the papers or seen on the telly: it was old news. But when she told him about her conversation with Steve and showed him the note on the back of the photo, she had his full attention.

'If I was back in Jamaica I'd get my gun, place it on my lap and wait for that bastard to come through the door.'

'We're not *in* Jamaica and you don't have a gun. Any more stupid ideas?' Victoria snapped.

'We could call the police.'

'And what could they do? We don't even know where Qasim is.'

'How about if we go to the press? We could tell them about Steve putting the bomb on the plane that killed Qasim's sister. That would soon get the cops on board.'

'Another brilliant idea. And what will you do when the cops come to investigate your claim and ask to see some identification? How many years have you been here illegally?'

Jermaine stared sheepishly at the floor. There was a long silence as Victoria caressed Anne's cheek as the baby lay cuddled in Jermaine's muscular arms.

'We're screwed,' she whispered. 'We really are screwed.'

Wearing a baseball cap pulled down to just above his eyes, and with his leather manbag hanging off his shoulder, Arlo entered through a trades' entrance at the rear of the hospital.

'Keep the bad guys guessing,' he mumbled as he dodged trolleys laden with boxes of cleaning fluid, dirty laundry and tightly wrapped, bulging black bin sacks. Once through two sets of automatic double doors, he headed for the men's locker room.

'What's with the manbag, Arlo?' Lorraine teased as he was about to push open the door.

Arlo stopped abruptly and closed his eyes. *I don't need this*, he thought.

'It's very European,' she said as she moved closer. 'What do you keep in there?'

Arlo lowered his arm alongside his body to cover the bag, raised his cap slightly and looked her in the eyes. 'I've got a handgun and a few rounds of ammunition. Bring on Spiderman.'

With his gaze fixed steadily on Lorraine, he watched as she back-pedalled slightly, thought for a moment then laughed out loud. 'Knowing you, it's probably a piece of fruit and a couple of tuna sandwiches. See you at the desk. The waiting room is packed, but you knew it would be.'

She walked away chuckling as she repeated Arlo's line about having a gun and ammunition, though he was confused as to why she was speaking in an American accent. He breathed a sigh of relief when she disappeared around the corner.

He put the bag in his locker and tucked the key deep in his pocket. A second tug at the metal door handle, followed by a third, confirmed the locker was secure. It was time to go to work.

As he left the room, he bumped into a colleague. 'Just the man I wanted to see,' Dr Gurminder Singh said.

'What's up?'

'Lorraine said you had a manbag. Can I see it? I'm thinking of getting one.'

'Sorry, no time.' Arlo didn't slow his pace as he turned in the direction of A&E. 'I'm needed.'

'No problem,' said Singh. 'We're on the same shift so I can check it out when you finish.'

❊ ❊ ❊

A frantic cry from Anne in the nursery down the hall woke Victoria from a sound sleep. The illuminated red numbers on the bedside clock announced it was 3.17am.

She rolled onto her back and waited but the sobbing continued. Lifting her head from the pillow, she saw that Jermaine was no longer in bed next to her. *Hmm*, she thought, *first time for everything.*

She lowered her head again, closed her eyes and turned on her side but the cries grew louder. She listened intently; there were no sounds other than those coming from the baby.

Reluctantly she sat up, slipped into her dressing gown and

went to the door. As her fingers clasped the handle, she stopped, turned around and crept towards the dressing table on the far side of the room. Taking a large pair of scissors from the top left-hand drawer, she held them in front of her face.

'Damn you, Steve,' she whispered.

She moved cautiously along the hall and looked to her right: the tiny kitchen was clear. Raising the scissors, she tiptoed to the living room. Also clear. Outside the nursery she took a breath, steeled herself, then barged through the partially open door.

The glow from a nightlight plugged into the wall gave enough illumination for Victoria to scan the room and confirm that Anne was alone. She picked up the baby and gently patted her back. 'Jermaine?' she called quietly.

When calm was restored, she returned the baby to her cot and went to the only room she hadn't checked. The bathroom door was shut; she knocked but there was no response. She opened the door and turned on the light. Another empty room.

'It's 3.30 in the bloody morning, Jermaine. Where are you?'

There was a towel on the floor and she picked it up, folded it and hung it on the rail next to the bath. As she turned, she caught sight of herself in the mirror and grimaced. She looked tired, dishevelled.

She ran her fingers through her hair and wiped the sleep from the corner of her eyes. Her gaze slid down to the white porcelain basin where there was a bar of soap, some cotton buds and a yellow plastic cup holding their toothbrushes and toothpaste. Something wasn't right.

She looked, then looked again. It was several seconds before she realised what it was: Jermaine's toothbrush wasn't in the cup. It had been there when she'd gone to bed – she remembered thinking that it needed a good scrub.

She scanned the white tiles on the floor and the area around the bath. After a moment's though, she moved to the tiny cupboard next to the front door. Jermaine's suitcase had gone.

Back in the bedroom, she emptied the contents of her handbag onto the duvet. Her wallet had gone, too. 'You bastard,' she shouted.

Stethoscope draped around his neck, Dr Singh pulled back the blue curtain and entered Consultation Room 4. Arlo seized the opportunity and immediately headed back to the doctor's locker room. With his manbag under his arm, he jogged to his car, about twenty-five metres away at the rear of the building.

Opening the driver's door, he removed the gun from the bag and started to shove it under the seat. A beam of light lit up the inside of the car, startling him. His hand jerked slightly and the weapon slid onto the mat, coming to rest next to the accelerator.

The voice was polite but firm. 'Please leave the gun where it is and move away from the vehicle.'

Arlo cursed silently but did as he was told. Steve appeared out of the shadows, picked up the weapon and tucked it into his belt. 'I can explain later,' Arlo pleaded. 'But I must get back to work.'

'Are you the doctor whose car I blocked with my van the other day?'

Arlo nodded and gestured impatiently towards the hospital.

100

'Call me when you finish your shift,' Steve told him. 'Here's my card.'

Four hours later, Arlo was waiting by his locker. When Dr Singh approached, he held up the manbag. 'Do you like it?'

'Yes, it's very nice.'

'Then it's yours.' Arlo placed the bag in the doctor's hands and hurried out of the room.

A cool breeze caressed his face as he stepped into the morning sunshine. Fresh air replaced the amalgam of cleaning agents, body odour and other smells that had assailed his nostrils during the past nine hours.

Once he was safely ensconced inside his car he closed his eyes for a moment, enjoying a silence that had not been available to him during the night. A tap on the side window startled him.

'You okay?' Lorraine asked. Arlo lowered the window and nodded. 'You gave Dr Singh your new bag. Was it something I said?'

'No, it wasn't anything you said. It just wasn't me.'

He started the engine but Lorraine didn't move away. 'I see you've stopped shaving and you're letting your hair grow. If this is your way of disguising yourself, it may help to remove your name tag.'

Arlo glanced down at the piece of plastic pinned to his coat.

'So, what are you doing about Spider?' she went on.

'Not sure. I thought I had the answer, but it turns out that wasn't me either.'

※ ※ ※

Still sulking because he'd been left out of the loop, Eddie spent the night shift working as far away from his father as possible. When it was time to meet up to cover the notorious Cramer Industrial Estate, where gangs fought and a teenager had fallen to his death from a sixth-storey window, he went AWOL.

Later that morning, breakfast at the Foley kitchen table was a tense affair. 'You didn't make it over to Cramer last night,' Steve remarked.

'I got delayed.'

'Must have been serious.'

Tight lipped, Eddie continued stirring his coffee. Steve's phone rang but before answering it, he made sure he had the last word. 'Fortunately, Eddie, I didn't need you. Lager had my back.'

Eddie lowered his head and gritted his teeth.

Steve picked up his keys and headed for the front door.

A blanket of threatening black cloud hung over the Red Dragon pub. In the distance, thunder roared a warning of what was to come. Arlo, feeling anxious about his ten-thirty meeting with Steve, stayed in his car, engine running. The windscreen wipers suddenly screeched as they brushed away the first tiny drops of rain, then the heavens opened without warning and the wipers doubled their pace.

With his car parked facing the only entrance to the pub, Arlo squinted through the water-covered window searching for Steve's van with the On Guard logo emblazoned on its side; he was also watching for anyone who might be watching him.

At exactly ten-thirty, Steve pulled into the car park. Arlo flashed his lights like someone in a spy movie then immediately regretted it.

The van backed into the space next to Arlo's and Steve gestured for him to come over. 'I guess one of us has to get wet,' Arlo said before hurrying to the passenger seat. He reached out his damp right hand and Steve responded with a grip that sent a shock wave up his arm.

Tanned, fit, back straight, and still sporting his marine number-four haircut, Steve looked much younger than his forty-three years. Arlo, slouched and pale, glanced at his bulging stomach and was aware of his own weak handshake. What had happened to that man in Mosul who had fought and killed a terrorist in a water tank? Would anyone believe him if he told the story now?

'So what's with the gun?' Steve asked.

'I bought it for protection.' When Steve didn't respond, Arlo knew who was supposed to do the talking.

Steve waited patiently as Arlo gathered his thoughts. After a long pause, the doctor gave a complete history of the events in Mosul in June 2014. The part where he drowned an ISIS fighter drew a raised eyebrow from his companion, but nothing more. After he'd finished, Arlo passed over his phone. As Steve scrolled through the photos and videos, his expression changed from curiosity to shock, and finally to anger.

'This was several years ago. Why do you need protection now?' he asked.

'Because I had to get revenge for Jen's death. I told her killer I had pictures of him committing atrocities and if he wanted them back he should come and get them.' Arlo lowered his head; not for the first time, he realised the stupidity and recklessness of his actions.

'Who is he?' Steve asked.

'He calls himself Spider. I don't know his real name.'

Steve's head jerked. The tension in his face disappeared and was replaced with a sinister smile. 'Why are you smiling?' Arlo demanded.

'I've heard of this guy – in fact, anyone who's ever set foot in Iraq or Syria knows about him. He's a legend. This is good news.'

Confused, Arlo protested, 'You sound like you're happy he's coming here to kill me!'

Steve didn't respond; instead he closed his eyes and seemed to be talking to himself. 'He's not strong or courageous, so when he comes he won't be alone.'

Even more confused, Arlo asked, 'What are you talking about?'

'Is it just a coincidence? Would Al-Qaeda and ISIS join forces?'

'I haven't got a clue what you're talking about!'

Steve opened his eyes. 'Someone is coming from Pakistan to kill me, my family and my friends. I've been told that person won't be alone.'

'Bloody hell. Sounds like you need the gun more than I do!'

The ringtone on Steve's mobile interrupted them. Even without the speaker, Arlo could hear the caller's words. 'Dad! Mum has just moved back into the house and she's got Baby Reggae with her.'

'Don't do anything stupid, Eddie.' Steve's words were a command, not a request. 'I'll be there shortly.' He cut the call, reached under his seat and offered Arlo the gun. 'Do you really want this?'

Arlo shook his head. 'I've spent most of my life trying to save lives. I can't start taking them now.'

'You're right. That's my job. Keep your head down and I'll think of something. I don't believe they're in the country yet so we have some time.'

'Anything else?'

'Send me those photos.'

Arlo swallowed hard, transferred the pictures then got out of the car. Hardly aware of the torrential rain that was bombarding him, he slowly returned to his own vehicle. He was assailed by doubts. *Did I just make a useful ally, or have I doubled my chances of being killed?*

11

It felt good to be back on dry land. Having survived the attack by Somali pirates, Spider and Qasim were anxious to get a flight out of the area.

They jogged from the beach and took cover in the trees about twenty-five metres from what appeared to be an abandoned single-engine airplane. Ten minutes passed before they moved in for a closer look. With his gun drawn, Spider glided silently across the grass to the tail of the aircraft. His eyes widened and his heart sank.

Fish Dady had been a pile of junk and this mode of transport was a close second. The Cessna 205 had been built in the early sixties; now parked in a neglected farmer's field, it looked like it was being held together with string and duct tape.

His right hand brushed over a metal patch botch-welded onto the body of the plane and memories of his mother attempting to sew denim patches on his ripped jeans while high on crack came flooding back.

While Qasim did as he'd been told and kept an eye on the perimeter, Spider opened the door beneath the wing. At first the interior appeared empty, but then the sound of snoring drew his attention away from the cockpit. The pilot, still clinging to an empty bottle of vodka, had passed out in the passenger seat.

It took several hours to get the man back on his feet and by then it was too dark to fly. At sunrise, Spider frogmarched the pilot down to the beach and chucked him in the water. His objective was twofold: sober the guy up and wash away the stench that emanated from his body. Next he carried out a thorough search of the aircraft but found no weapons.

With their bags stowed, the door shut and seat belts fastened, Spider glanced at the controls: the dial on the fuel gauge was hovering just above empty. Fuming, he stuck the barrel of his handgun in the pilot's mouth and waited.

As the man shook and sweat poured down his face, Spider asked calmly, 'Are we good?'

'Yes, yes! We good,' he stuttered.

'That's nice to hear because if we don't fly you die.'

The pilot kept nodding as he muttered, 'We fly, we fly.'

The first attempt to start the engine failed but finally the plane lifted off and headed for Yoboki. There they picked up food and fuel before crossing Ethiopia to Khartoum in the Sudan.

The journey was anything but pleasant. Searing heat, coupled with endless clouds of desert sand, permeated the cabin; turbulence tossed the lightweight aircraft around like a piece of paper in a hurricane. It was just as painful as being knocked about by massive waves on the Arabian sea.

Qasim, afraid to say anything that might endanger his life, stayed silent throughout the entire journey. He checked his phone and sent a text. *We're in Africa. Horrible trip.*

Five minutes later he received a reply. *Who is with you? I thought you were alone.*

Qasim winced, knowing he'd made a mistake.

The Cessna finally touched down on a narrow dirt road a

few miles from Khartoum. Once again it was good to be back on solid ground.

To avoid Libya and Algeria, the plan was to travel 2,300kms through Chad to the city of N'Djamena. They had a ten-hour drive in a forty-year-old Chevrolet pick-up truck to their next stop, Niamey in Niger. Satisfied there were no concealed weapons, Spider jumped into the passenger seat while Qasim had no option but to sit in the back where he was completely exposed to the elements. The driver offered his keffiyeh and Qasim accepted it gratefully, glad to be able to cover his head from the scorching mid-day sun.

Back home in Peshawar, Pakistan, Qasim had played in the midfield for the local football team. He'd been good though not the best; with no interest in sports, his focus had been on Pakistani politics. Despite training with Al-Qaeda, he was neither physically nor mentally prepared for this journey and with each stage he became weaker and more disillusioned.

For what seemed like an eternity he sat on the steel floor of the truck beaten, bruised and caked in dust.

The driver stopped for a toilet break on the outskirts of Niamey, the second in ninety minutes. Spider remained in the truck while Qasim climbed over the tailgate to stretch his legs. The driver headed for a bush at the side of the road, but instead of relieving himself he made a call.

When Qasim drew closer, the driver paused and asked him if he spoke French. The boy shrugged his shoulders, mumbled something in Pashto and went through a series of stretching motions before casually moving to the passenger window.

'I heard him speaking French on his phone,' he whispered to Spider while glancing at the driver in the distance.

'I know a few Arabic words but I never got the hang of languages in school,' Spider said. 'You speak French?'

'A little.'

'Do you know what he said?'

'*Araignée.*'

'What does that mean?' questioned Spider.

'Spider,' Qasim replied.

When the driver returned to the cab of the pick-up, he felt the cold steel of Spider's gun barrel pressed firmly against the side of his head. His eyes closed and his body slouched as Qasim whispered, '*Araignée.*'

Using the teenager's limited French, they learned that a trap had been set this side of Niamey: a diversion sign would take them along the southern edge of the city through a narrow one-way street in a residential area. With both ends of the street blocked and no side exits, they'd be surrounded. Ten American dollars was the payment for betrayal.

Qasim watched in horror as Spider pulled the driver into the bushes and forced him to his knees.

Spider gestured for the boy to join him then thrust a massive hunting knife in his hand. When Qasim hesitated, Spider turned the gun on him. It was kill or be killed and for the second time in just a few days Qasim did what he had to do to stay alive.

He wiped the blood from his hands and the blade of the knife on some tall blades of grass. When he returned to the truck, he flipped down the visor to shade his eyes from the sun and saw a photo of a woman hand in hand with two young girls on the underside of it.

His gaze locked onto the picture until Spider quickly removed it and threw it out of the window. 'Sentimentality will get you killed,' he snapped.

Qasim took a breath, pulled the driver's keffiyeh over his head and stared out of the side window.

A single act of disloyalty, although unacceptable, was expected in this part of the world where money was king but Spider knew that a second attempt on his life could mean only one thing: someone in ISIS or Al-Qaeda wasn't happy with this arrangement and wanted it to end badly.

The original plan had been to head south and change the vehicle and driver at the Burkina Faso border, but now the risk was too high. Spider and Qasim had no choice but to go it alone.

Nouakchott, Mauritania, where a tanker was waiting for them, was a two-day drive. Taking turns behind the wheel, they headed north over less-travelled back roads. They took few breaks, stopping at roadside fruit stands for food and siphoning diesel at night from parked lorries.

Spider barely slept; when he wasn't driving, he rested his feet on the dashboard and kept his gun on his lap. Qasim got his head down as much as possible, or at least pretended to snooze, to avoid engaging in conversation. The hunting knife, he'd used to kill the driver was once again tucked away inside Spider's backpack.

It was mid-morning when the Chevy approached the outskirts of Nouachott, and the road to the port was jammed. Overcrowded buses with commuters clinging to their sides, animal-laden trucks, horse-drawn wagons filled with fruit and vegetables, tuk-tuk taxis and motorcycles were moving in a chaotic dance through the city. A strong breeze rolling off the Atlantic helped to keep the soaring temperature bearable while at the same time tossing dust particles into the air.

Spider cursed the locals every time they cut him up while Qasim sipped constantly from a bottle of water. The temperature gauge on the pick-up hovered menacingly over the red zone; within minutes, steam was pouring from beneath the bonnet.

'That's it,' Spider shouted. Clutching his backpack, he opened the door and started walking through the traffic towards the port. Qasim removed the driver's keffiyeh, placed it carefully on the dashboard and followed.

The sound of angry drivers blasting their horns drew his attention back to the truck where two men were quickly claiming ownership of the abandoned vehicle. Qasim didn't care: he was happy to leave it behind. His body still hurt and the image of the young family in the photo was weighing heavily on him.

Thirty-five minutes later, he was staring through a chain-link fence at the *Ventura Star*, their transport to Cádiz in Spain.

Like a puppy following his master, Qasim was always a step behind Spider. He had no idea what was coming next and would have been the first to admit that if it wasn't for his psychopathic companion, he'd still be sitting cross-legged on the ground outside the port in Karachi. But he was annoyed and afraid: annoyed he hadn't asked more questions of those in charge in Afghanistan, and afraid of where this unhealthy union would lead him.

The ten dollars that Spider had stolen from the driver of the pick-up was all it took for a lone guard to facilitate their entry to the docks. 'Ten bucks appears to be the price of disloyalty in this part of the world,' Spider mocked as they marched towards the tanker. 'Makes you wonder what they'd do for double that amount.'

Unable to shake off the moment the driver had offered up the money to have his life spared, Qasim ignored him.

The journey from Nouachott to Cádiz was uneventful. Calm seas provided a welcome change from the uncomfortable conditions of the previous boat journey, and the varied, tasty menu designed to satisfy the international crew reminded Qasim of home. Most importantly, no one tried to kill the only two passengers not included on the ship's manifest. Even so, he struggled to adjust to this new way of life and death.

Although they shared a cabin, most days Qasim managed to keep a safe distance from Spider. The massive 200-plus metre long tanker offered plenty of places where he could keep to himself, think and plan. The photo of his sisters, Rana and Benazir, which he kept in his wallet, served as a reminder of why he was there. A string of missed calls from his father was a clear indication of how much he had changed since their passing.

Entering Europe through the port at Cádiz was easy. At 3am, a lorry arrived to replenish *Ventura Star's* food stocks. Just over an hour later, Spider and Qasim crept into the back of the now-empty vehicle.

There was no inspection when they left the docks, just a nod from a security guard at the barrier who was too tired or too lazy to do what he was paid to do. When the driver of the lorry told them that, Spider laughed. 'In Africa, money opens doors. In Europe, it's incompetence.'

They were taken to a derelict industrial estate on the AP-4 north of the town. A short distance away, a white Ford camper van with British plates was waiting in the shadows next to a barbed-wire fence. Spider collected his bag, removed his handgun and walked slowly to the van.

'There's no need to point that thing at us,' the man at the wheel of the camper van shouted. 'We've been asked to take you to England.'

Spider didn't respond. Keeping the gun pointed at the driver and his female passenger, he inspected the cab of the mobile home, Satisfied that the couple, who appeared to be in their seventies, didn't have weapons, he opened the door to the living quarters at the rear, climbed inside and checked around.

When the woman tried to introduce herself, he screamed, 'No names.' A deathly silence followed; visibly shaken, the couple sat motionless.

'I don't care who you are,' Spider added more quietly. 'And you don't need to know who we are. Your job is simple – get us to England.'

The old woman snapped back, 'Our job will be made a lot easier if you get rid of your long hair and that Osama bin Laden beard. You look like one of those terrorists we see on the television.'

Qasim, who was standing a few steps away, gave a loud gasp and for a moment Spider seemed lost for words. He gritted his teeth and glared at the old woman as a red mist descended. *If this was Iraq…* But it wasn't: it was Spain and he desperately needed transport to England.

'Shall I give you a trim?' she asked, holding a pair of scissors in one hand and a small makeup mirror in the other.

Spider gazed at his reflection and nodded reluctantly.

It was just over 1,000 kms from Cádiz to the French border, but a journey that should have taken ten or eleven hours turned into fourteen due to frequent stops for tea and to empty the old man's bladder.

Spider and Qasim stayed in the rear of the camper van, away from the window. Qasim played with his phone, drank Coke and ate cheese-and-onion crisps, while the newly groomed Englishman lay on his back and stared wide-eyed at the roof of the van. Conversation between them was non-existent.

When the vehicle came within two miles of the border, the old man stopped at a lay-by and the passengers climbed into their hiding places. Qasim, the smaller of the two, squeezed through a cupboard and slid into a space behind a purpose-built cooker that was barely half the depth of a normal working appliance.

Spider lowered himself into a box that doubled as a seat at mealtimes and a bed in the evening. A false bottom had been cut deep enough to hold Spider's sturdy frame but he was forced to lay flat on his back with his head tilted to the side. The backpack was crammed between his feet; the gun rested firmly in his right hand. A makeshift larder on a wooden shelf millimetres from his face was a disgusting mess for a reason: jars with jam and honey running down their sides, an open bag of flour, two cracked eggs in a ripped egg box, blackened bananas and sticky sweets would make a thorough search by customs officers an unappealing prospect.

For the first time in the journey north, they heard a loud clunking noise as the gears changed from high to low and the van slowed to a crawl. Qasim's heart beat faster as he heard French voices grow louder. If he was discovered, he assumed he'd be deported for trying to enter the country illegally but that would be it, nothing more. His name was most likely on a European stop list because of what his sisters had done, but he hadn't committed any crimes that the authorities would be aware of. No one in Europe knew or cared about what had happened in Africa.

But he was concerned about Spider. If discovered, the ISIS psychopath would not want to be captured and would come out fighting; with no exit route, their chances of survival were limited. Fingers crossed and holding his breath, Qasim waited and listened.

The van continued to roll forward and didn't stop as he'd expected it would. Several seconds passed and suddenly it picked up speed. The sound of the gears grinding and the engine roaring brought a smile to Qasim's face. 'Thank you,' he mumbled looking skyward. 'Thank you.'

The camper van eventually stopped north of Saint Jean-de-Luz, a small fishing village on the Atlantic coast. A roadside petrol station and restaurant with a car park that extended to the rear of the building was perfect for their needs; neatly sandwiched between two large lorries, their vehicle was impossible to see.

The old lady climbed into the rear of the Ford and shut the door. Qasim's backpack lay at her feet. She shook her head, slid open the cupboard door, pulled back the side of the cooker and waited for Qasim to wriggle out of his hiding place. She passed him his backpack.

'Sorry,' he whispered just as Spider emerged from his box.

The Englishman didn't look happy. 'I need a piss and something to eat,' he grumbled, and set off west across the car park.

The old woman waited until he was far enough away then made her feelings clear. 'He's not a nice man. I hope he's not going to England to hurt anyone.'

'What's in it for you?' Qasim asked her.

'What do you mean?' she replied.

'Taking us to the UK. Do you need money?'

She shook her head.

'You went to a lot of trouble to build places for us to hide in the van. Why would you do that? And grinding the gears at the border was genius. It worked. The border guards must have thought you were a couple of harmless old people.'

The old woman looked at her husband for support and he nodded reluctantly.

'ISIS have our son,' she said softly. 'He was working with a charity when they took him. If we get you to England safely, they said they'll let him go.'

'ISIS has been defeated,' Qasim objected.

'That's what the media tells us, but it's not true.' She thought for a moment then asked, 'Are you ISIS?' Qasim shook his head. 'And what about your friend?' she probed.

Qasim ignored the question and started to walk away but then stopped. 'You could go to prison for doing this.'

'We know,' she said. 'It's a chance we're willing to take.'

12

Present day

The journey through France was long and tedious. Conversation in the van was kept to a minimum, stops were frequent.

The old couple had decided some time ago to drive to Cherbourg and catch a ferry to Poole in Dorset, England because they believed security there would not be as tight as at other entry ports. Their reasoning was simple: a Google search revealed that twenty-five percent of the local population was over sixty-five, so a couple of septuagenarians heading in that direction would not arouse suspicion.

Qasim smiled when he heard their plan but Spider wasn't amused; he thought it was naïve and would put their lives at risk.

The old woman was quick to reply. 'Have you got a better idea? If you prefer, we can drop you off in Calais. I hear they're doing a roaring trade in rubber-dinghy crossings to Dover.'

Qasim sniggered. Spider, stone faced, leaned forward and whispered in her ear. A moment later he backed away and took his seat in the van.

'What did he say, Pat?' her husband asked.

'He reminded me that our son's life was in his hands.'

'So he must be ISIS?'

Pat nodded and moved around the van to the passenger seat.

‹ ❊ ❊ ❊ ›

Two hours later they reached the outskirts of Cherbourg. The van pulled off the D650 to a quiet spot and both passengers relieved themselves before being helped into their hiding places. Qasim remembered to squeeze his backpack between his feet and Spider kept his gun close.

The old man joined a short queue to the ferry and fidgeted in his seat as he edged nearer to the lady inspecting tickets at the barrier. A cursory glance at his boarding pass was followed by a wave of her hand. Within minutes he was parking his camper van on the ship's car deck.

Pat turned in her seat and quietly announced, 'We're on board now and will be going to the upper deck. The crossing will take just over four hours. Don't make a sound.'

Once the vehicle was locked, the couple went up to the restaurant where they ordered two cups of tea and a chocolate brownie to share. Sitting at a table tucked in a corner, the old man questioned their arrangement with ISIS. 'How do we know they will stick to their part of the deal?'

'We don't,' replied his wife, 'but we have no choice. What else can we do, Nick?'

He sipped his tea, looked up at her then whispered, 'What if we took them hostage and exchanged them for our son?'

Pat's eyes widened and her jaw dropped before she carefully studied the people nearest to them in the restaurant. 'Are you stupid?' she asked through gritted teeth. 'They'll kill us.'

'Maybe we could subdue them somehow,' Nick added nervously.

'Drink your tea,' she snapped. 'We have a plan, let's stick to it.'

When the announcement finally came over the ship's tannoy to return to their vehicle, Nick remained seated. Despite encouragement from his wife, he gripped the sides of the table, lowered his head and wrapped his feet around the legs of the chair.

'What are you doing, Nick?' Pat demanded.

'We're either going to die in a shootout or be arrested,' he mumbled as passengers shuffled close by.

'We knew this – we discussed it and we agreed it was our only option. Think of what our boy is going through. We're his only hope.'

A long pause followed. Nick eventually loosened his grip on the table and slowly raised his head as she continued to offer encouragement. 'We've come so far. Let's not stop now. Once we get through customs, our boy will be safe. Please, darling. *Please.*'

After another moment's hesitation, Nick stood up, took hold of his wife's hand and followed her down a flight of stairs to the van.

'Here we go,' Pat said to her passengers hidden in the back. 'No matter what happens, please keep quiet.'

As the camper van crawled slowly behind a red Mercedes SL 500, she collected the passports from the glove compartment and an onion from a plastic bag at her feet. She peeled the skin off the onion and held it until they were four vehicles from the immigration booth.

Nick reached out and bit into it like he was biting into an apple. His face contorted as its sharpness attacked his senses then he breathed hard in his wife's direction. He was ready.

Reaching the booth, he lowered his window, leaned towards the seated officer and handed him the passports. The officer immediately recoiled, did a quick passport check and returned the documents. 'Thank you,' Nick said as he moved the camper van forward.

A large lorry to his right was being searched by a uniformed customs officer, but to his surprise the way ahead was clear. With his foot gradually pressing harder on the accelerator, the van pulled away from the inspection area.

'Keep going, keep going,' Pat insisted as Nick, still holding pieces of onion in his mouth, started to gag. She opened the carrier bag, placed it on his lap and put a bottle of water in his left hand. Following a lengthy rinse, he spat liquid and onion chunks into the bag. As they moved slowly through the heavy traffic, he threw up.

'I didn't need to eat the bloody onion,' he said, coughing. 'The customs man was already occupied.'

As the camper van passed through the winding streets, Pat curled her right hand into a fist and gently punched the air. 'We did it,' she said softly. 'We bloody did it.'

Nick turned on the radio, placed his finger to his lips, then pointed to the rear of the van. 'What about them?' he mouthed. His wife looked confused then shrugged her shoulders. 'I don't trust them,' he added.

After negotiating several twists and turns in the road, they arrived at Poole train station. The old woman climbed into the rear of the vehicle and shut the door. When the panels and shelves were removed, Spider and Qasim appeared.

They barely had time to rub their eyes and stretch their limbs before Pat started issuing instructions. 'You're in England.' She held up her phone. 'We've kept our part of the bargain, so please keep yours. Send the text to this number saying you're here and tell them to release our son, Colin.'

Spider didn't bother to respond. He copied the number into his phone, typed in a message and showed it to her before pressing send.

'Thank you,' she said.

He and Qasim collected their bags and walked towards the station. Qasim, a couple of steps behind Spider, turned and gave the old woman the thumbs up. She forced a half-smile then returned to the passenger seat. Her husband was nowhere to be seen.

Several minutes later, Nick opened the door, sat behind the steering wheel and said, 'Buckle up, Pat. We're going to Bracknell.'

13

Eddie was sitting on the sofa, arms folded. His mother was in the kitchen sipping a cup of tea while baby Anne slept nearby in her pram. 'I can't live in the same house as that woman,' he shouted. 'Make her go.'

Steve rubbed his hand through his cropped hair. Like a referee in a boxing ring, he stood back, watched and listened.

'It's half my house,' Victoria replied, loud enough to be heard but not loud enough to wake the baby.

Steve inhaled and exhaled loudly as he approached the kitchen. 'I thought you were going to hide at a friend's place?'

Victoria glared at her husband as she slid the photo of Qasim's dead sisters across the table. 'Someone is watching me,' she said through gritted teeth. 'And it's all your bloody fault.'

Steve studied the photo and the comments on the back. His wife continued to vent her anger but kept her voice low. 'So I thought that if I'm going to die, I might as well do it in my own bed. Speaking of my own bed, I've moved your stuff into Tim's room. I need the big bedroom for Anne and me.'

'Are you kidding me?' Eddie yelled. He was now standing in the kitchen doorway. 'You can't just walk back into our lives! You left us for Bob Marley and Baby Reggae, remember? And speaking of Bob,' Eddie stopped, raised his arms, looked around the room then asked, 'where is he?'

※ ※ ※

The elderly couple drove their camper van into the pub car park across the street from Bracknell station. It was late afternoon and the place was deserted so it was easy to manoeuvre their vehicle to a space with an unhindered view of the exit door from platform one and the long line of taxis that snaked to the right of the building.

Drivers were standing beside their cabs, talking, waiting. With changes at stations in Basingstoke and Reading, the train from Poole was always going to take longer than the van to reach Bracknell: Nick had planned it perfectly.

After a leisurely stroll to the confectionery stall on the small concourse, he bought a couple of bottles of water and a packet of mints which he hoped would clear the taste of onions and vomit from his mouth. The electronic arrivals and departure board hanging from the ceiling confirmed the train from Reading was on time. He glanced at his watch then returned to the van.

'So, tell me again why we're doing this?' his wife asked.

Nick took a deep breath, kept his gaze forward and said softly, 'Because I don't believe for one minute these bastards will release Colin. If they keep their word then fine, but if they don't, at least we'll know where to find them.'

'And once you find them, what will you do?'

'I'll cross that bridge when I come to it.'

When the train pulled into the station, the camper van eased nearer the exit. The couple's eyes were fixed on the stream of passengers hurrying towards the station car park, the taxi rank and the short cut to town through the bus terminal.

Nick squinted as he watched the stream of people become a trickle. When the train left for Waterloo Station there were no more passengers passing through the gate and not a single taxi waiting. 'Bloody hell,' he shouted. 'Where are they?'

Five minutes elapsed before his question was answered. A black VW estate sped into the car park and stopped abruptly at the pedestrian area to the right of the building. Spider and Qasim appeared briefly from behind a staircase before diving into the vehicle. Within seconds they were gone.

'Go, go!' Pat shouted.

The camper van remained motionless as two cars passed then squealed onto the road. Nick took up a position close enough to follow the VW but far enough away not to be seen.

'Why all the cloak-and-dagger stuff?' Pat asked. 'Do you think they suspect something?'

Her husband shrugged his shoulders. For the next ten minutes they followed at a distance; on more than one occasion they lost sight of the black estate, only to spot it again waiting at traffic lights. A few minutes later, while driving through a maze of residential streets, it turned left down a cul-de-sac.

Nick tucked in behind a telecom van that was on the approach road and waited patiently behind the wheel. After three minutes, he slipped on a windbreaker and flat cap, got out of the camper van and moved slowly to the corner of the street. Peering out from behind a lush, overgrown hedge, he spotted the VW parked on Ellen Lane in front of the third house on the left.

Moving slowly along the pavement, he approached a young couple pushing a pram. They ignored him as he had known they would because old people were invisible.

He jumped when there was a sudden tug on his arm.

'What the hell are you going to do? Knock on their door?' his wife whispered.

Nick froze, lowered his head and said nothing.

'Let's go,' Pat said. 'We know where they live.'

Steve checked the locks on the windows and fixed three steel bars across the glass pane on the back door. Although the 1970s' red-brick detached house was locked up tighter than a drum, he knew that when the time came an attack wouldn't take place here; it would be on some deserted industrial site in the middle of the night. Even so, he wasn't taking any chances. Victoria and Anne were here and they needed protecting.

He removed two flashlights from a bag on the floor and gave one to his wife. 'Here,' he said. 'These are special. If you're about to be attacked, point this at the person's eyes, press this button then run like hell.'

'You must be kidding,' Eddie laughed.

Steve moved to the switch and turned off the light, throwing the room into darkness. When he shone his torch into Eddie's eyes, his son instantly raised his hands to block the beam and stumbled backwards.

Steve moved in quickly and placed the flashlight gently against his son's head. 'Temporarily blinded and then knocked out. It's a versatile weapon.' Turning to Victoria, he added, 'I don't expect you to hit anyone, but it'll give you time to get away while he or she is disorientated. I'll reinforce the bedroom door. You should be fine.'

With her baby safely cradled in her arms, Victoria started climbing the stairs. Halfway up, she stopped and said softly, 'I hate you for what you're putting us through.'

Eddie stepped forward as if to speak but was stopped by his

father's outstretched arm.

The old man let out a large sigh as his body sank into the double bed. 'This is nice,' he said.

Pat looked around the cramped bedroom on the top floor of the local B&B. An old mahogany wardrobe with one leg propped up on a school textbook stood against the wall, while a white plastic garden chair doubled as a bedside table. It was possible to touch all four walls when standing in the middle of the bathroom. 'It's marginally bigger than our camper van,' she complained.

'Correct,' Nick replied. 'But this bed is so much more comfortable than that inflatable mattress in the van. My back may never recover.'

'So how long are we staying here?'

'I booked us in for three nights. That should give us time to hear from whoever is holding Colin.'

'I don't understand you sometimes.'

'Huh?'

'One minute you're scared of being killed or arrested then the next minute you're acting like Rambo.'

He smiled and removed a photo of Colin from his wallet. 'Like you said on the boat, we must think of our son.'

'Well, I hope you know what you're doing,' she snapped.

'Darling, I haven't got a clue. I just pray something will come to me if I need it.'

Pat sat on the edge of the bed staring at her phone. When Nick asked if there was any news, she responded with a tired shake of her head.

※ ※ ※

Before work, Steve attached bolt locks to the top and bottom of his wife's bedroom door even though he had no idea who may be coming to kill his family or what type of weapon they might use. Was Qasim brave enough to try on his own, or had he joined forces with someone else? Could it be Spider from ISIS? Arlo had told Steve that Spider's weapon of choice was a chainsaw; if that was the case, the locks would be nothing more than window dressing.

Four small battery-driven spy cameras that linked to an app on Steve's phone were mounted discreetly on each side of the house. Had he done enough?

He was standing on the front porch when Lager arrived punctually at 9pm. It was dark with a slight chill in the air, and the ex-cop was wearing an On Guard sweatshirt instead of his usual short-sleeved T-shirt.

'Autumn is coming, then it'll soon be bloody winter,' he moaned as Steve moved into the passenger seat. 'You not bothered?' he asked, glancing at Steve's bare arms and the summer gear he was still wearing. There was no response. 'I like to wrap up as soon as the sun goes down,' Lager continued.

Silence. Ten minutes passed before Steve checked his pockets and finally spoke. 'I forgot my bloody phone.'

'Shall I turn around?' Lager asked.

'There's no time. We've got a job to do.'

Another couple of minutes went by. Curiosity eventually got the better of Lager. 'What's up Steve?'

'Victoria hates me.'

'But you knew that when she left you and had a child with another man.'

'What I didn't know is that I think I'm still in love with her.'

With his keys in his hand, Eddie left his room and walked to the top of the stairs. He paused when he heard an unfamiliar buzzing sound coming from Tim's room. The door was slightly ajar and it opened fully with a gentle push. On the bed, his father's phone was vibrating, the screen flashing violently.

Eddie's thumb pressed down on the green button at the top right-hand corner of the screen and instantly a video steeped in shadows started playing. In the background, his father's stern voice announced repeatedly, 'You have stepped on an explosive device, do not move. You have stepped on an explosive device, do not move.'

He studied the video closely as his father's voice continued unabated, but it was too dark to make out who was caught in their trap. Could this be their skinny black friend? A grin rolled across his face as he ran to his car in the street. Once inside the vehicle, he banged the steering wheel and shouted, 'Step aside, Dad. I got this!'

Ten minutes later he stopped at the gate leading to the run-down industrial estate. The barrier was shut but only a flimsy piece of wire held the metal structure in place. *Why bother?* he wondered.

Once inside, Eddie drove with his headlights off past a sea of damaged vehicles waiting to be brought back to life. The old furniture warehouse on his left had never looked better: the absence of any light hid the gaps in the wooden outer walls and the blotches of rust and paint on the metal corrugated roof. Cracks in several panes of glass were lost in the blackness of night.

The garage where Eddie had worked as a mechanic was opposite; that was a job he'd hated from day one. A few feet away he could hear the recording of his father's voice barking out his deadly message.

A slow and deliberate survey of the surrounding buildings confirmed that the place was deserted. Eddie's heart rate increased as he picked up the truncheon from the passenger seat. Switching on his flashlight, he stepped cautiously towards the garage door. To his right, a large Q painted in red defaced the On Guard banner. He'd hit the jackpot.

'Well, well,' he gloated as he circled the skinny black kid who was shaking nervously while desperately trying to remain still at the same time. 'You're the kid who broke into our house a while back,'

The teenager squinted at Eddie. 'And you're the idiot who threw me out of the first-floor window.'

Eddie laughed and turned on the overhead light as his father's voice continued to ricochet off the concrete walls and floor. He flicked a switch on the control box located on a cluttered work bench and instantly silenced the threatening command. 'That's better,' he said. 'Now let's talk.'

'Get me out of here first,' the teenager replied.

'You're in no position to bargain. You're standing on a pressure plate. If you step off it – bang.'

'And you'll be killed too!'

Eddie shook his head. 'My father was – and still is – one of the best bomb-disposal experts in the country. There's nothing he doesn't know about explosives. The device you're standing on is set to blow off your foot – but only your foot. However, if your feet are too close together it will leave you footless.' He chuckled. 'And if you spread your legs too far apart, you could lose your bollocks. It's your choice.'

There was a long period of silence during which the kid appeared to be thinking about his options. Eddie jumped in. 'I guess if you lose a foot, you can always become a para-Olympian. Can you run?' He laughed again before his tone turned serious. 'Why not start by telling me your name?'

There was no response. When the kid drew his phone from his pocket. Eddie immediately grabbed a broom that was resting against the wall, knocked it to the floor, swept it across the room and gently poked the boy in the back.

The kid screamed as he frantically tried to keep his left foot on the metal plate beneath him. 'What are you doing? Are you crazy?'

'As a matter of fact, some people call me Crazy Eddie. Now, for the last time, what's your name?'

'Denzel,' the boy replied reluctantly.

'That wasn't so hard, was it? The next question has two parts.' Eddie sounded like a teacher addressing students about to take an exam. 'Is Qasim in the country? And if he is, is he alone?'

Denzel looked down at the floor and wiped the sweat from his face with his right hand. Without missing a beat, Eddie placed the broom handle under his chin and slowly raised the youngster's face until they were eye to eye.

'I don't know.'

'You don't know if he's here or if he's alone?' Eddie demanded.

'Both.'

'What *do* you know?'

'Qasim sent me money to paint graffiti on the places where you work. He wanted to piss you guys off and let you know he was coming for you.'

Eddie took a deep breath. 'Did he ask you to vandalise my baby brother's headstone?'

Denzel shook his head and said quietly, 'I'm sorry.'

Moving to the far side of the garage, Eddie kicked a bucket into the air and swung the broom baseball style along the work bench. Two empty beer cans, some plastic water bottles and a handful of small tools flew across the room and onto the floor. 'You crossed the line, you son of a bitch. I should have killed you when I had the chance.'

At the sound of shuffling feet, he turned. His father and Lager were standing shoulder to shoulder in the doorway. 'You left your phone on the bed,' he stuttered as his father walked towards him. 'When I heard the alarm, I got here as fast as I could.'

'Why didn't you call Lager? You knew we were working together.'

Eddie had an answer, but it was one he didn't think his father would like. He watched as Lager picked the phone up off the floor and scrolled through the messages while his father instructed the kid to empty his pockets.

'His name is Denzel,' Eddie added, trying to stay ahead of the situation. 'And he says he doesn't know if Qasim is here or if he's travelling with someone.'

Steve opened Denzel's wallet and removed his driver's licence. 'His name is Jamal Swift and he lives on the Coniston Estate.'

Eddie grimaced.

Lager stopped scrolling. 'Here's a text from Qasim thanking Jamal and saying he should keep his head down.'

Eddie swore under his breath.

'I think it's safe to say Qasim is in the country,' commented Steve. 'But is he alone?' He turned to Jamal and repeated the question.

The kid tried to bargain but Steve shut him down. 'You're young and fit but you'll grow tired and your foot will develop pins and needles. When that happens, you won't be able to tell how much pressure you're putting on the plate. You'll become confused, angry and then… I'm sure you can work out the rest. See you in the morning. Maybe then you'll talk – if you can.'

Eddie watched his father and Lager head for the door. He hesitated then followed. 'Turn off the lights, son,' Steve shouted.

It was only a matter of seconds before Jamal was pleading for them to return. His eyes were red and he looked defeated. 'I'm not sure, but I think he's travelling with someone.'

'Go on,' Steve said.

'He wrote that they were in Africa and it was a terrible trip. I texted him back asking who he was with, but he didn't reply.'

Eddie tried to enter the conversation by asking where Qasim was staying but Jamal only shrugged his shoulders.

'Where's the list?' Steve asked.

'What list?'

'The list of those he plans to kill. You must have given him names and addresses – how else would he find his victims?'

Jamal looked confused. '*Kill?* He never said anything about killing people.'

'What did you think he was going to do?' Steve mocked. 'Take them out to lunch? If anyone dies, you'll pay. Big time.'

Jamal lowered his head and started to cry. 'I didn't know he wanted to kill anyone and I don't know anything about a list.

I was just told to piss you off.'

'You've already said that,' Steve retorted as he, Eddie and Lager moved to the back of the garage.

Steve tapped his number into Jamal's phone then pushed call so that he now had the boy's number. More importantly, by doing that he had also registered Qasim's number.

The three men were close to the door. 'Hey, what about me?' Jamal screamed.

'You're free to leave. Call me if you hear anything,' Steve replied.

Jamal stood motionless. 'Go on, bugger off,' Steve ordered.

'But – but – what about this thing?' The boy pointed to the device beneath his trainer.

Steve turned around, took three quick steps towards him and grabbed him by the arm. The youngster's face contorted and his eyes closed. 'No,' he begged. As his foot lifted off the floor, a loud 'click' echoed around the cold concrete garage. Jamal's legs buckled as the ex-marine loosened his grip and a foul smell exploded from his trousers.

Lager and Eddie started laughing.

Steve towered over Jamal. 'Tell your friend Qasim to keep his eyes open. Dog shit's not the only thing he could step on in this town.'

A knock on the door at midnight woke Arlo from a sound sleep and instantly sent shivers down his back. Moving quietly, he slid the duvet to one side and placed both feet on the floor. Without thinking, he reached under the bed to collect his cricket bat then opened the drawer of his bedside table and pulled out the scalpel.

Rubbing sleep from his eyes, he checked the time on his phone then wrapped himself in the dressing gown that was hanging on the back of the door. There was a second knock. Tiptoeing out of the bedroom, he crossed the living-room floor, drew the curtain back slightly and peered into the darkness.

'Bloody hell,' he moaned. He put the bat behind the curtain and slipped the scalpel into his dressing-gown pocket. 'Lorraine, it's the middle of the night,' he sniped as he opened the front door. 'Are you okay? What are you doing here?'

'I know what time it is, thank you very much. What I don't know is why you provoked a terrorist.'

'What's happened?'

'He called me again still pretending to be your friend Derek.'

'What did he want?'

'I don't know. When he said he was Derek I told him who he really was, that the police knew he was here and he should leave you alone. Then I ended the call before he could respond.'

Arlo glanced along the street, closed and locked the door then sat on the sofa staring at Lorraine. She looked dazed as she stood in the middle of the room. After a long period of silence, she commented, 'Looks like you're not the only one to provoke a terrorist.'

Steve, Lager and Eddie decided to adopt a more cautious approach after talking to Jamal. They were now convinced that Qasim was in the country and was not alone.

Eddie didn't appear to be concerned but Steve had come prepared: he'd packed one of his newly acquired special flashlights, two batons and a canister of pepper spray into a small bag.

Lager wasn't pleased. 'The cops will have our balls for bookends if they catch us with that spray.'

Steve didn't respond as he slipped a handgun into his pocket. Eddie's face lit up but Lager freaked out. 'Where the hell did you get a gun?' he shouted. 'Do you know we can go to prison for having that thing?'

'It's a long story, but it was given to me by Dr Arlo at Bramley Park – he was having second thoughts about carrying a firearm. He bought it because an ISIS psychopath called Spider is coming here to kill him and I think Qasim has hooked up with Spider. I know it's wrong, but it's better to have the gun and not need it than need it and not have it.'

'No, thanks,' Lager spat. 'I don't want any part of this.'

'So what will you do if Qasim comes at you wrapped in a suicide vest, or that crazy son of a bitch appears from nowhere waving a chainsaw?'

Lager just shook his head and walked away.

Eddie, though, was ecstatic; like a kid on Christmas morning, he giggled and wriggled with excitement. Within seconds, his mood changed: his face contorted and his eyes went cold and vacant as he glared into the distance. His voice was soft, unemotional as he said, 'Let the killing begin.'

With Lager gone and his son returning to his old ways of wanting to hurt people, Steve felt vulnerable and alone.

※ ※ ※

'I messed up.' Arlo said. 'I'm sorry I got you involved. Forgive me?'

Lorraine stayed silent as she sipped her coffee. Looking tired and pale she gazed into his eyes before slowly reaching across the kitchen table. Surprised but pleased, Arlo touched her hand. 'Thank you,' he said.

'Forgiveness comes at a price,' she said.

Arlo waited. He wasn't sure what she meant until she stood up and went towards the bedroom door. 'Lorraine—' he muttered before she interrupted.

'I wanted you long before Jennifer came on the scene. I still do.'

'I never knew.'

'How could you know? You only ever loved her and, unfortunately for me, you still love her even though she's gone.'

Arlo's half-hearted reply that he and Lorraine were friends and work colleagues fell on deaf ears. 'It'll do us good,' she said.

'How?'

'We might discover there's life after Jennifer.'

Arlo smiled. 'You didn't just come over here to scold me, did you, Lorraine?'

'No, I didn't. But there's no harm in trying to kill two birds with one stone.'

❊ ❊ ❊

The night shift was tense but ended without incident. With Lager gone, keeping safe while patrolling sites and protecting their vehicles was damned near impossible. Things had changed; the loss of that extra pair of eyes meant Steve and Eddie were exposed and they didn't like it. Steve knew Lager would return in a heartbeat if he ditched the handgun, but he also knew what he was up against if Spider was the opposition.

Back at the house there was tension of a different kind. They could hear Anne's screams as soon as they reached the front door.

Eddie stopped and did a quick about face. 'I don't need this,' he groaned. 'Fancy breakfast in town?'

As Steve shook his head, took a deep breath and opened the door a familiar feeling came over him. It was like old times; a crying baby and a mother desperately trying to placate her child brought back fond memories. Smiling and feeling better about life, he cruised into the kitchen. 'Boy, this takes me back,' he said.

'How would you know?' Victoria snapped. 'You were never here.'

Steve came crashing down to earth with a bump. With gritted teeth and feeling like he'd just been punched in the gut he turned, left the house and quickly caught up with his son.

'I take it things didn't go well?' Eddie tried unsuccessfully to hide the pleasure in his voice.

'I'm an idiot,' Steve muttered. Eddie looked confused. 'I thought we could get back together. When I saw your mother in the house last night it seemed so right. Talk about bloody rose-tinted glasses.'

'Dad, she had two kids with two different men while she was married to you. When are you going to believe that enough is enough?'

The sound of ringing ended the possibility of further

conversation and Steve instinctively reached for his phone. Malik's name appeared on the screen. 'Good morning,' he said.

'Good morning, Mr Foley,' Malik replied. 'I guess you know why I'm calling.'

'You want an update on your son, Qasim?'

'His mother and I are worried sick. He hasn't contacted us since he left home months ago and when I tried calling him yesterday he'd changed his number. Have you heard anything?'

'Hang on.' Steve passed Qasim's number to Eddie, who attempted to make the call. A shake of his son's head a moment later confirmed that Qasim's number was no longer in service.

Steve didn't hesitate to reveal what he knew; the pain in Malik's voice was proof that the man was genuinely hurting. 'We're confident your son is in the country.' A lengthy period of silence was followed by the question Steve knew was coming but didn't want to hear. 'Are you going to kill him?'

'Not if I can help it.'

'Thank you.'

Spending the night with Lorraine felt so right yet so wrong. A few intimate hours with the forty-four-year-old divorcee had helped Arlo temporarily forget the guilt he'd carried since Jennifer's death, but as sunlight burst through an opening in the curtains he started to regret what he had done and the guilt returned.

Lorraine's comment, 'It'll do us good,' had been spot on,

but he knew the woman asleep in his bed was not the one to help him move forward. She was a good friend and that was all.

It was just after 8am when Arlo poured himself a cup of coffee, put on his windbreaker and placed his car keys in plain sight on the table. Leaning against the counter, he watched impassively as Lorraine skipped into the kitchen wearing his dressing gown. She stopped suddenly, her smile vanished and she glared at Arlo. Then, head bowed, she turned towards the bedroom.

'Give me a minute to change,' she said.

Pat had stared at her phone for hours while her husband slept. She'd sent two texts during the night to the people she thought were holding Colin but there'd been no response. She'd used the number her son's captors had used to set up the deal that had brought Spider and Qasim to England. 'Why don't they answer me?' she mumbled. 'We did what they asked us to do.'

Nick rolled over on to his back and slowly opened his eyes. 'Darling, give them time. Maybe they don't have a signal or they're too busy killing each other to reply right now.'

'That's not funny, I'm worried sick.'

'I'm worried too, but let's wait a bit longer.'

'What if we don't hear from them, or it's bad news?'

Her husband sat up in bed and thought for a moment. Finally he said, 'The guys we dropped off at the station were sloppy. It could be they thought that because we're old we're also stupid. But we're not. We know where they live.'

'Okay we're not stupid, but we are old,' Pat argued. 'What can we possibly do against two young, fit men?'

The old man smiled. 'Leave it to me, I've got a plan.'

14

Qasim sat on the edge of a single bed, held his breath and listened as a car door slammed and the roar of an engine faded into the distance. The time was 3.55am.

After a long period of silence, he crept barefoot across the carpet and placed his ear next to the door. Still unsure if he was alone in the house, he gently turned the handle and moved into the hall, glancing left and then right before stepping quickly along the corridor to the next room.

With one hand gripping the doorknob, he considered his options. *If I just walk into Spider's room and he's there, I'm dead. But if I knock and he answers then I can say I heard a noise outside and wanted to alert him.*

Decision made, he stepped back before tapping on the door. His heartbeat increased as several seconds passed without a response. Eventually, he gathered up the courage to wrap his fingers around the doorknob. After counting down from three, he took a deep breath and pushed into the bedroom, which was partially lit by a street lamp outside the window.

The room was empty, the bed unmade and the closet doors wide open. Take-away food packaging littered the floor.

Qasim wasn't surprised; he'd suspected something was going on. Spider had become even more secretive and suspicious during the past twenty-four hours and on more than one occasion had moved to a different part of the house when he was talking on the phone. Even so, he was confused. Why would Spider agree to be his guardian angel then leave before anything started?

Wide awake and unsure what was happening, Qasim turned on the lights in the hall, the living room and kitchen as he passed slowly through the house. There was a note on the kitchen table.

Spider's message was brief and to the point: *Lock the doors, close the curtains, turn off the lights and stay in the house. Will call later.*

Qasim shivered as he looked around the room. The curtains were wide open, the lights were on and the chain on the front door was hanging freely. When Spider spoke, he always jumped and words scribbled on a piece of paper proved just as powerful as if the man were next to him.

Within seconds the house was dark and secure.

Qasim fumbled through drawers until he found a large carving knife then spent the next ninety minutes on his bed staring at his phone with the weapon close at hand. Too frightened to sleep and with time to reflect, he took a small family photo from his wallet and placed it on his pillow. The light from his mobile phone illuminated the crumpled picture – but instead of recalling better times with his father, mother and sisters, he saw the smiling faces of the family of the dead driver in the pickup.

'It was kill or be killed,' he mumbled unconvincingly. 'I had no choice. Besides, he was leading us into a trap.'

He shook his head to clear the image but it didn't work, and the longer he stared at the photograph the more depressed he felt. Finally, he screwed the snapshot into a ball, threw it across the room and buried his face in the pillow.

For a moment he found peace, but then light burst into

the room and the neighbourhood started to come alive. He crept to the window and looked through a crack in the curtains. The man next door got in his car and drove away. It all looked normal; there were no new cars on the street. Nothing suspicious.

A text announcing Spider's arrival sent Qasim scurrying through the house to open the front door. He recognised the black VW estate; it was the same vehicle that had collected them from Bracknell station. Then the driver had been wearing gloves, a mask and a hoodie. Spider was strong on protecting identities, but Qasim still tried to see who was driving by standing on his tiptoes.

Spider pushed him backwards into the hall then gently closed the front door. 'You still don't get it, do you?' he said. 'The less you know, the longer you'll stay alive.'

Head down, Qasim backed away.

'And speaking of knowing things,' Spider went on, 'I met your friend Jamal.'

Qasim's eyes lit up. He started to say something but was immediately interrupted. 'While you were announcing to the whole world that you were on your way here, I had eyes on Steve Foley and his messed-up son, Eddie. Jamal was never far away and he was easy to spot. Did you know that the Foleys and their sidekick, Lager, trapped Jamal and interrogated him?'

Qasim shook his head.

'That's why I left the house. I didn't know what Jamal told them because I didn't know what you told Jamal.'

Qasim lowered his head again.

'So, I met with your little friend and he assured me he knows nothing and he'd told them nothing.'

'I'm sorry,' said Qasim. 'I won't contact him again.'

'I know you won't,' said Spider. Then he added, 'Nobody will.'

Qasim didn't ask what he meant. He already knew.

※ ※ ※

Showered, shaved and wearing a shirt and a pair of faded jeans, Eddie bounded down the stairs. 'You off?' his father asked.

'Coffee with Carol.'

Steve looked his son up and down. 'You cleaned up, even put on a shirt with a collar. It must be serious,' he joked.

'It's not serious, Dad. It's called going out, meeting people and getting a life. You should try it.'

Steve gave himself a moment to regain his composure. Eddie had hit a nerve. 'Touché,' he replied finally. 'You're right. I do need to get a life.' He turned to look at Victoria breastfeeding Anne at the kitchen table.

Her response was immediate and scathing. 'Don't even think about it. We didn't have a life together when we *were* together, and we're not starting one now.'

Steve swallowed hard: two major put-downs in a matter of seconds. Taking the piss was a daily occurrence in the forces; no matter who you were, someone at some time would have a go at you. There were no boundaries: they could pick on your name, accent, body shape or the way you walked, and if you couldn't take it you didn't survive.

But these jibes felt different: they were personal and they were true. Steve had no defence, so he kept his mouth shut.

When Eddie headed for the front door, Steve followed him.

He spoke quietly so as not to alarm Victoria. 'Be careful, son. They're watching us and could strike at any moment. Keep to public places.'

'Of course. Have you any idea how we're going to get these guys?'

His father shook his head. 'By the way, what do you know about this girl you're seeing?' he asked.

'Dad, I've been out with Carol a few times now. She's fine. Her father was in the Scots Guards – she's one of us.'

'That's great. Maybe I know him – what's his name?'

Eddie grimaced. 'You don't trust me, do you?' Before his father could respond he went on, 'You don't trust me to do anything, not even find a girlfriend.' The door slammed and he was gone.

'That went well.' Victoria was now standing in the hall. 'I see you haven't changed one bit,'

'I'm just trying to keep him safe, that's all.'

'Like you did with Tim?' she mocked.

Eddie had half an hour to kill so he stopped at the cemetery to talk to his brother. Standing next to the grave, he lowered his head, said a silent prayer and then started a one-way conversation.

'Hey, Tim, it's me. Just checking in. How's it going? Sorry, that was a dumb question. Things here are going *so* well. Mum is back home with a baby from some guy who's done a runner and Dad is sleeping in your room. Qasim has come to kill us and the chances are he's brought some bloody ISIS headcase with him. Lager quit the company because Dad

146

has a gun, and these days Dad doesn't trust me to go to the loo by myself. I get so angry at times that I'm afraid I might do something stupid. But here's some good news – I met a girl called Carol. She's nice but obviously not very intelligent because she seems to like me.' He smiled. 'I'm having coffee with her in a few minutes, so I should go. I miss you little brother. Sleep tight.'

Acting on Spider's instructions, Qasim opened the curtains, turned on the kitchen light then made two cups of coffee and sat quietly opposite Spider, who was casually sharpened a large knife. He had so many questions but knew there was a good time and a bad time for talking.

Since their meeting in Karachi, Spider's temperament has been unpredictable at best. He drifted from mood to mood, from almost pleasant to bloody terrifying. Saying the wrong thing at the wrong time could be painful – even fatal.

Qasim waited and slowly sipped his coffee, avoiding the large chip on the edge of the mug. Then, after a discreet study of the man facing him, he took a breath and spoke. 'So you managed to find a safe place to go to?'

'Who are you?' Spider demanded. Qasim didn't understand the question. 'Who the bloody hell are you?' the Englishman repeated.

'Qasim.'

'Wrong,' Spider shouted, jamming the knife into the table top. 'You're nobody and that's why I left you here. The cops don't know you or want you. The worst thing that can happen is that you get picked up for being illegal and you get put in a four-star hotel.'

The boy sank deeper onto the chair, his lower lip quivering, his mind spinning. *If that's true, why tell me to secure this place?* After a split second, he realised. *The bastard was winding me up, controlling me, trying to scare me.*

'Get your act together,' Spider ordered. 'You're a fighter about to climb into the ring. Be prepared, concentrate. Concern yourself with who and how.' He pulled the blade out of the wooden surface and leaned across the table. The words that came out of his mouth were slow, staccato. 'Who – will – you – kill – and – how?'

He placed the knife firmly in Qasim's hand. 'So, who's first?' he added through gritted teeth.

A whimper escaped Qasim's mouth as Spider stood up and moved around the table. Towering over the youngster, he demanded, 'Show me your kill list.'

'I – I—' Qasim stuttered. 'I have Steve and Eddie Foley's address.'

'What about the guy they call Lager? What about Steve's wife? Do you know where they live? Because I do?'

Qasim shook his head.

'And what about this one?' Spider placed a piece of paper on the table.

Qasim studied the name written on it then looked up blankly.

'You're bloody useless,' Spider growled and tapped the paper. 'You boasted you wanted to do away with Foleys' friends and family? Well, here you go – your first kill.'

Still gripping the knife, Qasim watched Spider storm out of the kitchen, spewing obscenities as he climbed the stairs to his room. Not that long ago he'd been afraid to stay in the house by himself but now he longed to be alone, to be rid of the threats that controlled his life.

As a pained sigh drifted silently from his lips, he dropped the weapon to the floor, folded his arms on the table and lowered his head.

The Ugly Mug coffee shop was buzzing. A group of young mothers who'd just finished the school run occupied a long makeshift table down the centre of the room. Eddie was sitting alone next to the window reading the local newspaper. He was ten minutes early for his coffee with Carol.

His attention was drawn to an article on page one with the headline, *Bracknell man commits suicide*. A few words into the first paragraph, the victim was named as Jamal Swift. He stopped reading and put down the paper. 'Oh my God, we did this,' he said louder than intended. A quick glance around the room confirmed that no one had heard or cared about his outburst.

He carried on reading. Jamal's body had been found behind a dumpster, his lifeless hand clutching an empty bottle of pills. 'Son of a bitch,' he muttered.

A moment later he was on the phone. 'Dad, you're not going to believe this. Jamal topped himself – took an overdose. It's in the local paper.'

'Where are you?' Steve asked calmly.

'The Ugly Mug. Why?'

'Don't say any more. Come straight home when you're done.' The phone went dead.

When Eddie looked up, Carol was standing next to him.

'Good morning.' She smiled. 'Are you okay? You look flustered?'

Eddie stood, greeted her with a peck on the cheek then moved towards the counter. 'Coffee?'

'Please.'

With a cup in each hand, he returned to find her reading the paper. 'This is tragic.' She pointed to the article about Jamal. 'Did you know him?'

'I bumped into him a couple of times,' Eddie replied.

Carol reached across the table and touched his hand. 'I'm sorry for your loss. Did he say anything that suggested he was about to end his life?'

'No, he didn't,' Eddie replied sharply. 'And we weren't friends so there's no loss. Why do you ask?'

'It's my background in charity work,' she said apologetically. 'I've dealt with a few suicides so I'm curious to know if one could have been prevented.' She put the paper aside and sipped her coffee. 'So, what have you been up to?' she asked.

Arlo was sitting in his car staring at the hospital staff entrance. He didn't want to go inside; Lorraine was on duty today and he was ashamed about how he'd treated her. Before her frosty exit she'd said that he needed to get help.

I don't need help, he thought. *I know exactly what's wrong with me. If Jen had died in any other way and in any other place, then I'd be over her by now. But because I took her to Iraq and didn't protect her, it's my fault she died. And I live with that every day.*

A tap on his side window made him jump and reach for his

scalpel. When he saw it was Lorraine, he lowered the window. She was the first to speak. 'You planning to spend the day in your car? If so, I'll start wheeling your patients out to you.'

Arlo chuckled. 'I'm sorry. I behaved badly.'

'Yes, you did, but I still had a great night. How does that saying go? I saw, I conquered and I came.'

Arlo laughed.

'It's a shame I didn't get breakfast,' she added. 'That would have been the icing on the cake.'

Arlo quickly changed the subject. 'Any more calls from Derek?'

The smile disappeared from Lorraine's face as she shook her head. 'I'm scared, Arlo. I'm thinking of taking some time off and maybe going abroad. You should come, too.'

'And then what? He'll be waiting for me when I return. No, you go. I got myself into this and it's up to me to deal with it.'

Lorraine rested her hand on his shoulder. 'You're either very brave or very stupid.'

'It's kind of you to offer two choices,' he responded. 'If I were you, I'd have just gone with the latter.

15

Pat mumbled to herself as she pushed an empty trolley aimlessly up and down the supermarket aisles. Stopping frequently, she read the labels on the back of cereal boxes, cake-mix packets and jam jars, then moved on. Tired from lack of sleep, her face was ashen and her eyelids struggled to keep from closing. With her left hand clutching her phone, she listened patiently for the familiar pinging sound of an incoming text that she hoped would bring news of her son, Colin.

Earlier she'd sent two texts asking for information about him. There'd been no response. During the night she'd dispatched a further three texts and yet again heard nothing. Her hands were tied. With just one mobile number and no contact name, her only option was to carry on doing what she was doing. The mysterious man who'd promised to release her son if she drove two men from Spain to the UK was playing a cruel game.

'I'm naïve and an idiot for believing Colin would be returned to us,' she said as her husband approached.

'Then that makes two of us, my darling,' Nick said quietly. 'And I'd be happy to be both naïve and an idiot again and again because we trust and we hope. What will become of us if we don't?'

※ ※ ※

The front door opened and Steve stepped outside to meet his son. An unsettled look appeared on Eddie's face when his father snapped, 'Back in the van.'

'What's up? You and Mum have a fight?'

Steve ignored him until they were both seated and the doors were closed then said impassively, 'Jamal's death was not an accident.'

'What have you heard?'

'I haven't heard a thing, but it just doesn't make sense.'

'Dad, we literally scared the crap out of him. Maybe he panicked.'

Steve shook his head. 'We let him go, Eddie, told him to bugger off. No violence, no threats. Nothing.'

'So who do you think killed him?' Eddie asked. Steve stared at him in disbelief. His son appeared embarrassed before answering his own question. 'Qasim?'

'Possibly.'

'Why?'

'He's covering his ass, tidying up loose ends. It's interesting that someone got to Jamal right after we questioned him in the garage. I guess Jamal wasn't the only one spying on us.'

'I thought we agreed that Qasim was a pussy?'

'It was either Qasim or whoever he's with,' Steve replied. 'My money's on Spider. No matter how you dress up Qasim, he's not a cold-blooded killer.'

'But isn't that why he came here?'

'I met a lot of guys in the military who talked the talk until it came to actually sticking their heads above the sandbags.'

'Well, I hope that's true,' Eddie retorted. 'If it is, then we have one less son of a bitch to worry about.'

Steve pressed the lever below his seat and slowly moved back from the dash. With his legs fully extended, his head resting against the headrest and his eyes closed, he murmured just loudly enough for Eddie to hear, 'We know Spider's coming to murder Arlo and get hold of the doctor's photos, but why would he risk spending time with an amateur like Qasim? Surely he'd want to get out of here asap?'

'Are you serious? Whoever it is, he's here to kill you. Even if Qasim wanted to do it, it's out of his hands.'

Steve sat up, opened his eyes, stared at his son and let him talk.

'The kudos and publicity for killing a famous British bomb-disposal expert here in the UK would be worth more than a thousand headless bodies in Iraq or Syria. You're the guy who made headlines picking apart my suicide vest. You're the guy who planted the bomb on the Cessna that killed Benazir and her terrorist friends.'

Eddie paused, glanced at his father and then continued. 'Okay, we're both aware MI5 made sure it was reported as an accident, but do you really think Al-Qaeda believed that?'

Steve didn't respond.

'Spider has personal reasons for coming after Arlo,' Eddie added. 'The doctor is a "nothing kill" and won't make headlines, but your death would elevate him to God-like status amongst his head-banging followers.'

After a long awkward silence, Eddie looked into his father's eyes. The truth suddenly hit him. 'Dad, you haven't said a word. You knew this already, didn't you?'

'Yes, I did, and I'm glad we're now finally on the same page. This is serious, so when I ask where you're going and who you're seeing it's for a good reason. Okay?'

❖ ❖ ❖

Pat hung on to her husband's hand as he helped her climb the narrow stairs to their room at the B&B. Once the pillow was fluffed up, he slowly lowered her onto the unmade double bed and removed her shoes.

A single tear rested on her cheek. 'Colin is a good boy,' she whispered. 'All he tried to do was help others. Why would anyone want to hurt him?'

'I'm going downstairs to the kitchen,' Nick said. 'I'll make us a nice cup of tea.' He waited at the bottom of the stairs for a short time before calling up to his wife. 'There's no milk, love. Just popping out to the shop. Won't be long.'

He was lying: there was milk in the fridge. If there hadn't been, he'd have taken a five-minute stroll to the petrol station, but instead he drove off in the van in the opposite direction.

Ten minutes later he pulled over and stopped not far from the third house on the left on Ellen Lane. Slouched in the driver's seat, he focused his gaze on the place where his two passengers had taken refuge a couple of days earlier. The VW estate was no longer parked in front, but there were signs of people moving about inside.

He had to know if they were still there. A gap under the fence of the house next door gave him an idea. He needed a prop and found one in the glove compartment. After removing a stale biscuit, he exited the van and approached the fourth house along the road. A young boy responded to his knock on the door. 'Hi,' Nick asked. 'Is your mother home?

'Mum,' the boy shouted.

A petite woman in her early thirties arrived after a lengthy delay. She was still wearing oven gloves.

'Sorry, I can see you are busy,' Nick said apologetically, 'but my dog just ran under the fence into your garden. Is it alright if I get him?'

Somewhat annoyed, the woman looked him up and down then stepped aside so he could enter the house.

'Thank you. This shouldn't take long. I'm afraid he has a mind of his own sometimes and just runs off on a whim.'

'Do you have a lead?' she asked.

'I have something better,' Nick replied, opening his palm. 'His favourite biscuit. He'll come once he sees this.'

He stepped over the threshold and followed the boy to the back door. As expected, there was no dog in the garden even so but even so he shouted, 'Here, Buddy. Here, boy,' as he worked his way to the wooden fence at the side of the property. Pretending to be searching for his pet, he looked discreetly over the fence.

The teenager he'd smuggled from Spain to England was standing at the kitchen window, washing dishes. *Well, one of them is still there,* he thought. *Excellent.* Ducking down to avoid being seen, he returned to the back door. 'Thanks for letting me have a look. I'll check further along the street. He can't be far away.'

'Can I go with him, Mum?' the boy asked.

Before his mother could open her mouth, Nick said, 'No, you stay here and keep an eye out for my cute little black Lab. Remember, his name is Buddy. If you see him, call me. My number is on the tag attached to his collar.'

The boy smiled and returned to the garden, shouting the dog's name.

Back in the camper van, Nick squinted as he stared across the road at the third house on the left. 'Where's the other bugger?'

※ ※ ※

Eddie tapped gently on Tim's partially opened bedroom door and stepped inside. 'It's strange to see you in this room,' he said.

Steve laughed. 'There weren't too many options. What's up?'

'We need Lager.'

His father rose from the bed and stood opposite him. 'I thought you weren't a fan?'

'I'm not, but three's better than two,' Eddie said. 'He'll have our backs and his contacts with the local police could come in handy.'

'That's true. But what about the gun? We may need it, and we know how Lager feels about that.'

'I'd rather have a good man than a gun.'

Steve's eyes lit up. *Nice one*, he thought. 'Okay, so what should we do with it?'

'We could ditch it or give it to Mum,' Eddie joked.

'And what are you giving to Mum?' Victoria asked, standing in the doorway, hands on hips.

Eddie groaned at the same time that Steve jumped in and made a clumsy offer of the handgun for protection.

Victoria froze. 'Please tell me that's not the same gun that killed our son?'

Steve shook his head and explained how he'd got the weapon. She appeared relieved but still not happy about having it in the house. She stared at the weapon that was now in Steve's hand. 'If I was attacked in the house and used that thing to kill the attacker, what would happen?'

'He'd be dead, and you'd be alive,' Eddie declared.

'But you could face charges for possessing an illegal firearm, manslaughter or even murder,' Steve added.

'How long?'

'Not sure – five years, ten – maybe longer.'

'And if I was attacked and didn't have the gun?'

Steve waited, took a breath, then reluctantly admitted, 'You'd be dead.'

Victoria returned to her bedroom across the hall. A couple of minutes later she was back. 'I'll take it on one condition.'

'Really? what's that?' Steve asked.

'You have to promise to help me bury the body.'

Stunned, Eddie turned and whispered to his father, 'Is she serious?'

'Yes, Eddie. I'm afraid she is.'

When Nick returned to the B&B, Pat was sitting at the kitchen table sipping a cup of tea. As he stood empty handed in the doorway, he knew what she was thinking. After forty-one years of marriage it didn't take much to read her mind. 'I'm sorry,' he said. 'I went to the house on Ellen Lane to see if they were still there.'

'And were they?'

'I only saw the young one.'

'So what's your plan?'

Nick shrugged.

'Well, I've been thinking and I have a plan,' Pat said. 'If they hurt our Colin then we should go round there and throw a petrol bomb through the window when they're sleeping. You know, like those Molotov cocktails they threw at the army in Northern Ireland back in the day.'

'And what if we don't hear from the people holding Colin? Do we assume the worst? Do we wait another day? Two days?

A week? And what about the people next door? It's a row of terraced houses. We could kill the family with that lovely little boy!'

His wife's hand shook as she lifted the teacup. It didn't make it to her lips. 'I don't know,' she replied wearily. 'The only thing I know is that I'm tired and confused and I want to turn the clock back to the day before Colin left.'

'He's a grown man. It was his decision.'

'We should have tried harder to stop him.'

They didn't speak for the next few minutes. Pat picked up her phone and sent another text pleading for her son's release. Nick put the kettle back on the cooker and turned on the gas. 'Would you like a fresh cup of tea?' he asked.

16

Qasim sat on the floor, knees bent, his back resting against the bed. Staring at the blank wall opposite, he thought about the night ahead. His stomach churned and his palms were moist. A shiver vibrated through his body as the afternoon sun slowly disappeared behind the rooftops and his room grew dark.

The hour was drawing near; the time for talking and spreading threatening graffiti was over. Spider's kill list had one name on it; he'd said he'd add more names as and when required. That was how Spider maintained control and Qasim knew he had no way of fighting it.

Feeling helpless and alone, he tapped his father's number into his phone then stared at the green button. Reality hit hard. *What would I say to him?* he mused. Hi, Dad, it's me, Qasim. *Sorry I haven't been in touch, but I'm sure you'll be pleased to hear I'm about to kill someone I don't know.*

Making the call was a bad idea and his father's number disappeared across the screen as he pressed the delete button.

At the sound of footsteps climbing the stairs, he looked at the gap beneath the door and watched as a shadow approached, growing darker and more menacing with every step. Feeling like a prisoner waiting for the executioner to take him from his cell, Qasim held his breath. *It's too early*, he thought. *It's too light.*

He was right. The shadow drifted past the opening and

towards Spider's room.

The boy breathed normally again.

Spider kicked off his shoes, removed his T-shirt, bent over to touch his toes ten times then followed with twenty press-ups. As he flexed his biceps in front of the full-length mirror, a loud ping announced an incoming text.

He moved to his bedside table and drank from a bottle of water before reading the message.

Hi, just heard from our friend in Mosul. A journalist from Iraq is tracking you. Here's what he knows and doesn't know after talking to ISIS prisoners. You're English, white with black hair, and you're known as Spider because of your tattoo. He doesn't know your name or age, just that your father left when you were born and your deceased mother was a crackhead. He thinks you had no allegiance to ISIS and killed purely for the fun of it and the money. He said there are no known photos of you.

Spider texted back: *Anything else?*

Yes. *He said you're a psychopath and will burn in hell.*

Spider's eyebrows raised slightly. He texted back: *He's spot on except for the photo, but I'm working on it.*

After tossing his phone on the bed, he strolled across the room to the window overlooking the lawn at the rear of the property. A young boy standing by the neighbour's fence looked up at him, smiled and waved. Spider raised his hand to head height then opened and closed his fingers, just as he'd done on the morning his mother was carried from the family home in a wooden box. It was a gesture made without emotion: cold and hollow.

※ ※ ※

Head down, feeling like he was running out of time, Qasim paced the floor in his dimly lit bedroom, desperate to find some justification for what he was about to do.

His sister Benazir, wrapped in a suicide vest, had been killed before she could cause carnage in London, yet that truth had never entered his decision-making process. She was dead and Steve Foley had killed her, so the ex-marine's family and friends must suffer. Clear and simple.

Initially he had struggled to come up with an explanation he could live with. After dismissing a couple of scenarios, he'd settled on painting his first target as a behind-the-scenes facilitator, a murderer without the courage to pull the trigger or plunge in the knife, but just as guilty.

The more Qasim thought about it, the more he convinced himself that his reasoning was sound. His first victim was no longer an innocent. A feeling of calm finally washed over him. Now all he had to do was stay positive.

Wearing black boots, an On Guard sweatshirt and cargo pants, Steve walked down the hall, his hulking frame almost blocking out the light that passed through the open door ahead. Two steps behind him, with his backpack slung over his shoulder, came Eddie, a mirror image of his father.

Victoria couldn't help smiling. Two beautiful men. It was a pity they were so messed up. 'When are you going to show me how to use that thing?' she shouted.

Steve turned, thought about it for a moment, then walked

back to the kitchen. Reaching into the cupboard above the sink, he pulled the gun from an empty box of cornflakes.

Victoria rolled her eyes. 'Really?' she asked.

She watched as he demonstrated how to remove the magazine and place it back in position, then she listened intently as he laid down a few important rules. 'Always treat the gun as if it's loaded and point it towards the ground unless you plan to shoot. Only put your finger on the trigger if you're about to shoot and be careful of what or who is behind your target.'

'Yes, sir,' she snapped and saluted. Now it was Steve's turn to roll his eyes.

Without asking, she snatched the 9mm pistol from Steve and held it in her right hand, weighing it up as she would fruit in the supermarket. 'Is that it?' she asked.

Steve moved forward until his hip brushed against her leg. He wrapped his hands around hers and carried out an up-close-and-personal demonstration of how to hold and fire the weapon.

Victoria felt her heart beat faster and her cheeks warm. She'd have happily stayed right there – until Eddie jumped in. 'For God's sake, you two, get a room,' he snapped.

A period of awkward untangling followed as Steve released his hold on his wife while she took a step back. 'Well done,' he said, clearing his throat. 'You're ready.'

With the weapon still in her right hand, Victoria regained her composure. 'So are you telling me that after two minutes of show and tell I'm qualified to kill someone with this thing?'

It wasn't a rhetorical question, but even so there was no response.

❋ ❋ ❋

Steve and Eddie greeted Lager with a brief man hug at the entrance to the Pines Golf Club. Chat was limited to the job at hand. There was no mention of the gun; that conversation was done and dusted. There were no hard feelings, just respect.

Steve applied pressure to the gate fob, pointed it at the rusty metal box to his left and waited until the red-and-white-striped wooden barrier lifted to ninety degrees. It was 10.45pm; the restaurant and bar had closed for the evening and all the staff had gone home.

Sensor lights flashed on and off as they drew close to the main building. In the past security at the golf club had been an assignment for one man, and Steve's On Guard firm had it under control. There hadn't been a break-in or a report of criminal damage at the club since he'd taken charge three years ago. Now, because of threats from Qasim and the death of Jamal, it was a team effort. Safety in numbers was the new policy.

While Lager kept watch from deep in the shadows of the covered front entrance, the Foleys, carrying truncheons and a knockout flashlight, turned their phones to silent and circled the wood-panelled structure. In order to get Lager back on board Steve had agreed to ditch the handgun and his canister of pepper spray, but he felt naked and vulnerable. Facing an ISIS killer without proper firepower was pure lunacy.

At the rear of the premises, Steve checked the access to the kitchen and the up-and-over door leading to the space where lessons with the golf pro took place. Both were secure.

A heavy layer of cloud and a broken sensor light made the surrounding area darker than usual. As they rounded the corner, they could hear laughter from the direction of the eighteenth green but it was impossible to see what was going on from where they were standing.

'I got this.' Eddie marched towards the last hole on the course. Standing by the edge of a kidney-shaped sand trap at the top of the green, he watched as a bare-chested overweight man danced around the flag while a second man attempted to putt a golf ball into the cup using the rake from the bunker.

'Okay, gentleman, the fun's over. Time to go,' he announced.

'Get stuffed,' the fat man shouted. He was now clinging to the pin.

'Hush, this putt's for the win,' slurred the man with the rake.

Eddie walked around the bunker; the golfer was furthest away and he'd deal with him last. The fat man instantly went on the offensive, withdrew the flagpole from the cup and assumed a jousting position. Eddie approached him head on. As the fat man lunged with the pole towards his chest, he twisted, grabbed it and dragged his opponent with it. A split-second later, his forehead smashed firmly against the fat man's nose.

An agonising cry shattered the silence of the deserted golf course and interrupted the golfer's concentration. 'You bastard! You ruined my putt.'

With the fat man down on the ground clutching his face, the golfer sprinted across the green brandishing the rake high in the air and spitting threats and obscenities. Eddie stood firm, waiting until his attacker was about fifteen feet away before pointing the high-powered flashlight beam in his face.

The effect was almost comical. The golfer lowered both arms to shield his eyes, tripped over the rake and found himself pinned between the ground and Eddie's boot. The aggressors were down, their weapons discarded.

Eddie took a breath then turned quickly as he heard a massive thud a few feet away. A third man, still clutching a rock, was face down in the sand with Lager sprawled on top of him.

It was obvious what had just happened, yet it still took a while to sink in. Eddie glanced at his father, who was smiling, then turned back to Lager. Events appeared to be moving in slow motion and his mind started to wander. He'd always dreamed of being a marine like his dad had been and doing what they did, but although the adrenalin rush and the camaraderie presented such an inviting package, it wasn't to be. He didn't make it beyond the first hurdle. 'To kill Mussies' was not an acceptable reason for wanting to join the force.

But knowing Lager had just saved him from having a massive headache in the morning was a small taster of what might have been, and he was happy. Finally someone other than his father had his back.

Qasim cleared his throat, dipped his hand under the running tap and splashed cool water over his face. Smudges and cracks covered the bathroom mirror and partially hid the worry in his eyes. After wiping his hands on his trousers, he reached for the doorknob then immediately withdrew his arm.

He turned and rested his back against the door. Numbness flowed through his upper body; his legs were like jelly. With both palms facing his chest he closed his eyes and muttered an inaudible prayer. For a moment he found peace, but it was soon shattered when Spider's voice penetrated the slab of wood that was keeping them apart. 'It's time.'

Qasim stayed pressed against the door, unable to move.

'Did you hear me?' Spider shouted.

'Coming.' Qasim tiptoed across the bathroom floor to flush the toilet. The cold-water tap was fully open so that splashing sounds were audible.

'You got the runs?' Spider laughed as Qasim finally appeared. 'Don't worry. The more people you kill, the easier it gets.'

'Is that what happened to you?' the boy snapped then immediately regretted quizzing a psychopath.

'Absolutely,' Spider continued, much to his surprise. 'I'd never hurt anyone before I travelled to Iraq.'

Sensing Spider wanted to talk, Qasim asked delicately, 'How did you end up doing what you did?'

The man thought for a moment. 'I was bored, going nowhere just like you. It gave me a purpose and status in the community.'

A shudder ran through Qasim's body: being compared to a cold-blooded killer like Spider made him feel sick. There were so many things he wanted to say, like he wasn't a mass murderer and didn't kill those who hadn't threatened his life. But then he realised where he was going and what he was about to do.

No longer wishing to continue the conversation, he raised his hoodie, lowered his head and walked towards the car. *What have I become?* he wondered.

Sitting alone in the back of the black VW Estate, he clicked his seat belt into position and stared out of the window. The road ahead, partially lit by a flickering streetlight, was packed nose to tail with cars but there wasn't a single pedestrian in sight.

His attention turned to the empty driver's seat: the last

time he'd been in this car was when they'd been picked up at the station. On that occasion, it had all been very 'cloak and dagger': the driver was dressed in black, wore gloves, a hoodie, face mask and sunglasses. Nobody had spoken during the journey. All the interior lights had been removed and Qasim had been told to sit in the rear seat and keep his head down. That was no surprise because Spider was big on privacy: anonymity was key to his survival – but the longer Qasim remained in the dark, the more he feared for his life.

Spider climbed into the driver's seat and they moved slowly through the heavily built-up area of terraced houses. Unaware of the identity or location of his first kill in England, or even how it would be carried out, Qasim sat hunched and silent. It was a little after midnight so traffic was light, although a kebab van parked on a slip road adjacent to the Bagshot Road was doing brisk business.

As the car approached Bracknell town centre, the familiar surroundings triggered memories of the time Qasim had spent with Tim. On the left was the greasy diner where they'd shared a laugh and a full English. A few minutes later the car passed the football pitch, their first meeting place.

Qasim had calculated every get-together to befriend the youngster who was five years his junior. Every compliment and lie had helped him get into the Foley home so his father could plan Eddie's kidnapping. At the back of Qasim's mind, the question remained: if he had not agreed to help his father and had stayed in Pakistan, would Tim be alive today?

A series of roundabouts took them to the opposite side of town where temporary traffic lights funnelled the VW into a narrow one-way system. Movement was slow, and with every passing second Qasim grew more anxious. His chest was tight, his lips dry.

Needing fresh air, he pushed the button to lower the rear window. Spider snapped, 'Shut it, idiot. They're tinted for a reason.'

Qasim cowered in his seat. As they left the construction zone, Spider had more to say. 'Well, look who it is.'

Cautiously Qasim straightened his back and raised his head high enough to see Steve and Eddie's On Guard van waiting for the lights to change. 'So that's the enemy,' mocked Spider as he slowed to a crawl. 'Mean-looking couple of guys. I'm glad *I* don't have to kill them.'

Laughter filled the front half of the car but in the back seat there was an uneasy silence as Qasim put his trembling hands between his knees. Meanwhile, Spider continued to chuckle as he drove quickly from tarmac and overhead streetlights onto a dirt track where only a handful of dark, lifeless houses dotted the landscape.

Qasim's breathing quickened when the car stopped at the side of the road. Frozen with fear, he remained motionless as Spider spoke without turning around. It was a terse one-way conversation and the boy swallowed hard when a huge machete was passed to him between the seats.

'First house on the right,' whispered Spider. 'You know what to do. And you know what will happen if you don't do it.'

Qasim stepped slowly out of the car. Following Spider's instructions, he made no noise as he shut the door and avoided walking on the gravel path leading to the house. It was a cool evening, yet he found himself wiping drops of sweat from his face.

He studied the front door and the three windows that overlooked the road. The porch light was off and the curtains were drawn: there was no sign of life. Crouching, he inched his way along the lawn on the right side of the house. At the back of the building, his body lurched forward as his foot slammed into the edge of a raised patio. The machete slipped from his grasp and clattered on the concrete.

He grimaced, held his breath and waited.

With his body pressed firmly against a metal drainpipe, he counted to thirty. When he felt it was safe to move, he collected the machete and reached for the back door. There was no need to force his way inside: the door was open.

Something wasn't right. Qasim made a slow 360-degree turn, carefully scanning the shrubbery that enclosed the small garden to the rear, then focussing on the area leading back to the street. There wasn't a soul in sight.

Without making a sound, he crossed the patio to the far corner of the house. At the back door he paused; he had plenty of doubts about what he was about to do, but Spider had left him with limited options. Reluctantly, he carried on.

Using the tip of the machete, he pushed the door wide enough to slip through into the hall. His first step took him to an oversized door mat on which he stopped to wipe his feet. A series of large rugs placed on the tiled floor made it easy for him to walk silently around the house.

Following a swift check of the ground-floor rooms, he stood at the bottom of an old staircase wondering how much noise this wooden structure would make. It didn't take long to find out: a loud creaking echoed through the house as he placed his foot on the first step and forced him to retreat to the living room, where he held his breath through yet another lengthy count.

Once again, his suspicions were aroused. *This is crazy. No one could sleep through that.* Aware that the element of surprise might be long gone, he hurriedly creaked and clattered his way to the first-floor landing. To the left, four doors were open; to his right, at the end of the hall, a double door remained closed.

He marched towards it. Holding the machete in a striking position, he turned the handle, took two steps inside – then stopped abruptly. The lights were off, the curtains drawn, but he had no difficulty in seeing the horror show on the double bed in the centre of the room. A burning candle on the bedside table gave enough light to reveal a woman's twitching, bloodstained body.

Qasim recoiled. Unable to look, he thought about running, slipping out of the back door and disappearing into the night, but he knew that would never happen. Spider wouldn't allow it.

A creaking floorboard drew his attention to the bedroom door and there was Spider, standing tall. For a long, frightening moment he didn't speak then he whispered calmly, 'Finish her.'

17

The smell of bacon frying in the kitchen wafted into their first-floor bedroom. The old man opened his eyes, slid his white freckled legs over the side of the bed, stretched his arms and yawned.

'Still nothing.' Pat was propped up against the headboard.

Nick glanced at her and sighed quietly as she remained glued to her phone. 'Come on, Pat, put that thing down,' he said gently. 'Get dressed. It's time for breakfast.'

'Why won't they answer me?' she asked. 'I've sent more than twenty texts.'

Her husband shrugged his shoulders and shuffled quickly to the loo. A moment later Pat screamed, 'Nick, Nick! Come here! I've got a text.'

'What does it say?' he called from the behind the closed toilet door.

'They want to know who I am and what I want.'

Nick thought for a moment, pulled up his pyjamas then went back into the bedroom. 'Stop, Pat!' he shouted. 'Don't send anything.'

She lifted her fingers from the screen and glared at him. 'Are you crazy? I've been praying for this moment.'

He placed his hand on her shoulder. 'I'm not saying we shouldn't reply, just be careful what we say.'

She waited until he'd lowered himself onto the bed. 'Why are we being asked these questions?' he asked. 'If it's the same person who contacted us before, he knows who we are. Someone else may be involved. If we tell them what we did and it's the police on the other end, we'll be in serious trouble.'

'So, what *do* we say?'

'If it's the police, they're bound to ask how we got this number.' Another long pause followed as both Nick and his wife stared at the phone.

'What if Colin's kidnapper is testing us?' Pat whispered.

'What do you mean?'

'What if he's thinking what we're thinking?'

'Huh?'

'Maybe he's making sure *we're* not the police.'

'You could be right,' Nick said. 'Let's keep it simple. Tell him who we are and that we're trying to find our son, Colin Wells, a charity worker.'

Pat tapped his exact words into her phone and sent them on their way. Within minutes a response arrived asking for Colin's date of birth. 'Is that a good thing?' she asked after reading the text aloud.

'I'm not sure.' Nick's voice cracked with uncertainty. 'But there's only one way to find out.'

Pat hurriedly typed in Colin's details then, fingers crossed, she moved close to her husband, the phone resting screen side up on the duvet.

They waited for more than an hour, longing for a pinging sound that would bring them good news. When the text finally arrived Pat froze, her face showing no emotion.

Nick watched as her hands remained clasped on her lap, her eyes closed. He knew the moment she had prayed for was now the moment she was dreading. As he reached for the phone, she grasped his free hand and squeezed it tightly.

A moment of silence was shattered by a heart-breaking scream. Nick dropped the phone on the bed and started sobbing uncontrollably.

'No, he can't be!' cried his wife. 'He can't be!'

'The bastards,' Nick shouted. 'I knew we couldn't trust them.'

Unwilling to accept that Colin was dead, Pat picked up the phone and read the brief message aloud: *Your son, the infidel, was executed.* 'This can't be right! It must be a mistake.'

Her eyes filled with tears as she gave Nick the phone and dictated a reply: *This can't be right. Please check again. You promised if we helped get the two men to England you would let him go. You gave us your word.*

The couple waited then resent the text, but there was no reply. A third text was followed by another long period of staring at the phone. 'They're not going to answer,' Nick mumbled. 'Besides, nothing they say will bring Colin back.'

'They murdered him. We can't just do nothing!' Pat protested.

'We won't,' he promised. 'We won't.'

Qasim sat alone at the kitchen table sipping a cup of cold black tea. Through eyes red from lack of sleep he stared at his fingernails, which were covered in congealed blood. For a moment his mind went blank but then he spotted the machete leaning against the wall. He lowered his head as he tried to come to terms with what had happened during the night.

'What's up, killer?' Spider joked as he bounded into the room. Qasim remained still and silent. 'You did good last night. You should be proud of yourself.'

Qasim raised his head. 'Who was she?'

'No one special. An acquaintance of the main man.'

'She was half-dead when I got there. Did you do that?'

'We just wanted to make it easy for you.' Spider walked to the front door. 'Be grateful. Next time you're on your own.'

As Spider left the house, Qasim stood up, filled the kettle and flicked the switch. He went into the living room and gazed out of the rain-splattered window before moving trance-like back to the kitchen, where the kettle was starting to boil.

Something wasn't quite right. Suddenly the penny dropped. 'Spider said "we",' he announced out loud as a cloud of steam drifted in front of his face. '"*We* just wanted to make it easy for you".'

As Arlo drove into the hospital car park, Lorraine was walking towards the staff entrance. 'I thought you were going abroad,' he said as he pulled up beside her. She smiled, shook her head and kept moving forward. 'So what happened?'

'I changed my mind.' She pushed open the glass door and stepped inside the building. A moment later Arlo came face to face with her in the hall. He was about to speak when she interrupted, 'I decided not to go away because I'm needed here.'

'That's very commendable, Lorraine, but we have lots of nurses who can cover for you.'

'I'm not talking about the hospital.' Her gaze shifted to the floor.

'Then what are you talking about?'

'My goodness, for someone so qualified you're not very bright, are you?'

Arlo raised both his hands to signal his confusion. 'Enlighten me, then.'

Lorraine took a deep breath. 'It's obvious you can't do it yourself, so I'm going to take care of you.'

He chuckled. 'And just how will you do that?'

'I've arranged for us to stay with different friends and family every couple of nights. If you keep moving, he'll never find you.'

'Are you serious?' Lorraine took a step back and nodded as he continued. 'He knows where I work and he could be watching me right now. This guy is crazy and won't stop at just killing me. Do you really want your friends and family involved?'

As tears trickled down her cheeks, Arlo's tone softened. 'It's very kind of you to want to protect me and I really do appreciate it, but I got myself into this mess and it's up to me to sort it out.'

The Ugly Mug was packed. A young mother was pacing between the tables desperately trying to calm her screaming baby while those around her raised their voices to be heard.

Carol sensed she was grinding her teeth as she sat patiently, phone nestled in both hands on the table. She glanced at the clock on the wall behind the counter: it was 12.20pm and Eddie was twenty minutes late.

She'd decided she'd stay for another ten minutes just as he

came crashing through the front door. 'I'm sorry,' he said. He looked dishevelled. 'I overslept.'

'Eddie, it's the afternoon! Who sleeps this late?'

'We had a long night and I didn't get to bed until a few hours ago. Coffee, Carol? Croissant, cookie, cupcake, can of Coke?"

Carol shook her head and pointed to her half-empty cup, ignoring his attempt to make her smile with his deliberate use of alliteration.

A minute later Eddie returned to the table with a cappuccino, a toasted ham-and-cheese sandwich and a piece of chocolate cake. 'I'm starving,' he said with more than a hint of embarrassment.

'So you had a long night?' Carol asked.

'Yeah. We couldn't work on our own like we usually do.'

'Why?'

'There's a couple of crazies out there, so we're sticking together. Safety in numbers.'

'Do you know who they are?'

'We think one of them is a terrorist.'

'Could they be the same guys who killed a prostitute in Bracknell last night?'

'I haven't heard anything about that, but I doubt it.' Eddie stuffed the cake into his mouth.

'Why do you doubt it?' Carol asked.

'We think there's a hit list and a hooker definitely wouldn't be on it.'

'Are *you* on it?'

Eddie smiled and carried on eating but Carol wouldn't let it go. 'Eddie, how can you defend yourself against someone like that?' she probed. 'Do you have a gun?'

'That would be illegal.'

'What about the others you work with?'

He didn't reply, just carried on eating until eventually Carol changed the subject. 'Any chance we can go out one night like grown-ups? she asked. 'Or will we forever be stuck drinking coffee in this creche they call a cafe?'

'I'm in the security business. I work nights.'

'Great, Friday night it is then,' she replied, without seeking Eddie's consent. 'I'll choose a restaurant and let you know.'

Nick's heart sank as he stared at his wife's bloodshot eyes and tear-stained cheeks. Several hours had passed since the text had arrived yet her hands were still shaking. He felt so helpless: his words offered no solace, his embrace no warmth.

After closing the curtains in their small bedroom, he dimmed the lights and carefully placed a blanket over her, whispering that he was going downstairs to make her a cup of tea. She didn't respond.

In the kitchen he asked the landlady of the B&B if they could stay on for a few more days; business was slow, so she agreed immediately. When he asked for details of the nearest car rental agency, she hesitated, then looked at the camper van on the forecourt and waited.

'That big old beast is fine for long trips on the motorway,' Nick said quickly. 'But it's not great for seeing the sights on these beautiful, narrow, winding country lanes.'

She smiled as she handed him a double-sided laminated paper listing local points of interests and business names and numbers.

Nick thanked her and headed upstairs, clutching the cup

of tea. When he got to their bedroom, Pat was gone and the camper van keys were no longer on the plastic chair. Her phone lay on top of the blanket that had covered her just a moment ago.

He hurried down the stairs and out of the door onto the empty forecourt. 'Bloody hell,' he shouted.

Two minutes later, he was walking in the direction of the train station where he knew there was a taxi rank. The journey wasn't an easy one. After ten minutes pounding the pavement, his knees started to ache. His sedentary lifestyle had taken its toll on his seventy-three-year-old body, but still he marched on, perspiration dripping down his face, his heart thumping in his chest.

Facing an uphill climb, he stopped and sat on the curb. He was still there when he heard his wife shout, 'What on earth are you doing?'

Nick looked up and forced a smiled when he saw her in the van on the opposite side of the road. He tried to speak but he didn't have the breath. Finally, wiping a tear from his eye, he spluttered, 'I thought you were going after those two we had in the van.'

'To do what? Yell at them? I went to the church to say a prayer and light a candle for Colin. Besides, I got the feeling you were going to handle them, that you have a plan.'

Nick stood up slowly and crossed the street. 'You're right. I do have a plan.'

'And?'

'Let's go back to the room and I'll tell you.'

※ ※ ※

It was late afternoon when word spread around the hospital that a woman had been beheaded during the night and was now laying on a slab in the basement. A chill ran through Arlo when he heard the news. There could only be one person who would do that. Had it really happened? He had to find out.

Without telling anyone, he slipped away from A&E and went down the long corridor to the rear of the building. Using his pass, he opened the metal door, walked beyond a large service lift and descended the bleak concrete stairs to the morgue.

When he arrived at a second door, a small glass window enabled him to look inside the room that, much like the connecting hallway, hadn't been updated in years. A large stainless-steel table occupied the central space while a row of refrigerated cabinets stood tall along the right side. Huge air pipes and several fluorescent strip lights hung down from the rafters. The walls, covered from floor to ceiling in faded white tiles, made the space look exactly what it was: cold and clinical.

Arlo tapped on the door to alert the attendant. 'Don't tell me,' the man said with more than a hint of sarcasm. 'You're here to see the headless woman.' He paused for dramatic affect before adding, 'For professional and educational purposes, of course.'

Arlo ignored his theatrics but couldn't help feeling like a student being scolded by his teacher.

'You're not the first today and probably won't be the last,' the man went on. 'Fill your boots, doc. Third freezer, top row.'

Arlo walked hesitantly towards the cabinet, grasped the

handle and pulled the drawer open. After a deep breath, he removed a section of the white sheet covering the woman's body.

Images of the atrocities he'd witnessed in Mosul assailed him and he heard the pitiful cries and the roar of the chainsaw.

He'd seen enough. After replacing the sheet and closing the cabinet, he turned to leave the room. 'And that could be you,' Lorraine whispered. She was standing a couple of feet away.

Without looking at her or speaking, Arlo returned to the stairs then up to the corridor and back to A&E. Once he was inside an empty examination room, he tapped in Steve Foley's number. 'Have you heard?' he asked.

'Heard what?'

'I think Spider's in town.'

'Why do you say that?' Steve asked.

'There's a woman downstairs in the morgue. She was decapitated. It's got to be that sick bastard – normal people don't do a thing like that.'

'Does she have a name?'

'I didn't ask. Why do you want to know her name?'

Steve's response was clipped and without feeling. 'They've come here to kill us and it makes sense they'll start with a soft target. Since no one in my family died last night, I'm assuming it's a friend. Can you get me her name?'

Arlo agreed to call him back. Ten minutes later he had some answers, although they were not what Steve wanted to hear. 'They haven't been able to identify her yet.'

'What's the hold up?'

Arlo hesitated then said, 'She was found in a field, no clothes, no jewellery, nothing.'

'Tell me what she looked like. Young? Old? Blonde, brunette?'

'I can't.'

'Why not? You just bloody saw her?' Steve barked.

Arlo pulled the phone away from his ear. Then, with the coolness and calmness of a doctor revealing his diagnosis to a patient, he said softly, 'They still haven't found her head.'

Victoria was sitting alone at the kitchen table. The sun had set and the room was dark, yet she still hadn't turned on the lights. Tired, fed up and hungry, she sipped her first cup of coffee of the day and was about to bite into a peanut-butter sandwich when baby Anne began to cry. She waited, hoping her child would go back to sleep but it didn't happen. The cries became louder and more frantic.

'I'm too old to play this game,' she muttered as she trudged back up the stairs. When she was three steps from the top, the doorbell rang. Feeling torn, she glanced at the bedroom door then down at the front door.

Anne's cries intensified. The doorbell rang again. 'Hang on,' she shouted as she went back down again.

With both feet on the door mat, she reached up to release the lock – then suddenly withdrew her hand. She backed away from the door, crept into the living room to peek through the curtains. A young man wearing sunglasses, a baseball cap and a high-viz jacket was holding a parcel.

Why was he wearing sunglasses?

He appeared calm as he waited patiently on the porch. She couldn't remember ordering anything and she was confident that Steve didn't shop online, he was more of a hands-on kind of guy. Give him a bag of explosives and he could blow the hairs off your head without drawing blood, but he wouldn't use a keyboard to buy things.

She thought for a moment about retrieving the handgun from the cornflakes box then dismissed the idea. Instead she ran into the kitchen and picked up a large carving knife. Back at the door, with Anne still screaming upstairs, she called out, 'Yes, can I help you?'

'Delivery for Mr Foley.'

'Leave it on the porch, please.'

'Can't. I need a signature.' She could barely hear his voice above the incessant crying.

'I've had enough,' she sighed to herself. 'This is doing my head in.' Decision made, she turned the lock and partially opened the door, the knife tucked out of sight in the rear pocket of her jeans.

'Sign here, please.' The delivery man offered up his pen.

Still not entirely convinced she'd done the right thing, Victoria looked over his shoulder to scan the street. Next, she discreetly examined what the man was doing with his hands: one held the box and the other the pen. Everything seemed fine.

Steve had once said that you could tell a man's true intentions by looking into his eyes. Since she had no plans to remove the delivery man's sunglasses, that piece of advice was no help at all. Anyway, if he was going to kill her, he'd have done it by now.

Satisfied she wasn't about to die, she signed the paper, grabbed the parcel, stepped back into the house. *Is this what's going to happen every time someone comes to the door?* she asked herself.

With the package on the table in the hall and Anne

screaming for attention, she climbed the stairs cursing both her estranged husband and her ex-lover. 'Bloody men,' she shouted. 'They'll be the death of me.'

Steve punched the air as he left the magnificent new indoor go-kart and multi-room entertainment complex, and it wasn't because he'd won a race. He was ecstatic because he'd just secured a lucrative security gig. 'We're going to need more staff, Eddie,' he joked as they walked to the van. 'But it's a good problem to have.'

Once behind the wheel he turned on his phone and watched a short video in silence. His fists clenched.

'What's up?' Eddie asked.

'Your mum just had a visitor.'

Eddie took the phone and pressed the 'watch again' button. 'What the hell?' he yelled. 'Why did she open the door?'

Steve took back the phone and called Victoria. When she picked up, her mobile was on speaker and Anne was wailing in the background. 'Why is she crying?' he asked innocently.

Her voice laden with sarcasm, Victoria retorted, 'That's what babies do when they're hungry, have colic and are teething. But you wouldn't know. You were never around.'

'I'm having difficulty hearing you above the racket,' Steve said. 'Can you hear me?' There was no response. 'You just had a delivery,' he shouted.

'How do you know that?'

'I put up cameras and linked them to my phone.'

'That's great.' she mocked. 'If he'd been here to kill me, you could have watched. Perfect. I feel so much safer now.'

In addition to sarcasm, Steve could hear the stress and anger in her voice.

'I'm sorry,' he said. 'I was dealing with a new customer and turned off my phone.'

Either Victoria didn't care what he'd been doing or she didn't hear him because she talked over his explanation. For the next few minutes she went on an out-of-control rant about how he had ruined her life, screaming and cursing so loudly that Anne joined in and her cries reached a whole new level.

The noise coming out of his phone was agonising. Steve grimaced but stayed with the call and let her continue. When she finally stopped, he jumped in. 'Look, I said I'm sorry and I'll make sure it doesn't happen again. But next time you buy something online, get the time and date of delivery and I'll be there.'

'I didn't buy anything,' she snapped. 'It's for you.'

'What did you say?' Steve shouted. He repeated the question but all he could hear were Anne's screams and Victoria's desperate attempts to calm her down.

'I think she said the package was yours,' Eddie offered.

Steve shook his head, his mind racing. 'It can't be mine. I haven't ordered anything.' What the hell was going on?

Out of nowhere, Arlo's comment during their earlier telephone conversation resonated loud and clear. 'I think Spider's in town,' he said slowly then held his phone as close as possible to his mouth and yelled, 'Victoria, don't open the parcel!' There was panic in his voice.

'What's going on, Dad?' Eddie asked.

'Victoria, please answer me,' Steve pleaded. 'Put the baby down, pick up the damn phone and get it off speaker. And don't open the parcel.'

There was no response. Leaving the phone line open, Steve put his foot down firmly on the accelerator and headed home. Finally he heard Victoria's distant voice fading in and out. 'I'm changing Anne's nappy. Give me a minute then I'll have a look for you.'

'What did she say?' Steve asked his son.

'I think she's going to open it.'

Steve raced along the dual carriageway, down a slip road and into a school zone where yellow lights were flashing. The pavements on each side of the road were packed with schoolchildren and mums pushing prams. A lollipop lady stepped onto the road to block traffic.

'Get out of my way,' Steve moaned, slamming on the brakes. He tried again to get a response from Victoria and failed.

'Dad,' Eddie said, 'she's got her hands full – she can't talk now. What's so important about this parcel?'

At that moment, a series of blood-chilling shrieks filled the inside of the van.

Steve's closed eyes and rocked his head backwards. Oblivious to the lollipop lady waving him forward and the car behind him blowing his horn, he turned to his son and said, 'Now I'm really in trouble.'

Twenty minutes later, they arrived home. Despite numerous attempts Steve hadn't been able to speak to Victoria, but a review of the security camera video link confirmed there'd been no more callers. Even so, they were taking no chances.

Truncheons in hand, Steve and Eddie moved quickly towards the house. Eddie slipped down the side passage to the rear. His father's instructions were clear: do a sweep of the small outside shed, the kitchen and downstairs loo. Meanwhile, Steve opened the front door, stepped inside and paused. It was absolutely quiet and dark.

After checking the living room, he crept upstairs and tried to open the door to the master bedroom but it was locked. Steve knocked and called out but there was no response. Finally he took three steps back, charged forward and smashed the door wide open with his shoulder. A flick of the switch on the wall lit up the room.

Victoria was sitting curled up on the floor in the far corner like a frightened child. Her lip was quivering and her face pale.

'You okay?' he asked softly. 'Where's Anne?'

'Get away from me,' she screamed as Steve approached.

Ignoring her, he moved forward and reached out.

'I said, get away!'

'I just want to help you,' he pleaded, bending down on one knee. Then, as he rested his hand on her shoulder, she raised her right arm and jammed the handgun into his face.

She didn't need to say any more; her steely red eyes were proof enough that she meant business. She was on the edge and could easily tip over.

Lifting his hands in the stick-up position, he stood up and backed slowly away, watching as Victoria removed Anne from under the bed. Wrapped in a blanket, unaware of what was going on around her, the baby was babbling happily.

When Steve turned to leave the room, he came face to face with Eddie. A discreet shake of his head sent his son back into the hall. 'Is she okay?' he asked.

Steve shrugged; he wanted to put some distance between

himself and his wife before he spoke. Further along the landing, Eddie whispered, 'I've got something to show you.'

On the table was a cardboard box with Steve's name printed on the side in black felt-tip pen. There was no address.

The ex-marine took a deep breath; he was certain he knew what was inside, though not who. Gradually, and with respect, he separated the outer cardboard flaps followed by the pair on the inside. His heart sank as a bloodstained face appeared. 'Oh, Jesse, I'm so sorry,' he whispered.

'You knew her?' Eddie demanded. Steve nodded. 'But she was a hooker!'

Reluctantly, Steve nodded for a second time then added, 'It wasn't what you think.' Eddie stared at his father and waited. 'We talked, that's all. Your mother left me and I needed a shoulder. End of story.'

With those three words, Steve made it clear he wanted to change the subject and Eddie indulged him. 'So what do we do about this?' he asked.

Steve sighed. 'I'll take care of it.'

'What about Lager? Do you think he'll want to get the cops involved?'

'The cops are already involved. They just don't know we're involved, too. Let's keep it that way.'

'So, this didn't happen?'

'Exactly,' his dad snapped.

'One more question.' Eddie looked straight at him. 'If you hadn't backed off, do you think Mum would have pulled the trigger?'

'Your mother is fragile and very angry right now.'

'So that's a yes?'

'I'm afraid so.'

188

'Weren't you scared?'
Steve shook his head.
'Why not?' Eddie asked.
'The safety was on.'

18

Arlo's shift finished at 3pm but he stayed in the hospital. Sitting alone in a corner of the staff canteen, he pondered what his next move should be before quickly realising he didn't have one.

Staying with Lorraine and her friends was a bad idea; the chance of collateral damage was too strong. Jen's death had taught him that. Going home wasn't smart, either. The thought of being alone in his house with a cricket bat and a couple of strategically placed kitchen knives didn't exactly fill him with confidence now he'd seen the woman in the morgue.

He was screwed and he knew it. For a moment he considered calling Spider to trade his phone for his life, but he knew that was another dumb idea. Spider hadn't travelled halfway around the world to negotiate, he'd come to kill.

After a second coffee, Arlo rode the service lift to the basement. Walking in the opposite direction to the morgue, he arrived at a door a few feet from the hospital loading dock. Exhaust fumes from an ageing Luton van were pouring over the concrete surface as the vehicle reversed slowly into position.

With his hand over his mouth and nose, Arlo hurried through a door marked storage. Once inside, he turned on his phone light and carefully sidestepped a graveyard of damaged defibrillators, patient monitors, surgical tables, EKGs and ultrasound equipment. On the far side of the room he cleared a space, wrapped his arms around a mattress that was leaning against the wall and lowered it to the floor.

He took off his shoes, rolled his jacket up to make a pillow then lowered his head, turned off the light on his phone and closed his eyes.

Qasim sat on the floor with his knees bent, back resting against the side of the bed. After staring at his phone for a long time, he tapped a series of numbers into the keypad. Distracted by shuffling feet in the hall, he paused, waited, then carried on once he'd heard the front door slam.

After he'd pressed the final number, he put the phone on speaker and listened.

'Hello,' a voice said. Qasim remained silent. 'Hello.' A long pause followed. 'Qasim, is that you?'

The boy lowered his head, moved the phone closer but said nothing.

'If that's you, son, please talk to me. Your mother and I miss you terribly. We're worried about you. Please say something.'

In the background he heard his mother call, 'Who is it darling? Is that Qasim? Can I speak to him?'

'I'm afraid there's no one on the line, dear. Maybe they'll call back later.'

Hearing his mother's voice, Qasim immediately pictured her in the kitchen, her safe place where she spent most of the day. She'd be wearing the apron he'd bought her for her birthday when he was a child. Although it was somewhat threadbare, she always put it on first thing in the morning and took it off just before she sat down to dinner.

Down the hall in the living room, his father would be sitting in his favourite armchair, reading a book about the history of someplace he wanted to visit but had never been. They lived a quiet, simple life; they'd no longer been interested in socialising after the passing of their daughters, Rana and Benazir.

Qasim thought about speaking but couldn't; whatever he said would break their hearts. With tears rolling down his cheeks, he gently pressed the red button and ended the call.

❄ ❄ ❄

'Is it clear?' shouted Victoria from the landing.

'Yes, it's clear,' Steve replied.

'Are you sure?'

'Positive.'

She went back into the bedroom, cradled Anne with both arms and walked slowly down the stairs. Just outside the kitchen she hesitated, peered around the doorframe and scanned the table. The box had been removed, the table cleaned, and the baby basket made ready for Anne.

As she stepped past her husband, she snapped, 'I'm going shopping. Do I take the gun or do I get a bodyguard?'

Father and son exchanged glances before Steve reluctantly volunteered. Eddie put on his work jacket and headed towards the door but was quickly called back by his mother. 'You're babysitting until we get back,' she ordered.

Eddie glared at her and turned to his father for support, but Steve was already out the door.

They were barely two minutes into their journey when Victoria asked, 'Who was the woman in the box?' As Steve carried on driving, she carried on asking questions. 'You said someone was coming to kill our family and friends. She wasn't family and she certainly wasn't a friend of mine. So who was she?'

'She was someone I knew. Not really a friend, more of an acquaintance.'

'If she wasn't a friend, why was she killed?'

Steve didn't have the energy to do more than sigh and a shake his head as he pulled into the crowded supermarket car park. 'This place is mobbed,' he said. 'They'd have to be crazy to try something here.'

'And cutting off that woman's head doesn't mean they're crazy?' Victoria mocked.

Once inside, she went directly to the aisle stocked with baby food and nappies while Steve stood nearby. When she finished loading her trolley, she stopped and watched him for a moment as he checked out the other customers in the store. He looked every inch the war hero with his straight back, broad shoulders and strong jaw. *If I didn't know him, I could fancy him.* She turned and grabbed hold of her trolley.

At the checkout counter, a young woman scanned Victoria's purchases. She stopped when she took hold of the pack of nappies. 'You may want to exchange this pack,' she said. 'Someone's written something on the back.'

Victoria reached for the nappies, read the words and screamed. Steve was beside her in seconds, his massive frame towering over her. 'What?' he shouted.

Shaking uncontrollably, she pointed to the message: *You're next.*

'Bastards!' He grabbed his wife's hand and dragged her out of the supermarket.

Safely seated in the van, Victoria watched him call out to a supermarket employee who was collecting trolleys in the car park. After a brief chat, the young man ran into the store, then returned a few minutes later to continue the conversation.

Once he was back behind the wheel, Steve explained to Victoria she was in no immediate danger. 'That message was written some time ago.'

'How do you know that?' she asked.

'Every pack of newborn-baby nappies in there had the same two words on the back.'

Victoria thought for a moment. 'Am I supposed to feel good about that?'

'Why wouldn't you?' he asked.

'Because they know everything about me – where I live, where I shop and even what I buy – and now they're telling me I'm the next one to die!'

It was just after midnight when the clunking of metal doors and the screeching of trolley wheels woke Arlo from a fragmented sleep. He was aware that getting his head down a few feet from a concrete loading dock that operated 24/7 was not his best idea, but he was alive and that's how he wanted to stay.

There were so many questions to consider. How long could he hide here without being detected? What about clean clothes, toiletries, taking a shower? How many times could he eat in the canteen before the staff started asking questions? And what about Lorraine? If she knew what he was doing, she'd try to help. She was a good soul who meant well, but she was very naïve. Arlo's biggest fear was that she'd unintentionally lead Spider to wherever he was hiding.

He decided to do things one step at a time, and the first step was to get something to eat. Before leaving the room, he used his scalpel to take apart an electric plug and remove the fuse. With the fuse in his pocket, he crept past the loading dock and walked towards the stairway door.

A voice steeped in cigarette smoke called out from a shadow, 'Can I help you, doctor?'

Arlo turned and saw Kev, the massively overweight janitor with the bloodshot eyes. The elongated ash on his cigarette appeared to defy gravity. He wasn't in a good state.

'Just came down to steal a fuse from one of those broken machines,' Arlo replied, holding aloft the fuse and pointing to the storage room.

'Shouldn't the guys in maintenance do that?' Kev slurred.

'If I waited for them to fix things around here, all my patients would be dead.'

Kev laughed. 'You got that right.' He walked unsteadily back into the shadows followed by a cloud of smoke that drifted into the cool evening air.

As Arlo had expected at this late hour, the staff canteen was empty. He stocked up on sandwiches, snacks and bottled water without drawing attention to himself. His plan was to eat a big meal there as normal and use the food he'd just bought to get him through the time he spent in the storage room.

Next stop was the doctors' locker room where he put on a hoodie then stuffed a T-shirt and a pair of jeans into a carrier bag. Getting hold of a toothbrush, toothpaste, deodorant, razor and shaving foam was a problem: the nearest place selling those items was a mile away at the petrol station. Was going there worth the risk?

Arlo also had another problem: his car was parked in a doctor's space. If he left it there, it would suggest he was working in the hospital even when he wasn't, but if he hid it his eagle-eyed colleagues might ask questions. More importantly, what would Spider make of things if he were watching?

Arlo's head was spinning: he needed some fresh air. With his hood pulled over his head, he walked to the rear emergency exit and surveyed the car park through the reinforced glass panel. All was still.

After slipping through the partially open door, he stepped onto the tarmac and took a deep breath. A soft sprinkling of rain caressed his face. It felt good to be outside, away from the antiseptic-soaked rooms of A&E and the dank musty odours that permeated the basement.

His moment of peace ended abruptly when approaching headlights lit up the cars parked nearby. Arlo panicked and tried to re-enter the building but the door was locked. The screeching of brakes, compounded by the opening and closing of a car door, sent a shiver through his body.

Heavy footsteps drew closer as he froze to the spot. Aware that he'd run out of options, he pulled the scalpel from his pocket and turned around, holding the blade aloft ready to strike. Blinded by the vehicle's high beams, he squinted and shaded his eyes with his free hand.

'Drop that thing! I'm security,' shouted the advancing figure.

Arlo hesitated for a moment, recognised the voice and lowered the scalpel. 'Steve, is that you?'

'What the hell are you doing?' Steve snapped.

'I was getting some air when I saw headlights. I thought you were him.'

Steve glanced at the scalpel, raised his eyebrows and said coldly, 'Always be sure you have an exit route.'

Arlo viewed his surroundings. The door behind him was locked and there were two parked cars blocking the way to both his right and left.

'Are you working tonight?' Steve asked.

Arlo shook his head and then, slightly embarrassed, explained what he was doing in the hospital.

Steve showed no emotion when he suggested the doctor might want to leave town until this was over.

'Spider's been in contact with my friend, Lorraine,' Arlo said. 'He may use her as leverage if I disappear. I can't do that to her.'

'Fair enough.' Steve paused then added, 'I do have some good news.'

'What's that?' queried Arlo.

'You're not the next to die.'

'How do you know that?'

'Trust me, I know.' Steve put on a pair of gloves before opening the door and reaching into the back of his van. 'Just keep your movements to a minimum,' he added while gingerly removing a black sack containing an object about the size of a football.

Arlo did a double-take. 'What's in there?' As he stared at the sack, the rubber gloves fuelled his suspicions. Surely, it couldn't be… He looked and opened his mouth to speak.

Steve stopped him. 'I know what you're thinking and you're right.' There was sadness in his voice. 'I was fond of her and they knew it.'

'What are you going to do with it?' Arlo stuttered.

'When you go inside I'll put the sack by the dumpster.'

Arlo looked up at the building, searching for cameras. 'It's a camera blackspot,' Steve told him. 'Then I'm going to call 999 and in no time at all this place will be crawling with cops and a team from forensics. I'll show them what I found on my rounds and that'll be it. I know nothing more and you weren't even here.'

'I guess I won't be going to the petrol station to get a toothbrush then?'

'I'll bring you some stuff tomorrow. Try to survive without until then.'

After Steve had used his master key to unlock the emergency door, Arlo vanished down a dimly lit corridor, picking up a blanket and pillow along the way. Inside the storage room, he created a living space out of sight of anyone who might enter the room. He moved the mattress to the rear corner and pushed several machines forward to form a barrier. Anyone who tried to get in would have to crawl under the arm of a defunct x-ray machine. He propped a second mattress against the machine to provide additional cover.

He stood back and viewed his new living quarters, then his shoulders slumped and he gave a long sigh. *I've ruined everything. Why didn't I just keep my big mouth shut?*

Any further musing was interrupted by a gentle tap on the door. Arlo froze.

'Doc, it's me, Kev – the janitor. I know you're in there.'

Arlo opened the door a crack and gasped as he came face to face with the man: it was like he'd stuck his nose into an ashtray. Despite the strong odour, he held his ground and kept the dishevelled grey-haired man outside the room. Explaining to Kev what he was doing in the storage room at 2am wouldn't be easy, so he waited and let him do the talking.

'I know exactly what you're going through,' Kev announced as he wobbled slightly. 'The same thing happened to me.'

If only you knew, Arlo thought.

'My wife kicked me out two months ago,' the janitor announced as if he were the proud member of an elite club. 'Said I drink too much. Can you believe that? I spent a few nights on the bloody street. Now I'm couch surfing but I can't see that lasting much longer.'

Arlo nodded sympathetically.

'It was clever of you to find this place. Now I know where to come for a chat or – God forbid – if I find myself homeless again.' He peered around Arlo to examine the room. 'Hey, we could be roommates. I could tell you stories about some of those nurses you work with.' He leered as he waved goodbye.

Arlo watched him leave then shut the door. His secret was out and it was now in the hands of a couch-surfing drunk with a big mouth. Staying in the hospital was no longer an option – but where else could he go?

The police interview was over in less than an hour – Steve had known it wouldn't take long because the local cops respected and trusted him. He was a hero both at home and abroad, and he had a contract to provide security for the hospital. His history of detecting suspicious packages was well known: finding a severed head was just another day at the office.

A quick phone call to Eddie confirmed that all was well at the house, although predictably his son was pissed off with having to stand guard over his mother. Steve's second call was to Lager, who was waiting across town at a petrol station near a disused elementary school.

'Where've you been?' Lager asked. 'I been calling you for over an hour.'

'Sorry, I had to go to the hospital. They found the woman's missing head.' The ringtone on Steve's phone saved him from having to explain further. 'I'll see you in twenty, Lager. I gotta take this.' He seamlessly switched calls. 'Malik, you're up early.'

'I'm afraid sleep is a luxury my wife and I no longer have.'

'How can I help?'

Malik cleared his throat and took his time. It was obvious he was having difficulty saying what he wanted to say. 'I read on the BBC online news that a woman was decapitated near you.'

Steve immediately sensed the man was in pain and needed help, so he took over. 'I don't know, is the answer. Your son Qasim threatened my family and friends. This woman wasn't a friend but I knew her. I suppose it could be coincidence.'

'We think he called us the other day,' Malik said. 'He didn't speak, he just listened to his mother and me talking.'

'That's a good sign. Maybe he's having second thoughts and wants to go home. As soon as you know something, call me. I'll do the same.'

'Thanks, Mr Foley. You're a good man.'

The call ended as Steve stopped at a red light. Squeezing the steering wheel with both hands he murmured, 'You won't think I'm a good man if I find out your son was responsible for Jesse's murder.'

Nick slumped in the front seat of the Renault Trafic van, his cap pulled down to his eyes. To kill time, he played with the dials and switches of his newly acquired rental vehicle, which was much more comfortable and technically advanced than his old Ford camper van. Bluetooth, what the hell was that, he wondered.

As he slouched even lower in his seat to avoid being spotted by a lady walking her dog, he unscrewed the top of his thermos flask and carefully poured himself a cup of tea then placed the flask back on the floor between his feet.

His phone vibrated on the dash and his wife's face appeared on the screen. 'Nick, are you there yet?'

'Yes, darling. I'm parked across the street.'

'What can you see.'

'Not a lot right now, but it's early. I'll call you when there's movement.'

'Promise me you won't do anything silly.'

Nick sighed. 'That ship has long since sailed. Don't worry – I'm old but I'm not senile. I just want to see if the Englishman is still living here.'

'Do you think the Renault is big enough?'

'Pat, it weighs over 3,000 kilos. Trust me, it's big enough.'

Forty-five minutes later, he watched as the front door opened and the young man they'd smuggled across Europe stepped outside. 'That's one of them,' he whispered to himself. 'Now where's the one with the charisma bypass?'

The movement of an upstairs curtain drew Nick's attention to a window at the far corner of the house. Someone was checking the street. A short time later a second person left the house and headed for the VW estate parked on the street.

'That's him,' Nick mumbled. 'They're both still here. Great.'

Spider signalled to the waitress for a second coffee then turned to Qasim who was sitting opposite him. 'Try the bacon,' he mocked. 'It's really tasty.'

Qasim ignored him and carried on eating his French toast.

'Do you know how difficult it is to get this in Syria and Iraq?' Spider asked, lifting a rash of crispy bacon with his fingers and dangling it in front of Qasim's face. 'And alcohol. I missed that too. How the hell do you people get through the day?'

'I'm not from those countries, I'm from Pakistan,' Qasim said softly.

'It's all the bloody same,' replied Spider.

They said nothing more until after the waitress had placed the bill on the table. Spider turned it over, wrote a name on the back and slid it across the table.

Qasim looked surprised. 'What's this?'

'Your next kill,' Spider whispered.

'But I thought it was—'

A wide, sinister grin covered Spider's face. 'That's what I wanted everyone to think.'

19

Arlo woke feeling rough, his head hurting from lack of fresh air. The lumpy hospital mattress beneath him had taken its toll on his back and he rose to his feet like a man twice his age.

Once dressed for the day ahead, he tucked his food and clothes into a carrier bag and quietly left the room. He crept across the concrete floor past the loading docks and up the stairs to the staff locker room. Happy to have avoided Kev, he cleaned himself as best he could at a sink and squeezed out enough toothpaste from a discarded tube in a rubbish bin to finger-brush his teeth.

'Feeling almost human again,' he said to himself sarcastically and stepped back out into the hall.

Lorraine was waiting, arms folded. 'I hear you've moved into a room downstairs after being kicked out of the house by your wife,' she said, desperately trying not to laugh.

'Well, that didn't take long. I guess the whole hospital knows.' Arlo didn't sound surprised.

She nodded. 'What's next?'

He hadn't thought that far ahead; his focus was on staying alive and getting through the ten-hour shift in A&E. As Lorraine carried on asking questions, his mind wandered and her voice faded into the background. 'I should've kept the gun,' he murmured.

Lorraine's eye lit up. 'What gun?' she asked.

He tried to cover his mistake. 'Nothing. Just thinking out loud. I should have bought a gun.'

'No,' she snapped. 'You said, "I should've kept the gun".'

Arlo dismissed her with a 'whatever' and walked away, knowing that he'd just made a massive blunder that would fuel her curiosity and get her more deeply involved in his life.

Eddie was twenty minutes early, and he'd found a new coffee shop called the Brew Crew. He was trying to get his act together. He knew Carol wasn't happy meeting him at the Ugly Mug. She hated the place; it was crowded and noisy with screaming babies and out-of-control toddlers. He hoped the new spot would allow him breathing space to so he could postpone their night out but still keep the relationship alive.

His plan didn't get off to a good start. Carol entered the small, brightly lit café with a face like thunder. Refusing an offer of coffee, she sat opposite Eddie and waited.

'There's been a threat against my mother,' he said. 'I need to protect her until this is over.'

'I'm sorry, I didn't know that.' Neither of them spoke for a moment then Carol suggested, 'Why can't your father take over for a few hours while we go out? I promise to have you home by midnight,' she mocked.

Eddie thought for a moment. 'That'll leave Lager exposed.'

Carol shook her head, stood up and slowly pushed her chair closer to the table. 'Maybe we should call it quits. I like you, Eddie, but I can't see this going anywhere if we can't spend time together other than in a bloody coffee shop. This problem you and your father are having with terrorists, or whatever they are, may never end. Life's too short. Call me if you change your mind and want to do what normal people do.'

She left the Brew Crew without looking back.

Eddie felt numb. He thought about chasing after her, but what would he say? He couldn't reveal anything without clearing it with his father first, which he found unacceptable. Asking for permission to do something really pissed him off, and knowing Carol was aware of this made it worse. He agreed with her: why couldn't his father stay home and protect his wife? And why couldn't Lager be alone for a few hours? He was a big boy, ex-military.

Eddie made up his mind. He wasn't going to ask his father, he was going to tell him.

A&E was packed when Arlo walked through the double doors. There had been a couple of stabbings and a hit and run in the early hours of the morning, and those in need were already receiving priority treatment. The waiting room was filled with patients with the usual sprains and broken bones, signs of a stroke, headaches and skin infections. One elderly lady, still wearing pyjamas and dressing gown, had been hanging around for more than ten hours.

Arlo looked down the list and, like most days, wondered why they chose to sit in a crowded hospital rather than visit their local GP or pharmacist. Seamlessly, he slotted into the system and went to examine a man in his mid-thirties with a huge cut over his right eye. Lorraine had already cleaned the wound, so it was down to Arlo to stitch him up and send him on his way.

Once he'd administered a local anaesthetic, he began suturing. As he was tying a knot on the fifth and final stitch, his phone rang; Steve. Without comment, Arlo left the patient and Lorraine in the blue-curtained examination area.

'Please tell me you got him,' he said as he hurried to a quiet corner away from staff and patients.

'Good morning to you, too.'

'Sorry, I'm feeling even more stressed than usual today. I'll try that again. Good morning, Steve.'

'You still sleeping in the basement?'

'No. Why do you ask?'

'I have a plan.'

'That's good to hear?'

'Not really,' Steve responded.

'Why?'

'Because it involves you, and you're not going to like it.'

Eddie stormed into the house and marched down the hall to the kitchen where his father was sitting at the table. 'We need to talk,' he said.

Steve, sitting with both hands wrapped around an oversized mug of tea, didn't reply so his son continued. 'I know we're going through a difficult time but I need a social life. I work nights all week. I want to go out and do what normal people do.'

'Boy, that sounds familiar,' Victoria sniggered as she entered the room.

Steve looked at her with more than a hint of disdain then

returned his gaze to his mug of tea. 'Okay.'

Eddie was stunned: he'd not been expecting that, and his head was still full of points to make in his well-rehearsed defence.

'So how's it going to work?' Steve asked.

Eddie wasted no time. 'You stay here and provide protection while Lager looks after the safer, non-derelict sites like the hospital. I'll be back at work no later than midnight.'

'When?' Steve asked.

'Friday.'

His father's nod was all Eddie needed. He ran upstairs and called Carol. 'Are we still okay for Friday?' he asked.

'Sure – but what about your work?'

'I've sorted it out. Dad's looking after Mum.'

'What about the guy you call Lager?' Carol asked. 'Will he be safe?'

'Yes, he'll be fine. He'll cover the hospital and a couple of other sites where people gather. He won't be alone.'

'Then it's settled. I'll see you Friday at the Black Swan, eight o'clock.'

Eddie was puzzled. 'Don't you want me to pick you up at your place?'

'Thanks, but you don't need to. I have a couple of things to do first so I'll go straight there.'

Eddie returned to the kitchen to make a sandwich. His parents were sitting in awkward silence at opposite ends of the table. Finally, Victoria spoke. 'So what's her name?'

'Carol,' Eddie replied.

'Carol who?' asked Victoria.

He didn't know but he wasn't about to make that public. Only Carol's first name had appeared on the dating app and he hadn't bothered to ask for her surname. He kept his head down and carried on making his sandwich.

'Is she local?' Victoria continued.

Eddie nodded, then realised he didn't know Carol's address either. He started to feel uncomfortable. When his mother asked what Carol did for a living, he exploded.

'What the hell? You sound like Dad!' he shouted. 'Get off my back. It's just a date with a girl. And stop trying to be my mother. You resigned from that position years ago!'

With the sandwich in one hand and a can of beer in the other, he hurried back to his room and slammed the door. It took a few minutes for him to cool off, but when he did he started thinking. Carol knew everything about him, yet he knew nothing about her. Why?

Arlo peeped through a narrow crack between the curtains in his living room as he'd done at least ten times in the past hour. He'd checked and re-checked the lock on the back door and moved the key from plain sight on the tabletop to underneath a plant in the hall. The cricket bat had been joined by a newly purchased hammer, and his scalpel remained within touching distance.

Being home didn't fill him with confidence; the basement storage room at the hospital was musty and uncomfortable but he'd felt safe there. After Kev appeared, however, coming home had been inevitable – and it was where Steve wanted him to be.

During their telephone conversation, Steve had been blunt when he'd asked Arlo to act as bait to catch Spider. 'Stay at home when you're not working,' he'd instructed. 'If he comes, it'll be at night because the street is too busy for a daytime attack. Don't worry, I'll be parked outside your house.'

Don't worry! What a joke. Arlo made another visit to the living-room curtains. *How can I not worry? I've seen with my own eyes what this crazy son of a bitch can do.*

'I've just hired an ex-army buddy, Terry Black,' Steve announced from the foot of Eddie's bed. 'With you here at home and me at the doctor's house, we needed someone to back up Lager. I had second thoughts – it's not fair sending him out alone with this going on.'

Eddie nodded agreement. 'What's Black like?'

'Cool headed, quiet. Nice guy. Married, with a baby girl on the way.'

'What happens Friday night when I'm out with Carol?'

'The doc has arranged to do some night shifts at the hospital when we need him to, so I'll be here with your mum. When you finish your night out, you take over and I'll link up with Lager and Black. Okay?'

Eddie didn't respond; instead, he stared blankly at his hands resting on his lap.

'What's up?' his father asked.

'I've got to get out of here, get my own flat. This place is doing my head in.'

Now it was Steve's turn to be silent as he thought about what Eddie had just said. The Foleys were broken and had been for some time: Tim was dead; Victoria wanted a divorce, and Eddie was tired of being part of a dysfunctional family. Steve blamed himself; he'd never been around, and even when he was he'd spent his time trying to save the world. Those were Victoria's words, not his, but he still felt responsible.

He phoned Lager, hoping he could provide an update on Jesse's murder. Through his ex-colleagues on the police force, Lager could only ascertain that the beheading had been carried out in two stages, possibly by two attackers. That was it: no fingerprints, no footprints, no hairs, no fibres and no suspects.

Steve thanked him, ended the call and crossed the hall to his room. A moment later he returned and tossed a package on Eddie's bed. 'What's this?' his son asked.

'A stab vest.'

'Will it stop me losing my head?' Eddie asked sarcastically.

Steve's face hardened as he gazed into his son's eyes. 'Only your preparedness will prevent that.'

Nick was sitting on the edge of the bed, his belly pushing his blue cotton long-sleeve shirt to the limit. Sweat was dripping from his temples on to his cheeks until it eventually disappeared inside his collar.

'You alright?' Pat asked. 'You don't look well.'

'I'm fine,' he said through gritted teeth. 'Just a bit warm in here, that's all.'

Pat opened the window and passed him a small bottle of water. It took all his strength to undo the cap. After a small sip, he started to talk about the many things that needed to go smoothly for his plan to work.

'There must be no witnesses – that's why this can only happen after dark. It's important we're next in line because

210

otherwise I'll be coming from an angle, which may not work. Next, the Englishman must get out of the car. I believe he's the main man – if we want to, we can deal with his Pakistani friend later. Finally, we really need to do it twice to be sure. We must be quick.'

Pat shook her head. 'There's not much room for error, is there?'

Her husband wiped the perspiration from his forehead then ran his hand through his thinning hair. He felt frustrated, inadequate; this was his best – and only – plan, but it had it holes big enough to drive a truck through. 'You're right,' he said, 'but we agreed that we can't do nothing.'

Pat paced up and down the small room. She looked tired and her shoulders were stooping; news of Colin's death was weighing heavily on her.

'You're not convinced,' Nick said.

'Whether the plan works or not, there's still a bigger question.'

'What's that?'

'Can we kill?'

As soon as the question left her lips, Nick responded without hesitation. 'Anyone can kill,' he said confidently. 'Anyone.'

※ ※ ※

It had just turned dark and the streetlights outside the house cast a strong glow over the pavement that fronted the row of symmetrical houses on Ellen Lane. Qasim's mind wandered for a moment, allowing him to picture a man in a building down town adjusting the light timings to coincide with the frequent changes to sunrise and sunset.

He smiled when he thought about the streetlights in Pakistan that rarely came on despite the miles of wires that hung like balls of spaghetti from teetering wooden poles. He missed the traffic chaos, the houses perched on top of each other and the smell of food being cooked on the street. He missed his friends. He missed his parents. Sitting alone in the house, he dreamed of going home – and today was the perfect opportunity to do just that.

Spider was nowhere to be seen. Qasim knew he could run and, with help from his father, possibly make it all the way back to Peshawar. Barely a day went by when he didn't consider it, but he also knew he would never be safe. Spider was ruthless, his contacts were ruthless; if Qasim ran, his life and most likely the lives of his parents would be over. He had come too far, done too much. The only way out was if Spider were dead. And barely a day had gone by when he hadn't considered that, too.

On Qasim's bedside table a ten-inch zombie knife with both a sharp cutting edge and a serrated cutting edge sat menacingly, waiting for its next victim. It was a lethal piece of kit that Spider had bought on a local estate and proudly presented to him at breakfast.

The teenager finally knew who and how, but he didn't know when or where. Spider's mind games continued.

The landlady at the B&B was waiting at the bottom of the stairs to greet Nick and Pat. The old man knew something was wrong because her arms were folded over her food-stained apron and she wasn't wearing her normal 'nice to see you face'.

'I have guests arriving tomorrow and you're taking up two parking spaces.' Her tone was far from friendly.

'Sorry,' Nick, replied. 'I'll park the van on the street.'

'I thought you wanted a rental that was smaller than your camper van so it would be easier to get around the country lanes.'

She was right: he had said that. His eyes shifted to Pat for support, but she lowered her gaze and started searching for something in her bag. He was on his own. Thinking quickly was never his strong point, he liked to mull things over while having a cup of tea, but now there was no time. He thought about telling the old witch to mind her own business then quickly dismissed the idea.

'We decided to go antique hunting instead,' Pat announced without looking up. 'So we need a van with more room inside. Our camper has got everything in it, including the kitchen sink.'

A smile crossed the landlady's lips, her eyes lit up and suddenly her arms were no longer folded across her chest. 'There are a couple wonderful shops in the next town,' she said. 'I hope you find some lovely things.'

Nick nodded politely, took Pat by the hand and stepped outside to the car park. 'Nice one,' he whispered. 'Where did that come from?'

'No idea. I just blurted it out.'

'And what do we do if we buy a van load of antiques that we can't fit into our camper?'

Pat shrugged her shoulders. 'Didn't get that far. I was too busy worrying about tonight and how we're going to get away with murder.'

※ ※ ※

The front door brushed quietly over the thick bristle doormat, allowing the cool night air to filter into the hallway. Feeling nervous, Arlo cautiously poked his head through the opening and surveyed the street.

The rather large lady two doors down was conveniently staring at her phone while her dog did his business on someone else's lawn. The couple directly opposite were unloading shopping bags from the boot of their Land Rover following a trip to the supermarket. It wasn't a child-frenzied Saturday, but there were people around and Arlo felt confident he wouldn't die if he stepped outside. Steve had assured him an attack would happen at night and he was certain that the ex-marine meant while he and the rest of the neighbourhood were asleep.

It took him fewer than ten steps to reach his car. Once next to the door on the driver's side, he dropped his keys, knelt as if to pick them up then scanned the underside of his vehicle. Steve had insisted he do this before he drove anywhere. 'Look for anything that shouldn't be there,' he'd instructed.

If it had been a body on a gurney Arlo wouldn't have had a problem, but his knowledge of what went on under the bonnet was minimal and what happened underneath the car even less. 'Looks fine,' he whispered unconvincingly before returning to his feet.

'I hope you're not that clumsy when you've got a needle in your hand,' joked the large lady.

Arlo smiled half-heartedly, opened the door and sat behind the wheel. He thought for a moment then lowered the window. 'I hear there's been a spate of burglaries in the neighbourhood. Have you seen anyone suspicious lately?'

'No, but I'll keep an eye out,' she replied, 'I'm always aware of who's doing what around here.'

Closing the window and smiling at her, Arlo muttered, 'I bet you are.'

Feeling pleased with himself, he pulled away from the curb. Job done.

It was just after 8pm and traffic was light. The Renault, with Nick at the wheel, moved unhindered across town. In the passenger seat Pat fidgeted nervously with her phone while her husband hummed some unrecognisable tune.

It wasn't easy to stay calm: what they were planning to do was way out of their comfort zone, but betrayal had left them with no other option. During sleepless nights at the B&B they had talked about the possible consequences. Without hesitation, they had agreed to accept whatever was thrown at them, just as they'd agreed to do when they'd smuggled two unknown individuals across Europe.

'It's here. Turn left,' Pat instructed as they approached Ellen Lane.

'I know where it is,' Nick snapped as he eased the Renault into the turn.

'Sorry.'

The lane was packed with cars parked nose to tail. There was no way he could squeeze in behind the black VW. 'Damn,' he said through gritted teeth before driving to the end of the road.

'What do we do now?' Pat asked softly.

'If we double park, some nosey neighbour will spot us and think we're up to something. We'll stay here. Maybe a space closer to their house will become available.' He turned off the engine.

They unfastened their seat belts, slouched down in their seats and waited. Nick yawned, cracked his knuckles and started tapping his right foot. Pat turned to him. 'Take a deep breath,' she whispered. They didn't speak again.

Twenty-five minutes later, Nick spotted the red glow of tail lights further along the lane. In no time at all, he was heading towards the freed-up space. 'It's our lucky day,' he said. 'Look, we're right behind the VW.' He backed the Renault into position, leaving about three meters between the van and the black estate. 'Show time.' He sounded like a bad actor about to go into battle in a movie. 'Strap yourself in, darling.'

Pat ignored his theatrics and rested her hand on his knee. He turned his head and watched as she took a slow deep breath. Once again, they fell silent. It was 10.35 pm. Within a few minutes, they were both asleep.

At 11.17pm, Nick awoke when he heard someone trying to open the rear door. In his side mirror he spotted a grinning youngster. 'Little bastards,' he murmured. Without hesitating, he started the engine, slammed into reverse and only stopped when he heard a loud scream.

'Wanker,' yelled the youngster. Nick watched him limp across the road and disappear between the houses.

Startled awake, Pat cried, 'What's happening?'

Nick laughed. 'We just had a trial run – and it worked.'

She sat upright, smoothed her hair and looked at the road ahead. It was completely quiet. 'Did you kill someone?'

'No,' her husband replied. 'But I've got a taste for it.'

※ ※ ※

With his ear pressed against his bedroom wall, Qasim listened as Spider went through his regular evening workout. Announcing each exercise aloud as if he were performing in front of an audience, the Englishman counted down twenty-five push-ups, fifty sit-ups and fifteen squats until he eventually arrived in a plank position that seemed to go on in silence forever. Only a loud exhalation signalled the end of his routine.

Sitting back on the bed, Qasim stared at the zombie knife. His thoughts were all over the place; not knowing what was happening was messing with his mind.

Feeling he had nothing to lose, he walked down the hall and tapped gently on Spider's door. His heart rate increased as self-doubt took control. *Was this a mistake?*

An icy, unwelcoming stare greeted him and he took a step back. Sweat was dripping from Spider's unshaven face down his neck and over his bare chest. The clearly visible tattoo of the eight-legged creature sat menacingly on his left shoulder. It was a calling card that had spread fear throughout Syria and Iraq, but it was also a source of identification that seemed at odds with the man's obsession with anonymity.

'Tomorrow night,' he announced before Qasim could open his mouth. 'I'll take you there, then the rest is up to you.'

Qasim waited but there were no more details. At least now he knew when it was going to happen, but he was growing tired of the games.

With an unpleasant smile Spider added, 'Soon it'll be my turn. If I could, I'd put things right tonight and get the hell out of this place, but unfortunately my deal is to babysit you until you finish what you came here to do or you get killed trying.'

A moment's silence followed. Qasim swallowed hard. He had ended three lives: two of the victims had already been only a heartbeat from death, and the third was a man on his knees waiting for the fatal blow. They'd been easy kills, put on a plate for him, and there'd been no chance of retaliation. Now, though, things had changed and it showed on his troubled face.

Spider gave a laugh that was forced and over the top. As he slammed the door, he shouted, 'Welcome to my world.'

Qasim hurried back to his room and threw himself face down on the bed. This was it; in less than twenty-four hours he'd be going it alone. 'A lamb to the slaughter' was the phrase rolling around his head. Despite his best efforts, he couldn't block it out.

Reluctantly he picked up the knife and ran his fingers along the double-edged steel blade before clutching the handle. Standing up, he moved to the long thin mirror leaning against the wall. On a silent count of three he stepped forward and pretended to plunge the weapon into an imaginary target. His attempt to accompany the move with a frightening growl fell flat, and the mirror captured his every pathetic move.

He sat back on the bed, placed the knife on the table and muttered despairingly, 'I'm screwed.'

The lights inside the third house on the left on Ellen Lane went out just after midnight. The late-night dog walkers had returned home and put their pets to bed, and the neighbourhood was finally still.

'Let's go,' Pat pleaded. 'I'm tired and my bum is sore from

218

sitting for so long.'

Nick checked his watch then glanced in the wing mirrors. 'Darling, this is such a great spot. It might be days before we can park here again.'

'Then we'll have to take that chance. We have no idea when they'll leave the house, and from here it looks like everyone is asleep but us.'

'What if I take you back to the B&B and I spend the night here?'

'I thought we were in this together?'

He nodded, started the engine and drove back down the lane. 'Same time tomorrow?' he said.

'Same time tomorrow,' she replied. 'But with tea, sandwiches and a pillow.'

20

Qasim's thumb brushed against his iPhone screen and immediately the device lit up to tell him it was Friday, 4.23am. He'd lost count of the number of times he'd checked it since getting his head down just after midnight; despite closing his eyes, fear and anxiety had prevented him from falling asleep.

Down the hall Spider was having no such problem and the paper-thin walls separating their bedrooms did nothing to stifle the roar of his constant snoring. 'The benefits of being a serial killer,' mocked Qasim.

Draping a blanket over his shoulders, he tiptoed downstairs into the kitchen and made a cup of tea. In the living room, he stretched out on the sofa and scrolled through the contacts on his phone before eventually stopping at his parents' number.

Sipping the black tea, he thought about what life would be like for them now that he and his sisters were no longer there. He knew it would be a lot less noisy first thing in the morning. Gone would be the familiar sound of his father's call to get out of bed, the slamming of bedroom and bathroom doors and footsteps pounding down the stairs to the breakfast table. Sibling arguments about who did what to whom and discussions regarding politics and just about everything else had been lost. There would be no inviting aromas coming from the well-used pots and pans on the Aga in the kitchen. Without her children to feed, Qasim's mother would make salads instead of the family favourites like *peshawari karahi* and *chapli kabab.*

After confirming his phone was on speaker and the 'No Caller ID' settings, Qasim pressed the circle next to his parent's number and waited.

'Hello,' his father said softly.

Qasim mouthed the word back to him.

'Is that you, son?'

The teenager nodded.

'Are you alright?'

He gently shook his head.

'Please come home,' his father begged. 'Your mother and I miss you so much. It doesn't matter what you've done, we just want you to come home.'

The sound of footsteps crossing a wooden floor and a door closing indicated that his father had moved from the hall into the living room. Qasim sensed he wanted to talk in private. 'Qasim, are you still there? I need to tell you something.'

The boy didn't know what to expect and he waited while his father cleared his throat.

'People in Peshawar are saying you're in England to get revenge for your sisters' deaths. I think you know that Eddie had nothing to do with the attack on Rana – he was in Kabul at the time. His English friend Roadkill and the three Germans were responsible and they paid the ultimate price.'

Qasim stared at his phone, unmoved,. After a long silence, his father continued. 'There's something else. You're aware that your sister Benazir and a few others wrapped in vests packed with explosives boarded a small plane to skydive onto targets in London. Many innocent people would have been killed had the plane not exploded on take-off. I'm sure you know that Eddie Foley's father, Steve, planted the bomb that killed everyone on board. What you don't know is…'

The sentence ended abruptly. Concerned, Qasim studied his phone. He heard several deep breaths before his father carried on, his voice frail. 'What you don't know is that I pushed the button. I detonated the bomb.'

At first Qasim didn't believe him. It didn't make sense. He rocked back and forth, shook his head and mumbled 'no' as he struggled to understand his father's words. His head started pounding as if it had been hit by a hammer. It was too much to take in. How could his father have killed his own daughter?

'Benazir was going to die – it was just a matter of time. That was her mission,' continued his father. 'If I hadn't pushed the button, Steve would have done it. I felt it was the right thing to do because it was my responsibility. I didn't want our family forever linked to a mass killing.'

Still in shock, Qasim paced the room. He raised his arm to throw his phone against the wall though he didn't release it.

'Steve did our family a favour. The authorities had no idea what your sister and her friends were up to. An act of terrorism on that scale would have been catastrophic and it would have been shattering for us. Thanks to Steve's influence, the official report stated the explosion was an accident and that a group of skydivers died because of a leak in the fuel line. Benazir will not be known as a terrorist.'

And Steve won't be held accountable for planting a bomb on a plane, thought Qasim.

'So,' said his father, 'if you want to hurt someone, hurt me.'

As the last few words came over the speaker, the door opened. Spider was standing there, grinning from ear to ear. 'What now my little Paki warrior?' he asked.

Startled, Qasim fumbled with his phone but it took three attempts before he successfully pressed the red button.

'There's nothing like a one-way conversation with your father, is there?' Spider mocked.

Qasim froze. Spider pointed to his left and grinned. 'Thin walls.' Then, as if a switch had been flicked, the teasing stopped. A shard of morning light slipped through the partially closed curtains and highlighted the sudden change in his expression. His jaw tightened and his eyes turned steely, though his voice was calm.

'Nice speech. Quite a dilemma for you, huh? Pity it's too late.' He smirked, appearing to revel in having Qasim against the ropes. 'When you contacted Al-Qaeda, you boarded a runaway train.' He took a couple of steps closer and whispered in the boy's ear. 'And now you can't get off.'

The night shift had finished but Arlo had remained in the canteen sipping his third coffee. Doctors, nurses, admin staff and just about everyone else employed in the hospital walked by his table near the entrance.

The queue for flat-white, Americano and cappuccino takeaways stretched out the door, and Arlo chuckled inwardly as he wondered if any of the patients on the wards received treatment during breakfast time.

Head down, eyes glued to his phone, he scrolled through emails, Facebook and the news. There was nothing he wanted to see; it was just a way of wasting time until his street was buzzing with neighbours going to work and parents taking their children to school. Safety in numbers.

A quick glance at his watch confirmed he'd have to stay in the canteen a bit longer. He closed his eyes and for a moment he shut out the noise around him.

The sound of feet shuffling next to his table was followed by a polite request, 'Is this seat free?'

Arlo nodded but didn't look up. Someone placed a cardboard coffee cup gently on the table in front of him. The metal chair opposite squeaked as it was pulled across the floor.

'You a doctor?' the stranger asked.

Arlo hated that question because it was usually followed by: 'My wife/ husband/ relative has a rash/lump and I wondered if you could tell me what it is.'

He kept his eyes down but nodded politely. The man slurped his drink, placed the cup on the table and stood up. 'Nice talking to you, doc,' he said before walking away.

'Who's your friend?' Lorraine asked as she sat on the newly vacated chair.

Arlo shrugged his shoulders and raised his head. 'You look tired,' she added.

'Night shifts are a killer.'

'I know why you're doing them.'

Arlo half-smiled. 'Just trying to stay alive.' He stood up slowly, collected his empty cup and gestured for Lorraine to hand him the one the man had left on the table. She reached for it then stopped; visibly shaken, her eyes widened and her faced turned pale.

'What?' Arlo asked.

Lorraine lifted the cup and gradually rotated it until the customer's name written in black ink was visible to him. Her voice quivered as she announced, 'You just had a visit from Spider.'

Arlo glanced over her shoulder then moved toward the canteen door. 'What did he look like? What was he wearing?' he demanded frantically.

'I don't know – I wasn't looking at him, I was looking at you!'

'For God's sake, think,' he shouted, waving his arms. 'Fat, thin, short, tall?'

Lorraine didn't answer, instead she quietly called his name. 'Arlo. Arlo.'

'What?' he hollered before turning to face her. A slight movement of her head was all it took to stop him saying anything further. Every eye in the room was fixed on him; people were standing frozen to the spot as if they'd been caught in a photograph. Only the noise of the coffee grinder behind the counter disturbed the uneasy silence.

Arlo wanted to get out of there as quickly as possible but there was nowhere to hide, and if he ran he would look even more foolish. For the briefest moment he thought about making a statement, explaining things, but who would believe him?

It was yet another dose of humiliation to add to the story circulating about him sleeping in the basement because of a fight with a wife he didn't have. Arlo closed his eyes. *They must think I'm mad.*

Victoria brushed breadcrumbs off the kitchen table onto the floor before sitting down with a cuppa. Anne was sleeping nearby on a padded mat underneath a pair of criss-crossed arches that supported a handful of colourful hanging toys.

Finally there was peace. The baby was teething and she'd been awake most of the past four nights. Victoria's nerves were on a knife edge: she was tired, pissed off with just about everyone and everything, and it didn't help being trapped in the house with a husband she loathed and a son who loathed her.

She took a couple of deep breaths then sipped her tea, glancing constantly at Anne and grateful for every minute her baby slept. For the first time in days, she had time to unfold a newspaper, spread it over the table and catch up on the news.

She'd barely finished the headline when her moment of 'me-time' ended abruptly as a knock on the front door sent her into panic mode. Concerned that Anne might wake if the knocking continued, she hurried into the hall, completely forgetting about the threat to her life. At the same time Eddie crashed out of his bedroom clutching his phone to his ear and bounded down the stairs yelling, 'Don't open the door! Dad says it's an Asian kid. Could be Qasim.'

Victoria stepped aside and stared at her son. There was fire in his eyes. He was the mirror image of his father, fearless, with the same gung-ho attitude – but unlike his father, he didn't know when to stop.

'Are you expecting a delivery?' he whispered. Victoria shook her head.

Eddie repeated his father's words as they came through the phone. 'Baseball cap, sunglasses, package in left hand, something black in his right. Red 4x4 in front of house.'

Passing the phone to his mother, he removed the door chain, lowered his right hand and gently clasped the doorknob. Stepping back slightly, he turned the knob and yanked open the door.

Victoria looked on in disbelief as he sprang forward and

grasped the delivery man by the throat. Within seconds the man's feet were off the ground, his eyes were bulging and his arms flailing wildly. The parcel tumbled to the ground. 'You're choking him!' She screamed into the phone. 'Help! Steve, help!'

'I can't – I'm ten minutes away,' he hollered. 'Get your keys.'

Victoria grabbed her keys from the side table and slotted the large house one between her first and second fingers. With her fist tightly wrapped around the rest of the bunch, she hurried to the porch and punched her son as hard as she could in the side of the head.

Eddie shrieked, released his grip from the delivery man's throat and clasped his head. Blood started flowing from a small gash just below his temple. 'What the hell?' he shouted, glaring at his mother.

'You were killing him, for God's sake.'

Eddie stared at the key poking between her fingers. 'Dad taught you that, didn't he?'

Victoria almost smiled then she looked down at the man slumped on the floor. His sunglasses, cap, phone and parcel lay scattered on the porch. 'Is that Qasim?'

Eddie shook his head.

'The parcel is for the lady next door,' she snapped as she read the address label. 'He came to the wrong house and you almost strangled him.'

Eddie reached for the man's hand to help him to his feet, but the gesture was rejected. 'Fuck you, then,' he groaned. He turned to go back inside only to find his way barred by his mother's outstretched arm. She rubbed her thumb and index finger together. Eddie understood the gesture but failed to react.

His mother spoke softly. 'Police? assault?'

Reluctantly Eddie opened his wallet and took out a £20 note. Victoria signalled for more and he pressed a further £20 in her hand. 'Now apologise,' she demanded.

'You must be kidding,' he snarled before entering the house.

Disappointed, but not surprised, Victoria handed the cash to the delivery man who was huddled on the floor rubbing his neck. 'I'll take the money, but I'm still calling the police,' he said.

'That's fine. I'll tell them I saw the whole thing.'

'Thank you,' he muttered as he stood up.

'And I'll say that when I answered the door you grabbed my breasts and tried to rape me. Thankfully my son intervened.'

It was obvious the delivery man wasn't expecting her to say that. With a face covered in confusion and shock, he stared into her eyes as if waiting for her to say she was only joking.

'Who do you think they'll believe?' she asked confidently.

'There's a camera on the wall that'll show what really happened!'

'The video is being erased as we speak.'

The man shook his head in disgust. Without saying another word, he gathered his things and walked away.

Back in the house, Victoria sat at the kitchen table and placed her head in her hands. Tears filled her eyes. 'What's wrong?' asked Eddie. 'I heard what you said and it was brilliant.'

'That's what bothers me,' she cried. 'It was so easy. God help me, I'm becoming just like you and your father.'

❋ ❋ ❋

The drive home from the hospital was stressful. With one eye on the road and the other constantly glancing at the rear-view mirror, Arlo pushed his car over the speed limit when the traffic allowed. A white van overtaking him on a bend forced him to brake and think the worst was about to happen.

Filled with negative thoughts, exhausted from a long night shift and still shaking from knowing Spider had been within spitting distance, he was desperate to get home even though he wasn't sure what he'd find there.

He drove twice past his house; Steve had told him to look out for suspicious vehicles and that's what he was doing, although Arlo had never really understood what that meant. Was the white van parked at the end of the street suspicious? It was just like any other tradesman's white van, but also like the one that had almost forced him off the road.

After slowing down to a crawl, he stopped alongside the van and peered into the cab. It was empty. His imagination went into overdrive *It's the perfect vehicle for carrying a chainsaw. Where's the driver?*

'Get a grip, Arlo,' he hollered before parking in a space not far from his house. Once out of his car, he walked swiftly to the rather large lady with the dog. Unlike those who surveyed the street discreetly through parted curtains, she made a point of standing out front where she could easily be seen, the self-proclaimed queen of the street watching out for everyone's best interests.

'Good morning,' he said. Desperately trying to keep it low key, he added, 'Any strangers in town?'

She smiled politely, looked up and down the street and replied, 'Just one.'

Arlo glanced at his house then turned and waited.

'A woman put something through your letter box.'

He shifted his weight, spun around and stared directly at his house. 'Was she a courier?'

'Doubt it. She had long red hair, white blouse, blue jeans, brown cowboy boots and sunglasses. Looked rather smart, not like any courier I've ever seen – and I've seen quite a few on this street.'

The woman's attention to detail was scary and temporarily distracted him. He pictured her behind a one-way mirror viewing a line-up at the local police station; she'd be a cop's dream and a criminal's nightmare. The image of her acting the model citizen disappeared as quickly as it came into his head.

Curious yet suspicious, he turned and headed up the short path to his porch but instead of unlocking the door, he pushed back the flap on the letter box and studied the brown padded envelope on the floor. There was no address, just his name written in bold, black, felt-tip letters. That was strange.

'What's up, doc?' chuckled the woman. 'You locked out?'

Arlo smiled slightly to acknowledge her comment then quickly unlocked the door and stepped inside the house, making sure he stayed clear of the envelope. His next move was to call Steve.

'Hi, Arlo. You okay?'

'I met Spider today at the hospital.'

'You *what?*'

'It's a long story. Can you come over and I'll tell you about it?'

'Can't you tell me on the phone?'

'I'd like you to look at a package that's been put through my letter box. No address, no postage, just my name.'

'Black felt-tip pen?' Steve asked.

'Yes.'

'Don't touch it. Move to the rear of the house. I'm on my way.'

Steve was parked outside his house when he ended Arlo's call. Leaving the motor running, he raced inside and headed for the cupboard under the stairs.

'Great,' Victoria snapped. 'Now that you're here, you can talk to your son. You know he almost strangled that delivery man, don't you?'

Ignoring his wife, Steve grabbed a brown leather hold-all. The sound of metal wrenches, screwdrivers and keys clinking together made his heart rate increase and memories of his time in the service came flooding back. Hardly a day had gone by when he hadn't had to deal with a tripwire in a school or children's play area, or IEDs buried near places of worship and markets.

'He won't talk to you now,' Eddie said. 'He's on bomb patrol.'

Victoria stepped in front of her husband as he marched toward the front door. 'Off to save the world again?' she mocked.

'Can I come?' Eddie asked.

Steve brushed past Victoria then turned to Eddie and told him to stay home and look after his mother. As Eddie mumbled incoherently, Victoria, looking tired and defeated, returned to Anne in the kitchen.

With the bag on the passenger seat, Steve slammed the van door, pressed his foot hard on the accelerator and drove to Arlo's. He arrived fifteen minutes later, adrenaline still rushing through his body.

'Like old times,' he muttered as he strode through the open front door and looked at the package.

After checking out the immediate surroundings, he assessed the drop from the letterbox opening to the floor to be about one meter, a distance that could possibly trigger some device. He ran his fingers gently over the padded envelope, searching for anything solid that resembled a triggering device. Nothing.

Reaching into his holdall, he took out a respirator mask, chemically resistant gloves and a Stanley knife. With the mask and gloves in position, he used the knife to cut a small slit at the end of the envelope.

He removed the mask and called for the doctor. 'Is it safe?' Arlo asked as he walked timidly towards him.

'Someone's messing with your head. The envelope is filled with pieces of red fabric.'

Recognising the fabric, Arlo moved into the living room where a small piece of the same material had been cut from the bottom of his curtains. 'He's been in my house!'

Steve's heart sank but he was quickly distracted when a memory stick tumbled out of the envelope. 'Put this in your laptop,' he said abruptly.

Once the stick had been inserted, they studied the screen. There were no pictures just an audio clip: a moment of silence followed by the unnerving sound of someone starting a chainsaw. After two false starts the saw roared, and they heard pitiful screams and cries for help in the distance.

Steve pulled the stick from the laptop.

Arlo closed his eyes and wept.

❊ ❊ ❊

After Steve left, there was an uneasy silence. Victoria sat at the kitchen table, periodically glancing at the small device monitoring Anne who was fast asleep upstairs. With her elbows on the wooden surface and both hands supporting her head, she looked lost, alone and badly in need of a hug.

Meanwhile Eddie carried on as if there was no one else in the house. He fried two eggs while a couple of slices of wholewheat toast popped up and waited patiently in the toaster. He poured boiling water onto the instant coffee in his mug. Sitting at the opposite end of the table, he scooped up his breakfast with one hand and scrolled through his phone with the other.

He didn't look at his mother. When he wanted the salt and pepper that were in front of her, he got out of his chair and picked them up himself.

After a long period, Victoria spoke. 'Do you hate me?'

'I hate what you've done, not once but twice.'

'I'm sorry, but…'

'Too late,' Eddie interrupted. 'The damage is already done.' He rose from his chair and started washing up. 'I'm going out in a few minutes to look for a place to live. Don't worry about being alone. Terrorists usually attack at night.' A not-so-subtle giggle followed as he headed back to his room.

Victoria watched him leave then placed her hands on her lap. She looked around the room before raising her hand to table height and wrapping her fingers tightly around the handle of the gun. She scowled.

'I'm not worried. I'm not alone.'

※ ※ ※

After a thorough room-to-room check of the house, Steve returned to the living room.

'He knows everything about me,' Arlo moaned. 'Where I live, where I work, even what bloody shift I'm on. Now he knows how to get inside my house. What the hell can I do?'

'You can start by fixing that broken window catch in the kitchen. You made it easy for him.' Steve didn't have much to say that would reassure the doctor and he knew it. 'I've contacted local estate agents to see if anyone has rented to these guys, but nothing has come up. I'm pretty sure someone else made the arrangements before they arrived in the country. I've also got some of the local police and my old army buddies looking out for me.'

Steve hesitated. He was struggling to sound confident. 'There isn't a camera in the canteen. I'll check the one in A&E. Who knows? Maybe he was stupid enough to walk through there.'

Arlo lowered his head. 'I'm dead,' he muttered.

'Stick to the plan.' Steve tried to sound upbeat. 'Only go into areas where there are lots of people. After your shift finishes in the morning you'll be back on days and I'll be outside your house every night waiting for him. He'll show up some time – he can't keep hanging around forever. The longer he's here, the more anxious he'll become and that's when he'll make a mistake.'

'Why are you doing this? Why are you helping me? You hardly know me.'

'My soon-to-be ex-wife says I'm trying to save the world.'

'And?'

'Maybe she's right. If I am, I might as well start with you.'

※ ※ ※

As Eddie lowered his backside on to a steel folding chair, his elbow brushed against the large water-stained windowsill where insects of all shapes and sizes had gathered to die. He grabbed one of the many out-of-date, dog-eared magazines littering the coffee table and swept the tiny creatures onto the floor.

A skinny female secretary with a silver nose ring and bright red hair kept her eyes on her computer while an elderly assistant collected a folder from his desk and placed it on the table next to Eddie. 'This is all we have in your price range,' he said apologetically. 'Two flats on a nice estate in Bracknell, and a flat on the upper floor of a large house just outside town.'

After a cursory glance at the photos of the estate, Eddie dropped the papers on the coffee table. There was no such thing as a nice estate. 'The flat in the house looks okay,' he said. 'Who lives on the ground floor?'

'A lovely Indian family.'

Eddie grimaced as if he been punched in the gut and immediately handed the sheet with the letting details back to the assistant. This was his third visit to an estate agent in just under three hours. Although unhappy at home, he was fast becoming aware of how good it was there.

Fed up with listening to agents gushing over second-rate accommodation, and tired of sitting in their soulless offices, he stood up to leave.

'I've got a two-bedroom terraced house on a nice quiet street,' the agent said hurriedly. 'It's a little more than you want to pay but worth it, I think.'

Eddie stopped at the door. 'What's the catch?'

'Someone's living there. The place is being rented by the

week. I think the tenant is on a short work assignment, so I'm not sure how long he'll be around.'

'Can I see it?'

'Let me contact the tenant.' The agent returned to his desk, tapped a few keys on his keyboard then picked up his phone and made a call. 'Hello, is that Pierrepoint?'

Spider stood at the top of the stairs and shouted down to Qasim, 'Open the curtains, hide the knife and take all that Paki stuff on the coffee table up to your room. Don't make a sound or come out until I tell you.'

'What's happening?' Qasim asked.

'The estate agent is bringing someone round to look at this place.'

'Why?'

'Why do you think? He wants to rent it after we leave.'

As he gathered his belongings, Qasim asked why he had to hide in his room. 'Because a white man alone in a house with a Pakistani boy may raise a few eyebrows and get people talking,' Spider retorted. 'Also, you appear to have forgotten that the Foleys are known in this town and your threat to kill them and their friends has made you a target.'

Head bowed, Qasim moved slowly out of the living room. Before climbing the stairs, he turned and mumbled, 'I'm not a boy.'

Spider wasted no time in replying. 'We'll see what you are tonight.'

Clutching his *tasbih* beads, a magazine from his home country and the zombie knife, Qasim disappeared. Ten minutes later there was a knock on the front door.

The estate agent was the first to greet Spider. Eddie crossed the threshold a moment later and Spider did a double take; having seen Eddie in his van a few nights ago, he was fully aware of who he was. The agent's introduction confirmed what he already knew. 'Pierrepoint, meet Eddie Foley.'

'Thanks for letting us look around,' Eddie said.

'No problem. Just do me a favour and stay out of the first bedroom on the right. My girlfriend is in there and she's not feeling well.'

Both men nodded and did a quick tour of the house. Before they left, Spider heard Eddie say the place was perfect, just what he wanted.

He watched from the window. When their car pulled away from the curb, he yelled, 'I don't believe it.' He heard a creaking sound from the stairway. 'I thought I told you to stay in your room!'

Qasim appeared in the hall looking sheepish. 'I heard the door shut so I thought it was safe to come down. What's going on? Why were you shouting?'

Spider paused to savour the moment. He expanded his chest, and for the first time in a long time he smiled. 'I know you don't care, my little Paki friend, but Christmas is about to come early.'

Pat watched closely as her husband stood with his back to the wall in the tiny bedroom, his eyes focused on the floor as he muttered, 'Five steps one way and five steps back.'

She laughed. 'What did you expect?'

Her question went unanswered; his concentration was fixed on the threadbare carpet. With his arms outstretched as if holding a car's steering wheel, he walked forward. 'Crunch,' he said as his nose pressed gently against the wall.

Looking over his left shoulder, he went through the motions of making a gear change before quickly stepping back to the opposite wall. Another fast gear change and he moved forward again. 'Crunch.'

Pat placed her phone on the plastic chair, sighed and shook her head. She raised her weary body off the bed and snuggled up to her husband. 'I do love you,' she said. 'But do you really think you can practise running over someone by walking into a wall in your bedroom?'

Nick managed a smile. 'I'm just killing time.'

'You nervous?'

He appeared hesitant as he ran his fingers through his thinning hair. 'No, I just want to get it done.'

Sensing he wasn't being totally honest, she placed her hands on his shoulders, turned him slightly and peered directly into his eyes. 'What's really wrong?'

Nick stepped back and avoided her gaze. 'Actually, I'm worried about you. I've been thinking about it all day. There's no need for you to be there. I'll be okay.'

'Absolutely not,' Pat snapped. 'We already agreed that you and I would do this together. Besides, what would I have to live for if both you and Colin were no longer around?'

Her husband nodded. As far as Pat was concerned, the discussion was over. In forty-one years of marriage, they had always done things together and nothing would change that now. He offered to make coffee and headed to the kitchen.

As soon as he left the room, Pat picked up her phone, sat

on the bed and scrolled through her texts, WhatsApp and missed calls. She was in denial and she knew it, but she didn't care. Some people turned to religion, others took drugs, but hoping for a miracle was her crutch, her way of dealing with the horrible truth.

When her brief search ended, she placed the phone on her chest and closed her eyes. A short time later she fell asleep.

A gentle knock on the bedroom door was all that was needed to bring her back to the real world; deep sleep was a luxury she hadn't experienced since Colin went missing. After wiping her eyes and straightening her clothes she went towards the door but stopped when she spotted two full cups of coffee on the table. A second knock forced her forward.

'Sorry to bother you,' said the landlady. 'I just wanted to know how much longer you'll be with us.'

'Not sure,' Pat said. 'I'll ask my husband and let you know later.'

'That's fine. I would have asked him earlier if he'd not shot off in the van.'

Pat scanned the room before she closed the door. Two untouched cups of coffee should have told her everything, yet she continued to look for the keys to the hire vehicle and the camper van. Both had disappeared.

She started to cry. 'Nick, we agreed. How could you do this to me?'

Today had been a good day for Eddie: he'd set the wheels in motion to move out of the family home and he was about to go on a dinner date with Carol. Singing in the shower seemed like a good way to celebrate – until his mother knocked on the bathroom door. 'What?' he shouted.

'Can you keep the noise down, please? I'm trying to get Anne to sleep.'

'Bloody hell! Take her downstairs. She can't hear me if she's in the living room.'

'I've done that and we can still hear you.'

'I bet she wouldn't complain if I sang something by Bob Marley.'

'Please!' Victoria begged.

The singing stopped, together with the sound of water crashing on the ceramic tray beneath Eddie's feet. 'You happy now?' he snarled. There was no reply, just the sound of footsteps on the stairs.

A moment later, wrapped in a large towel, he left the bathroom. His phone came alive as he pushed open the door to his room; there was no caller ID so he let it ring out. He threw himself on the bed and scrolled through his phone. Four missed calls appeared in his recents, none with a number attached.

'Someone is anxious to get hold of me. Probably wants my bank details,' he muttered then laughed. As he scrolled through Instagram, he paused. 'But scammers usually give up after a couple of calls.'

The words had barely left his mouth when his ringtone echoed around the room. Eddie stared at the screen: another No Caller ID. He waited as the ringing persisted until curiosity finally got the better of him. 'Hello?'

'What took you so long, Eddie?'

'Who is this?'

'It's Qasim. Remember me?'

'Yeah, I remember you. You're the Paki bastard who faked a friendship with my brother to get at me.'

Qasim remained silent for long time before replying. 'I liked Tim. He was gentle and kind, everything you're not.'

'Stop it,' Eddie mocked. 'You're hurting my feelings.'

'I'm going to hurt more than your feelings,' Qasim snapped. 'I've already killed one whore and I'm going to kill another one. Your mother. Tonight.'

Eddie laughed. 'You're so brave attacking women. And who's going to hold your hand? Spider Man?'

Qasim stopped talking. Stuttered breathing told Eddie he'd hit a nerve.

The call ended abruptly.

❊ ❊ ❊

Eddie met his father Steve at the front door and quickly ushered him into the kitchen, holding a finger to his lips and pointing to the living room. Steve nodded then listened as his son told him about the conversation with Qasim. 'Why would he announce that he's going to kill Mum tonight?' Eddie whispered.

Steve thought for a moment. 'He's been threatening us for a while now, but he's never said anything specific. It could be a trick to get us to look in the wrong direction.'

'So, what do we do?'

'We tell your mother.'

'And what do you tell me?' Victoria asked as she crept into the kitchen.

Father and son exchanged glances before Steve explained. He didn't pull any punches, and Victoria didn't seem to mind. 'I'm glad this is happening,' she said. 'I'm tired of waiting in this bloody house. Let them try – I'll be ready. And don't worry, I'll take the safety off this time.' She smiled and motioned to leave, then turned to face Eddie. 'By the way,' she asked. 'How come Qasim has your phone number?'

Eddie shook his head and shrugged his shoulders. He had no idea.

21

It was early evening and most of the roadside parking spaces on Ellen Lane were taken. Nick had arrived in the afternoon and systematically moved his van over a two-hour period until he was within striking distance of the VW estate. With his cap pulled down over his forehead, he slouched in his seat and locked his gaze on the front door of the third house on the lane, his engine idling quietly. On the passenger seat his phone vibrated non-stop with a trail of missed calls from Pat.

'Okay, boys,' he declared. 'I'm ready when you are. Come outside and let's play dodgems.'

Arlo couldn't remember how many times he'd checked the locks on the windows and doors before taking a bath, but he knew it was more than three. He recalled the excessive security checks his father had carried out each night before going to bed; dementia had taken his father down that road, but for Arlo it was fear. In addition to the points of entry, he double-checked the various weapons stationed around the house. Would he use them? He tried to convince himself that he would.

He looked at his watch and sighed. It was almost time. Every staff member had to do their share of nights in A&E; the hospital had a strict rota system, although some regularly swapped their day shifts to work the unsociable hours. Back when his life wasn't being threatened he avoided working after sundown if he could; not only did it mess with his body clock but the daylight stint seemed to attract a better class of patient.

With the autumn light fading and the streetlights on, Arlo thought about what Steve had said a few days ago: 'If he comes for you, he'll come at night.'

A sudden urge to go to work early came over him but no one showed up an hour before their shift started unless they were a trainee. The protocol was simple: be there in time for the handover and no more.

As he weighed up his options, voices in the street drew him to the curtains which had remained closed 24/7. Peering through a small gap, he spotted the large lady talking to a neighbour.

His eyes lit up and he started moving towards the front door. *Get a grip*, he thought as he stopped short of turning the doorknob. *Do you really think a psychopath would spare your life because you're standing next to someone?*

He returned to the living room, sat on the sofa and turned on the television. His left hand slid down the side of a cushion until it rested on the handle of the carving knife. His right hand was already clutching the scalpel.

'I don't bloody believe it.' Steve banged his fist on the kitchen table. Eddie, just about to leave the house, turned and waited. 'Terry Black quit.'

'How could he quit when he hasn't even started?'

'He got a better offer.'

'What a prick. So, what about tonight? Should I call Carol and cancel?'

Steve shook his head. 'I'll get in touch with Lager and tell him to hang out at the hospital. I'll join him when you come home.'

Victoria appeared in the kitchen as Eddie left the house. 'Just the two of us then, it'll be like old times,' she said with more than a hint of sarcasm. When her attempt to rile him failed, she tried again. 'Oh, I forgot, it's never been the two of us because you were never here.'

Steve thought for a nano-second about keeping quiet, then didn't hold back. 'It's never been the two of us because you were always out screwing someone else.'

Victoria took a deep breath and her face hardened. She was poised to return fire when she was distracted by Anne's crying. Watching her stomp upstairs, Steve felt relieved that the sorry episode was over – for the moment, at least. He hated arguments; he'd confront the Taliban laden with weaponry all day long, but when it came to domestic issues, he didn't want to know.

Once Victoria had slammed the door and shut herself away in the bedroom, he carried out a thorough check of all downstairs doors and windows and made sure the cameras were working properly. He felt relaxed as he made himself a coffee and put his feet up on the kitchen table.

He turned his eyes towards the floor above. 'I pity the poor bugger if he gets past me tonight.'

※ ※ ※

Voices stirred Nick from a short but much-needed snooze: the moment he'd been waiting for had finally arrived. The two men he and Pat had smuggled into the UK were walking down the path as if they were off to the pub.

His mouth went dry.

Still in a slouched position, he pressed the clutch as far as it would go; this was no time for grinding gears. With his left hand wrapped over the top of the black and chrome gear knob, he guided the stick into first gear. As both men settled inside the VW, he sat up and moved his right foot onto the accelerator.

'Here I go,' he said softly. 'Just like in the room. Crunch and crunch again.'

As he gradually pressed harder on the pedal and the roar from the engine increased, a gentle tap on the side window suddenly forced him to raise his foot.

'Hey, mister, did you find Buddy?' Nick was not expecting to hear a child's voice. Confused, he studied the boy for several seconds before realising who he was and what he was asking.

Lowering the window, he turned his head slightly and spoke through gritted teeth. 'Yes, thank you, he's at home tucked up in his bed. Isn't that where you should be? It's very late?'

'It's my birthday. Mum and I went for pizza.'

'Happy birthday, young man.'

Nick raised the window, abruptly ending the conversation. A call from the boy's mother drew the kid away from the van. Now facing forward, the old man sighed when he spotted the VW's tail lights disappearing into the night.

'Shit!' he hollered. 'Shit, shit, shit!' With each obscenity he slammed his fist down on the steering wheel. *That was stupid,* he thought, as pain shot through his fingers.

Following a brief period of calm and some serious hand rubbing, he scanned the neighbourhood. The street was empty, all was quiet. Finally, he closed his eyes, folded his arms and sat back. They had to come home some time and when they did he'd be waiting.'

As Arlo went in to A&E, he was immediately confronted by Lorraine who was obviously in a playful mood. 'Another night shift?' She laughed. 'People here are starting to talk but don't worry – your secret is safe with me.'

Her comment, although tongue in cheek, made him think about what his colleagues knew or thought they knew. Just when it appeared that staff had moved on from Jen losing her life in Mosul, he was surrounded by negative vibes again. Sleeping in the hospital basement and his erratic behaviour in the canteen had started the rumour mill churning again. Stares lasted too long and whispers behind his back followed him everywhere.

'Do people think I'm crazy?' he asked.

'You're a good doctor and that's all that matters,' Lorraine replied.

'That was very diplomatic. You should have been a politician.'

She touched his hand. 'If I was going through what you're going through, I'd be a bit weird, too.'

'That's more like it,' Arlo said, walking towards his first patient of the shift. 'And you know what's really messed up?' he continued. 'I've put my life in the hands of Steve Foley, a man I don't really know.'

Lorraine pulled back the blue curtain where an eight-year-old boy was waiting to be examined after having been mauled by a rottweiler. 'Then you know how this young lad feels. We all need to trust someone at some time in our lives.'

'Jen trusted me and look what happened.'

Lorraine tugged his arm as she said softly, 'Jennifer has been dead for ten years. When will you let her go?'

'When Spider's heart stops beating. That's the least I can do for her.'

As on all his journeys with Spider, Qasim hunched out of sight in the back seat of the VW estate. Separation was one of the keys to survival, according to the gospel of the man at the wheel.

For the most part, conversation was limited and one-way, although Qasim had come a long way since their first meeting in Karachi. Tonight, though, he was particularly quiet because he was terrified, dry mouthed, and couldn't have spoken if he'd tried.

For months he'd boasted about getting revenge. An Al-Qaeda training camp and a hook-up with an ISIS psychopath were all that he'd thought he needed, but what he really needed was the stomach to go the extra mile. Killing those who couldn't fight back was easy, especially when Spider put him in a do-or-die situation by holding a gun to his head. But was he ready to progress to the next level?

That question would soon be answered. The steel blade of the zombie knife resting against his leg was a reminder, if one was needed, that he was on a solo kill mission and there was no back-up. If it didn't go as planned, he would either die or be caged like a wild animal in a concrete six-by-eight-foot cell for the rest of his life.

His left leg was shaking with nervous energy as he gazed out of the rear side window from his low-level vantage point. Streetlights, illuminated office buildings and neon signs were eventually replaced by a black, cloud-covered sky when the VW left the town centre. The deliberately slow pace of the journey had nothing to do with traffic; in fact, there were few cars on the roads. Qasim knew that Spider was just being careful because that was what kept him alive.

The VW meandered through narrow residential streets to avoid CCTV cameras then stopped in a layby a short walk from a dimly lit underpass. Qasim placed the knife in a carrier bag, stepped out of the car and walked hesitantly towards the concrete tunnel.

He was on his own. He knew the time for talking was over, yet before entering the underpass he turned his head and glanced back at the car, hoping for a thumbs-up or a flash of the headlights. He got neither: Spider had already disappeared into the night.

Nick's phone continued to vibrate every few minutes with Pat's name constantly appearing on the screen. 'I'm sorry, darling. I'll explain everything when I get home,' he said without answering the call. Then, as if reality had suddenly smacked him on the back of the head, he whispered, '*If* I get home.'

Time was dragging on: it had been more than an hour

since the boy had tapped on his window. A huge yawn was followed by a couple of futile arm stretches. Lifting his right bum cheek off the seat and then his left did nothing to relieve the pain he was experiencing in that area. Tired, fed up and hungry, he looked at his watch and decided to give it another half an hour.

He closed his eyes and tried to make himself comfortable, but barely five minutes had lapsed when headlights from an oncoming car lit up the street. As the vehicle approached, Nick turned the key in the ignition and slumped further down in the seat.

Peeking above the dashboard, he recognised the VW but could see only one person inside. He hoped it would be the main man, the Englishman. A three-point turn enabled the VW to back into the space about two metres from where Nick was parked.

Sitting tall, Nick moved into first gear, stepped on the accelerator and released the clutch, sending his van crashing into the rear bumper of the VW. 'Crunch,' he shouted before quickly reversing.

With the gear lever back in first gear he sat and waited, his right foot twitching on the accelerator. The driver's door on the VW flew open and a clean-shaven man jumped out. 'What the hell?' he hollered.

'It's him,' Nick mumbled while at the same time shielding his face.

He watched as the Englishman moved to the rear of his car to inspect the damage then, with a deep breath and a huge growl, Nick shot forward at speed and sandwiched the man's legs between the vehicles.

'Crunch,' he mocked. 'That's for our son Colin, you bastard.'

An agonising scream shattered the calm of the evening. Intent on inflicting as much damage as possible, Nick backed up the van then raced forward, smashing the 3000kg machine into the man's crumpling body. This time there were no painful cries.

Nick reversed the van and stopped, waiting and listening, his heart thumping uncontrollably beneath his sweat-stained shirt. It was dead quiet, save for the rumble of the van's turbo-diesel engine.

Several anxious seconds went by before he slowly raised himself off the seat to peer beyond the dash to the tarmac below. There was a popping sound from his back and a sharp pain shot through his right knee. His white knuckles stood proud on the steering wheel as his chubby fingers steadied his wavering frame. With his knee about to give way, he scanned the street in front of the van.

Dropping back into his seat, he shrugged and mumbled, 'Where the hell is he?'

It didn't take long for him to find out. A bloody right hand came out of nowhere and clung to the driver's wing mirror while a left hand in a similar state locked onto the door handle.

Nick froze. Had he locked the door? He wasn't sure. He reached for the lock button but it was too late: a fierce tug from outside opened the door. Nick grabbed the interior handle and wrestled to pull it back. Realising that, despite his injuries, the man hanging on the side of the van was much stronger than he was, he let go of the handle and shifted into first gear.

Engine roaring, he sent the van hurtling forward and twisted the steering wheel, forcing his vehicle to lurch to the left and avoid the parked car. He may have just missed the rear bumper but the van door smashed into the VW, tossing the Englishman into the air like a child on a bouncy castle.

Nick stopped a few feet down the lane, leaned over and tried to close the crumpled door. Broken glass covered his lap and tiny shards pierced his shirt and dug deeply into his arm.

A quick glance back down the lane didn't tell him much, but seeing a motionless man with his face in the dirt made him feel a whole lot better. Unable to shut the door, he removed his safety belt, wrapped it through the interior handle and pulled it as close to the van as it would go.

A few minutes later he stopped on a side street, turned off the ignition, removed the key and walked away.

The underpass, damp and smelling of piss, stretched for about twenty metres beneath a busy road filtering vehicles in and out of town. Once inside it, Qasim placed his hand over his mouth and nose and quickened his pace until he heard voices echoing off the concrete surroundings. Because of the poor lighting and a slight bend in the tunnel, his view ahead was hindered.

Spider had chosen this route so Qasim could go unnoticed, but he hadn't planned for people hanging out in an underpass in the middle of nowhere.

It was decision time. Turning around and finding another route was one possibility; the other option was to face his fears, stick out his chest and walk past like they weren't even there – they might just be kids sneaking a cigarette or downing a beer.

He waited too long. By the time Qasim had made up his mind, a couple of teenagers were standing only a few feet away. They were no more than fifteen or sixteen years of age, cocky, with bottles of beer in hand. 'What's in the bag, my little coloured friend?' asked the taller one.

Qasim ignored him, moved to the side and tried to carry on walking. The second boy, who was much shorter and heavier, stepped out from behind his friend and placed his hand on Qasim's chest. Like something out of a bad movie, he necked his beer and growled, 'My friend John asked you a question.'

Qasim knew he was no longer invisible; he also knew what Spider would do in this situation and quickly rejected it. Once again, he tried to walk away but for the second time they stopped him.

'Give me the bag,' John yelled.

Qasim was cornered; he'd run out of options. 'Okay,' he said calmly. 'Come and get it.'

Taking a short step backwards, he slipped his arm inside the bag and took hold of the knife. As John reached forward, Qasim let the bag fall to the ground. Both boys stood like statues, open mouthed, their gaze locked on the massive blade.

Qasim felt the power roll through his body: he was in control and loved it. 'You still want the bag?' he asked playfully. All they could manage was to frantically shake their heads. 'Are you sure?' This time they nodded, not a word or murmur. 'Then go. Get out of my sight before I chop you into little pieces.'

The boys ran. Qasim picked up the bag and placed the knife inside it. He was buzzing, full of confidence, but he knew this was just a sideshow, not the main event.

He was also aware that his cover had been blown. The boys in the tunnel wouldn't have any difficulty remembering a Pakistani kid waving a zombie knife. Would they join the dots if his mission was a success and was played out on the evening news? He didn't know and didn't care. If he went back to the house having done nothing, Spider would kill him so it wasn't worth worrying about. Time to move on.

Once out of the underpass, he turned right along a dirt path. After about two hundred metres he climbed a wire fence where it met a telephone pole then crossed a large muddy field.

There was still some distance to go and deep inside he was cursing Spider. Why couldn't he have picked an easier route that was closer to the target? Was this a test? Was the Englishman messing with Qasim or just trying to keep him safe? The boy had so many questions, but again it didn't matter.

With his shoes caked in mud and his socks soaking wet, he continued to follow the directions he'd memorised. Nothing had been written down, another Spiderism to keep him safe.

Finally, after a long trudge cross-country, he arrived at the edge of a copse. Looking through the trees he saw his target and suddenly everything got real. Qasim stopped and breathed slowly and deeply three times. He was now as relaxed as he would ever be.

Placing the bag on the ground, he took out a white doctor's coat and put it on, then hung a stethoscope around his neck. Gripping the knife as well as the carrier bag, he walked towards his victim who was casually strolling across the car park wearing his On Guard jacket.

'Evening, Doctor,' the man said.

Qasim nodded, forced a smile, walked two steps beyond him then stopped. With his back to the man who'd just greeted him, he released the bag, spun on his heel, raised the knife and sliced it into the guard's neck. No second strike, no hanging around: a quick, immediate exit was the plan.

Still clutching the bag and knife, Qasim disappeared quickly into the trees then removed the white coat. Seconds later, he was retracing his steps to the underpass. Somewhere along the way he ditched the coat and buried it in the mud; after wiping the stethoscope, he threw it high into the branches of an old chestnut tree. He put the knife, also cleaned of prints, blade first into a ditch and stamped on the handle until it vanished in the mud.

Once back in the tunnel, he lit a match, set the plastic bag on fire and watched it turn to ash on the ground. With smoke gently caressing his face, he drifted into a moment of calm. His hands had stopped shaking for the first time since he'd arrived at the edge of the car park; his throat was no longer dry and his breathing no longer hurried.

It bothered him to feel normal, unmoved, after what he'd just done. It bothered him more than he cared to accept.

They were finally meeting in a gastro pub at night, not in a coffee shop packed with parents and screaming babies in the middle of the morning. Carol had called it a date for grown-ups; she'd thrown Eddie a lifeline that would allow their relationship to progress and he'd grabbed it. He was excited: this was an opportunity to get to know her. Although he hated to admit it, his mother was right: he knew very little about the woman he'd been seeing, even though she knew everything about him.

Dressed in a clean pair of blue jeans and a button-down collar, pale-green shirt, he stood patiently at the sign that told him to wait to be seated. The Black Swan was bright, noisy and full of people his age. It felt good to be spending an evening somewhere other than in a disused factory or on a building site.

Unfortunately for Eddie, that feeling didn't last long.

'Are you Eddie Foley?' asked the girl standing just inside the main door. Eddie nodded, surprised. 'Someone called Carol left a message for you. Said she couldn't make it – something about a family emergency.'

Eddie understood the message but was still confused. Why hadn't she called him? She'd got his number. He stepped outside and rang her, but the call went to voicemail.

As he finished leaving a message, his dad's name appeared on his screen. 'Hey,' Eddie said.

'Can you get home right away? I need you.'

'Sure. What's up?'

'Lager's dead.'

Nick stood outside the B&B holding his right arm. He'd removed most of the tiny slivers of glass although a few remained. Spots of blood covered his trousers and torn shirt sleeve, and perspiration was dripping down his face, his neck and onto his chest. Drained and exhausted, he needed help.

Pat's bedroom light was on upstairs – and so was the light in the landlady's room on the ground floor. The chances of not bumping into the woman of the house on his way upstairs were slim, so he called his wife. A couple of minutes later she joined him in the camper van carrying a large bag. Before she arrived, he'd removed his shirt to reveal a slightly swollen arm covered in blood. He played the sympathy card and it worked: Pat forgot she was angry – for now.

After a lengthy explanation of what had happened on Ellen Lane, he cleaned himself up and changed into the fresh clothes Pat had brought. His next task was to call the police and report the hire van stolen.

Despite the long walk home after ditching the van, he was still on a high. 'I'm hoping no one saw what I did, but a young boy spoke to me about an hour before it happened. If the bloke is still alive he won't contact the police, but if the boy and his mother are questioned I'm screwed. And that, darling, is why I had to do it alone. It made sense. If both of us went to prison, who would visit us?'

Pat managed a smile. 'What do we do now?'

'Contact the hire company in the morning then check out of the B&B and go home.'

His wife hesitated and looked out through the side window as if she were checking to see if anyone was listening. 'What if he's not dead?'

'I squashed him twice like a bug, then hit him so hard he flew in the air and landed face down on the street. If that didn't kill him then I don't know what will.'

'So let's assume he's dead,' Pat whispered. 'What about his friend?'

'What do you mean?'

'Are we letting him walk free after what they did to Colin?'

'Pat, are you saying what I think you're saying?'

'Absolutely.'

✳ ✳ ✳

Eddie had never seen his father so distraught. Steve was a rock, an unflappable man who had frequently witnessed death and destruction in the Middle East and Afghanistan, yet here he was hunched over the kitchen table with his head cradled in both hands.

'You okay?' Eddie asked.

'It was my fault,' his dad muttered.

'No way!'

'When Black quit, I should have told Lager to stand down until I could join him at the hospital. It was a mistake to leave him on his own.'

'That's just part of it,' added Victoria, who was standing at the bottom of the stairs. 'You got sucked in to believing I was next to die.'

Eddie's faced turned red and his jaw tightened. 'You son of a bitch,' he shouted.

'They fooled you and you know it,' she shouted.

Eddie slammed his fist down on the table and moved within inches of his mother. Steve held up his hand and the room fell silent. 'Your mother's right. I messed up.'

'Lager was a professional soldier,' Eddie protested. 'He had eyes in the back of his head. Being alone on a hospital car park was hardly the most dangerous thing he'd ever done.'

'Then he must have been distracted,' Steve said.

Eddie gritted his teeth, shook his head and walked towards the stairs.

'Look after your mother,' Steve ordered. 'I'm going to the hospital to see what I can find out.'

Victoria resisted. 'I don't need a babysitter. Take him with you.'

Eddie punched the air as he marched down the hall alongside

his father. With his hand on the doorknob he turned to his mother, smiled and said, 'Shall I leave the door open?'

Two minutes later his phone rang: it was Carol. 'Hey, are you okay?' he asked.

'Sorry about tonight,' she said. 'My brother had an accident and I'm on my way to see him in hospital in London.'

'No problem. I hope it's not too serious.'

'Not sure yet, but I'll let you know. Where are you?'

'Dad and I are going to Bramley Park. Lager was killed there tonight.'

'That's terrible news! I'm so sorry, Eddie. Please pass my condolences to your father.'

'I will.'

The call ended just as he and his father pulled up to the staff car park at the back of the hospital. There were cops everywhere and the place was awash with blue flashing lights. Nobody would tell them what had happened until Steve spotted a cop he knew who revealed off the record that Lager had received a blow to the back of the neck, most likely from a large knife or machete.

The cop wouldn't let them go beyond the tape. 'Sorry,' she said. 'No one is allowed to go in or out of the hospital.'

Like most evenings, A&E was utter chaos and the police lockdown had made the situation even worse. All the chairs in the waiting room were full, so those already triaged or waiting to be seen sat on the floor while two of the more adventurous snatched wheelchairs that were sitting idle in the hall. Cries, groans and a man shouting in a language no one could understand just about drowned out the abuse coming from those wishing to leave or be prioritised.

Lorraine zig-zagged her way around a toddler vomiting into a plastic bag his mother was holding open. Two more nurses and a hospital porter pushing a gurney were close behind her. She raced through the exit to a man crumpled on the ground outside. Covered in cuts and bruises, with his shin bone sticking out of his trousers, he was groaning as he lay motionless in a pool of blood. Those unable to leave the area looked on as they huddled in the forecourt.

'How long has he been here?' Lorraine shouted as she started checking the man's vital signs before administering first aid. 'Anyone see what happened?' There was no response and none expected. 'One thing's for sure,' she said to herself as she examined his broken leg, 'he didn't walk here.'

After deciding his injuries weren't life threatening, she slid a transfer board beneath his body and, with help, raised him onto the gurney. The porter wheeled him inside the hospital and parked him behind the curtains in the first available consultation room.

Scissors in hand, Lorraine sliced open and removed the man's trousers then cut away what was left of his shirt. Then she gasped. It couldn't be – but it had to be!

She stepped outside the curtain and rang Arlo. 'I need you urgently.'

'I'm with a patient,' replied Arlo. 'What's wrong with Manbag Singh, or is he still at that incident in the car park?'

On any other day Arlo's comment about the manbag would have raised a smile but not today; Lorraine was too frightened. She whispered, 'I think Spider is here.'

There was a long pause before Arlo spoke, his voice no

longer light-hearted. 'Why do you think that?'

'Because there's a man in a cubicle with no ID but a huge tattoo of a spider on his left shoulder.'

'Seriously? What's his condition?'

'Broken leg, possible other fractures. He needs to go upstairs, but I thought—'

Arlo interrupted. 'Keep him there. I'm on my way.'

Seconds later Lorraine heard him running down the corridor. She stood with her back to the curtain, blocking his entry to the room. 'Take a breath,' she said, moving her palms in a calming motion.

'Why?' demanded Arlo.

'Because I don't want you to do something you'll regret for the rest of your life.'

'You mean like kill the guy who murdered Jen and countless others?'

'Exactly.'

'Okay, what would you do?'

'I'd do precisely what you want to do – but not now. Think about it, plan it and, above all, cover your ass.'

'Whatever happened to "I shall never intentionally cause harm to my patients, and will have the utmost respect for human life"?'

Lorraine forced a smile 'Read the small print. The oath wasn't written to protect murdering psychopaths.'

Arlo took a deep breath, stepped through the opening in the curtain and looked down at the man on the bed.

Lorraine could only guess the cocktail of emotions swirling inside her friend's head. This was the man he hated, the man he feared, the man who'd ruined his life and the man he so desperately wanted dead. She watched as he instinctively clenched and raised his fist, but her hand resting gently on his shoulder reminded him that this was not the time or the place.

Arlo turned away, removed his phone from his back pocket and scrolled through his photos. 'What do you think?' he asked, holding up the picture of a bare-chested Spider in Mosul next to the man on the bed.

'It's not a great photo. It's difficult to tell with that scruffy black beard and long hair covering parts of his face.'

'But the tattoo is the same, isn't it?' Arlo pleaded with more than a hint of desperation in his voice.

Lorraine nodded then added that it was time to transfer the patient upstairs.

Arlo refused to step aside. Instead, he took a photo of the man then placed his mouth next to the patient's ear and whispered, 'Spider, open your eyes. I know it's you.' There was no response.

Lorriane was getting annoyed and tried to move him away, but Arlo was too strong. She could only look on in amazement as he pressed his hand firmly on Spider's broken leg, forcing a loud, agonised cry.

A moment later Spider opened his eyes. With his face just inches away, Arlo whispered, 'You said in Mosul that if I surrendered you would do me a favour and kill me quickly. Well, I want you to know that I will do you no such favour.'

He stepped aside and Lorraine called for a porter.

Slouched in the back seat of the VW, Qasim hadn't been able to see much except for treetops, lamp posts and tall office buildings so he had no idea where he was when he returned to the spot where Spider had dropped him off. But against Spider's advice, he'd smuggled his phone out of the house and he used Google maps to navigate the trip they'd previously made by car.

Although uneventful, the journey to Ellen Lane was long and wearying. Back at the house, he was looking forward to a hot meal, a hot bath and a good night's sleep.

Everything changed when his phone rang and No Caller ID appeared on his screen. 'Hello?' he said.

Qasim shuddered when the caller spoke; the voice was channelled through some sort of distorted voice enhancer. It was weird, disturbing and neither male nor female. 'Spider has been attacked and is in hospital. The Foleys are checking out your good work. Congratulations. There's a small window to finish your next assignment, so hurry. Take the stuff in the package on the table.'

He wanted to know who was calling, but he was quickly shut down. 'Go,' was the last thing he heard before the call ended.

Once again Qasim responded like an obedient child and went straight for the package. Inside he found a black cap and the keys to the VW parked out front. There was also a sleeveless high-vis vest and a clear-plastic badge holder attached to a yellow and black lanyard. The ID card inside the badge holder showed the photo of someone similar in appearance to Qasim; on closer inspection, it looked like it had been cut from a magazine.

After he'd put on the cap and vest and placed the lanyard around his neck, he reached deep into the package and pulled out the remaining item: a handgun. Just as he'd done with the zombie knife, he went through the motions of a mock attack. This time there was no awkward fumbling body movements or pathetic howls. Qasim was firm on his feet with both hands on the weapon. He looked and felt comfortable.

Even though he had no idea why Spider was in hospital, a clearer picture started to form when he saw the state of the VW and the debris on the lane. There were several dents and cracks on the bumper and boot, and broken glass littered the ground together with different coloured chunks of steel and aluminium. A massive gouge ran from the passenger side doors to the back-wheel arch where black paint had been stripped away to reveal bare metal. Blood, probably Spider's, was splattered everywhere.

Shaken by what appeared to have been a forceful collision, Qasim thought again about running. It was the perfect time: he had a car, a gun, and Spider was incapacitated. And that was the problem. The caller had said he was in hospital, not dead; if he were alive, Spider still had a long reach no matter where he was or what shape he was in, and Qasim knew he could get to him and his parents.

The idea was a non-starter, so he moved on. A quick inspection of the vehicle revealed the headlights and taillights were intact, which was crucial because a broken light would certainly attract the wrong kind of attention.

Once at the wheel, he started the car and pulled away, his rear tyres crunching loudly as they rolled over the wreckage on the tarmac. As he drove through town, the warning of a 'small window' played on his mind. He wondered if the window was still open.

※ ※ ※

Arlo watched as Spider's bed was pushed into the corridor towards the lift. Suddenly he felt relieved. 'There is a God,' he said softly to Lorraine. 'And God wants me to live.'

'And there's a room full of people needing treatment,' she retorted. 'And God wants them to live as well. Shall we get back to work?'

Even though his mind was elsewhere, Arlo walked back into A&E reception and collected details of his next patient. 'Can you work with me?' he asked Lorraine, his voice a little shaky.

'I've already made some rota changes. I'm not sure I should leave you alone today.'

As they pushed the curtain aside, they saw a gaunt man in his eighties on the bed spitting and coughing. 'We need to get him a private room,' Arlo announced.

Lorraine looked surprised as she moved closer to the bed. 'You haven't even examined him yet.'

'No, not him,' Arlo said, looking at the old man. 'I'm talking about you-know-who.' He pointed upwards

'Why?'

'Because I need to be alone with him. I can't do what I want to do with other patients just a few feet away.'

'And dare I ask what you're planning to do?'

'I've got some ideas. Can you speak to someone about it, please? I know you have friends in high places.'

'What's in it for me?' Lorraine asked.

'Whatever you want.'

Somewhat surprised, she responded, 'You really are desperate, aren't you?'

※ ※ ※

Qasim did his best to avoid the main streets of town. The large unsightly scrapes and dents, together with the strange creaking noises coming from the rear of the VW, left him with no option but to take a circuitous route to his destination. Darkness provided some cover, but still he sniggered at the thought of Spider repeatedly telling him to stay invisible. It wasn't easy: he'd had to show his hand to protect himself in the tunnel, and now he was forced to drive around in a car that looked like it had been pushed off a cliff.

A fifteen-minute journey took twenty-five, but finally he was almost there. Two streets away from his target he turned off the headlights and drove into a cul-de-sac. When space became available, he did a U-turn and neatly positioned the vehicle for a quick getaway. Leaving the car unlocked was a no-brainer – fumbling with a key fob while running for his life could cost him his life. Spider had taught him that.

Walking along the pavement in front of a row of houses was stressful. There was nowhere to hide, no hedges, no fences. Streetlamps lit up the way ahead, while interior lights and TV sets cast a warm glow across the well-mowed lawns to his right. He quickened his pace, praying that the dog walkers had retired for the night. Where was the thunder and rain like in the movies, he wondered.

As he got closer, he had no time to reflect on what he was about to do. Standing at the end of the path leading to where he hoped he would find his next victim, he turned and surveyed the street. The neighbourhood was still but he knew it wouldn't stay that way for long.

The sound of gentle breathing coming from the baby monitor was music to Victoria's ears. It had taken her nearly forty-five minutes to get Anne to fall asleep and now she was in desperate need of some down time. Too tired to cook, she settled for a cup of tea and a digestive biscuit then walked slowly into the living room where the comfy sofa had her name written all over it.

Kicking off her slippers, she was about to lower herself onto a plumped-up cushion when she realised she'd left the gun next to the kettle. Shoulders slouched and eyes barely open, she went back to collect it then returned to the living room with the weapon dangling from her thumb and forefinger.

Finally, with her cuppa, biscuit and the handgun laid out on the coffee table, she sat down – but the doorbell rang almost at the same time as she pressed the red button on the TV remote.

Her eyes widened, her senses now alert. Still clinging to the remote, she rose slowly to her feet then stopped, put it back on the table and picked up the gun. She crept silently to the window and looked through a small crack in the curtains.

Although the porch was in darkness, it was easy to spot the man wearing a bright yellow jacket. Bizarrely, a feeling of calm came over her even though her husband had told her that the best way to hide in plain sight was to put on a high-vis jacket. 'They look like they are on their way to fix things so they get a free pass,' he'd said.

Even so, Victoria felt a lot better than when she'd first heard the bell. As she walked towards the front door, her phone rang. It was Steve. 'I know,' she said before he could speak. 'There's someone at the door.'

'Stay away from the door,' he shouted.

Victoria froze. 'Why?'

'Never mind, just do as I say.'

His tone angered her and she remained in the middle of the room with her phone pressed against her ear.

'I want you to shout "I'm coming", then go to the wall to the right of the door,' Steve instructed. 'Put your finger on the light switch then move an arm's length away. Keep your back to the wall.'

The doorbell rang again. 'Why am I doing this?' Victoria demanded. 'Am I in danger?'

'I'm not sure. I'll let you know when you turn on the porch light. No matter what happens, stay still and don't say a word.'

'Steve, you're scaring me.'

'Get ready. One, two, three – shout.'

Following a deep breath, she called, 'I'm coming,' then walked to the right of the door and stretched her arm until her fingertips reached the light switch. With her back to the wall, shoulders hunched and eyes closed, she turned on the light.

'It's Qasim,' shouted Steve. 'He's spotted the camera. Don't move.'

Seconds after the porch lit up, four shots came through the door. Splinters of wood flew into the air as bullets ricocheted around the house digging deep into the wall at the end of the corridor and the carpeted staircase on the right. A multi-coloured vase shattered into pieces, covering the floor with slivers of plastic and the remnants of dried flowers.

Victoria dropped both her phone and gun, covered her ears with her hands, slumped to the floor and started shaking like she was having a fit. Distorted cries from the baby monitor replaced the gentle breathing.

Through tear-soaked eyes she glared at her phone a short distance away. 'You bastard, Steve! I wish you were dead.'

Arlo sat at a vacant table in the canteen and picked up a coffee-stained magazine laying in front of him. With his left hand, he discreetly lowered the rolled-up magazine over a salt shaker, squeezed the pages together, grabbed a handful of paper napkins then left.

With the shaker transferred to his trouser pocket, he climbed the stairs and started searching for Spider. It was too soon after his admission for him to have a room, so Arlo combed the hallways; due to lack of bed space, patients with non-life-threatening injuries were often parked in corridors until a bed became available. It was degrading but commonplace and made it easy for Arlo to find his man without involving members of staff.

Standing at the end of Spider's bed, Arlo glanced casually over the notes attached to a clipboard. 'Unknown male' was written at the top, along with a unique NHS number. When it was clear to do so, he released the brake and pushed the bed down the hall and around the corner to a quieter part of the hospital.

Once there, he jammed several napkins into Spider's mouth, pulled back the adhesive surgical dressings covering two large wounds and poured salt on the open sores. Spider's eyes widened, his body contorted, but his muffled screams went nowhere.

Arlo leaned over him. 'How does it feel to have a taste of your own medicine?' He didn't expect a reply and he didn't wait for one; he was high on revenge and wanted to continue inflicting pain.

He walked to the corner, peered down the hall then returned to Spider. 'Your notes say that you have a couple of cracked ribs. I bet they're painful,' he teased, playfully running his index finger over Spider's bare chest. 'Right about here.' He pressed down firmly with an open palm.

Spider grimaced then the back of his blood-covered hand swung wildly, smacking Arlo on the jaw.

Arlo responded by pounding his fist on to the damaged rib cage. As his victim writhed in agony, he removed the tissues from his mouth. 'Let's keep this little visit between the two of us a secret. If you say anything, I'll spread the word that you killed Jennifer and then I won't be the only one around here queueing up to hurt you.'

'You don't know how to hurt me,' Spider said through gritted teeth. 'You're a pussy. If you want to torture someone, cut off a finger, a whole hand or even their dick. Hang them by their wrists for a few days and when they're cut down, their hands won't work and many of their joints will be dislocated. Electric shock is fun – I use a car battery but I bet your defibrillator paddles on the side of the bed would make an impression. Waterboarding is another favourite. For you, killing is easy – just inject potassium chloride because it's difficult to detect. Need I say more?'

Arlo stood motionless. He was aware his mouth was open and tried to disguise it by rubbing his fingers over his lips.

Spider appeared to savour the moment before looking into his eyes. 'Doc, you took an oath, but more importantly you don't have the balls to torture, let alone kill. Salt in my wounds and a punch in the chest? Fuck off and send in a real man.'

※ ※ ※

Steve turned onto his street and was shocked by what he didn't see: there were no cops, no crime-scene tape preventing his approach to the house, no crowds. The street was quiet, save for a couple of elderly ladies talking nearby. 'Evening,' he called. 'Everything all right?'

'I guess you didn't hear that bloody car backfiring, did you?' one of the women said.

Steve and Eddie exchanged glances. 'No.'

'Frightened the life out of me,' the other woman added.

Steve responded with a polite smile as he hurried up the path while Eddie went around the back. Bullet holes riddled the front door. Before Steve entered the house, he called out, 'Victoria, it's me. I'm coming in.' There was no response.

He opened the door slowly and worked his way along the hall. A muffled cry from baby Anne drew his attention upstairs. With Eddie a step behind, he hurried to the bedroom.

Once again Victoria was tucked between the wall and the bed, sheltering Anne with one hand and holding a gun in the other. Her eyes were bloodshot, her cheeks covered in mascara and her voice shuddered as she spoke. 'If either of you say one word or move one step closer, I'll shoot you both and then I'll shoot Anne and myself. I don't care. I've had enough. I can't live like this anymore.'

Steve raised his arms and backed away. He knew better than to chance his luck with Victoria pointing a gun at him for a second time. Besides, this time she'd turned the safety off.

※ ※ ※

With his phone buzzing and his pager illuminated, Arlo walked swiftly back to A&E. Lorraine, hands on hips like a mother about to scold her child, greeted him and demanded, 'Where the hell have you been?'

She was annoyed and he could see why. The waiting room was chaos, doctors, nurses and porters were darting between stations and he'd gone AWOL.

'I thought I could do it, but I couldn't … and he knows it.' Arlo stared at the ground. Eventually he lifted his gaze, saw the look on her face and knew that she knew.

'It's nothing to be ashamed of,' she replied. 'It just means you're a good person.'

'Jen deserves more. I let her down in life and now I've let her down in death.'

Lorraine moved a step closer, discreetly placed her hand on his and whispered, 'His day will come.'

Steve shook his head as he stared at the holes in the front door. Had his wife been standing behind the door, the four bullets would have struck her below the waist.

'He's not a very good shot, is he?' Eddie remarked. 'Maybe he missed that class at the Al-Qaeda training camp.'

Steve was in no mood for humour. His friend Lager was dead and his wife had been shot at. He wanted answers.

After a long period of silence, Eddie chipped in, 'I think we're being watched.' Steve motioned for him to continue. 'How else would they know that Lager and Mum were alone tonight?'

Steve nodded. 'It's a possibility, but something's bothering me. The cop at the hospital told me that the back of Lager's neck was slashed. If you attack someone from behind with a knife, wouldn't it be easier to stick it in their back? Why aim for the neck? If it was Qasim then it's even more confusing because he's much shorter than Lager.'

Eddie studied his father's face and eventually the penny dropped. 'They knew he was wearing a stab vest.'

'Exactly. Now who knew that Lager and Victoria were alone and that Lager was wearing a vest?'

Steve moved into the kitchen with Eddie. At that moment, Victoria descended the stairs. She ignored her husband and turned her head to look away as she approached Eddie. His eyes widened and his face hardened.

Five minutes later, with a bottle of warm milk in her hand, she went back to her bedroom. There hadn't been a word or a glance while she was in the kitchen.

'What's with that strange look on your face?' Steve asked.

'It's Mum.'

'What's Mum?'

'She knew everything,' Eddie muttered, glancing upstairs to see if his mother was listening.

'Don't be crazy! She wouldn't do that, and besides Qasim just tried to kill her.'

Eddie wouldn't let it go. 'What's the last thing we heard her say after Qasim blew holes in our front door?'

Steve shrugged his shoulders.

'She said, "You bastard, Steve. I wish you were dead."'

As the VW sat idling at a red light, Qasim stared straight ahead wondering if his mission had been a success. Now that

Jesse, Lager and hopefully Victoria were dead, he needed a plan to get to Steve and Eddie. But with Spider injured he was on his own, no longer guided by his 'guardian angel'.

A tap on the roof of his car interrupted his train of thought. A man in greasy overalls was standing next to his side window and shouting through the glass that the taillight on the VW was flickering. 'The cops will stop you for that.'

A thumbs-up sent the man back to his lorry. The light turned green and Qasim sped away. A few minutes later he pulled into a layby when his phone rang. He knew it would be important because only two people had his number: Spider and someone connected to Spider. He checked his screen. No Caller ID.

'Hello,' Qasim said hesitantly.

Once again, the voice was distorted. 'Don't go home.'

'Why, what's happening?'

'A neighbour heard the crash and called the police. They've only just arrived. They'll be gone soon because they won't find anything. Wait until morning.'

'Anything else?' Qasim asked.

'Yes. Spider needs to know if you hit your target.'

Qasim hesitated and the caller repeated the question. 'I think so,' he replied without conviction.

'You *think*? Why don't you know?'

'I shot through the door. I'm not sure if I hit her.'

The call ended abruptly, leaving Qasim feeling unsure about his future. If the woman wasn't dead, was he safe?

With his forehead resting on the steering wheel, he turned his gaze and looked at the handgun on the passenger seat. A dark cloud pressed heavily on his shoulders and images of his sisters Rana and Benazir flashed through his mind as he placed his fingers on the steel barrel. One pull of the trigger and he could be with them.

In the next instant his parent's faces appeared on the big TV screen in his head and quickly removed any thoughts of self-destruction. 'Get a grip,' he mumbled.

Moving the gear lever into drive, he pressed the accelerator and pulled out of the layby; it was time to get this wreck off the road. With no credit cards and just a couple of pounds in his pocket, checking into an hotel was not an option so a small car park next to a council football pitch became home for the night.

Wrapped in a tattered blanket, he curled up in the back of the VW estate. He had only two rounds left in his handgun. *That's okay. One for Steve and one for Eddie.*

The atmosphere in the Foley house was tense. Sitting alone on the sofa, Steve struggled to find any positives in his life. Lager, his army mate was dead, as was Jesse, his shoulder to cry on. His wife hated him, his son hated his mother, and there were people out there trying to kill him and his family. He couldn't make this shit up if he tried. He wasn't a religious man but on more than one occasion during the past weeks he'd said under his breath, 'Come on, man, give me a break.'

When a break finally came, he took a second to look up and say thank you even though it came from Arlo down here on earth.

It was just before midnight when the doctor called from the hospital. 'First, I'd like to offer my condolences. They haven't released a name yet, but I heard one of your employees was killed in our car park tonight.'

'Thank you.'

'I'm sorry we couldn't do more for him.'

Steve didn't feel the need to reply.

'Now, guess who's here?' Arlo went on.

Tired, and not wanting to engage in games, Steve's reply reflected his mood. 'Who?'

Arlo got straight to the point of his call. 'We've got Spider in A&E. Actually, he's just gone upstairs for surgery.'

'Are you serious?' Steve's voice was so loud that Eddie immediately came into the room.

'Yes,' Arlo replied. 'He was hit by a car then dumped at the entrance to the hospital. We've had a chat and it's Spider alright. I'm sending you his photo now.'

Eddie sat beside his father. When the photo arrived, he couldn't contain his excitement. 'That's him! That's the guy who's living in the house I'm going to rent! Son of a bitch – I shook his hand.'

'Do you think he knew who you were?' Steve asked.

'Definitely – we were introduced. Can't remember his name, though. And you know, I bet Qasim was there too. I had a look around but was told not to go into the second bedroom where Spider said his girlfriend was resting.'

Steve wasted no time saying goodbye to Arlo. He went to the closet and pulled out his military holdall, suddenly back in his happy place. Without saying a word, both men retreated to their respective bedrooms and changed into black combat trousers and hoodies that no longer carried the On Guard logo.

Clutching a balaclava, Steve met Eddie at the top of the stairs. 'Let's go find Qasim,' he growled.

※ ※ ※

Nick sat on the edge of the bed, his wife sound asleep beside him. They'd been arguing for more than two hours. Pat wanted to kill the young man they'd smuggled into the country, Nick wanted to go home.

Her plan was simple: knock on his door, throw acid in his face and strangle him while he was disorientated. Nick had asked what she'd do if the man didn't open the door; Pat had replied that she would think of something. He didn't bother to ask who would do the strangling.

It would have been easy to ridicule her, but she was hurting beyond belief and believed that only revenge would ease her pain. In the morning he'd try to change her mind. He wasn't very hopeful.

Maybe he could come up with a Plan B.

※ ※ ※

Steve looked back at the house as he pulled away from the curb. 'You worried about leaving her alone?' Eddie asked.

A shake of the head was followed by a huge sigh. 'Your mother spent most of our marriage alone, so I can't blame her if she doesn't want me around now. Besides, Qasim won't come back. He had his chance.'

Steve's tone was clipped, without emotion. It was clear to Eddie that his father didn't want to talk about Victoria, so he moved the conversation on. 'If we find Qasim, what will we do with him?'

'Good question. I'm sure he killed Lager and at least had a hand in Jesse's death so, he's got to be punished. Unfortunately, if we turn him over to the police he'll most certainly tell them I planted the bomb on his sister's plane.'

'Dad, it was a plane full of suicide bombers on their way to blow up London! Anyway, MI5 shut the inquiry down. It's officially an accident.'

'I know that. I'm just worried it could start a fresh investigation. Who knows what that could reveal.'

'So, what do we do with him?' Eddie repeated.

'There's only one thing we can do.'

Eddie smiled: he knew exactly what that meant. His heart rate increased and he clenched his fist but somehow he held it together and refrained from punching the air.

Motioning for his father to turn left and slow down, Eddie checked his watch; it was 12.25am, time to get serious and concentrate on the job at hand.

Ellen Lane was two streets away. Before leaving the vehicle, Steve went through his holdall and took out the tools he didn't need. Eddie stuffed a couple of nylon zip ties into his pocket before unscrewing the van's interior overhead light bulb. He slipped a truncheon into a loop on the side of his trousers.

His father, now wearing a balaclava and black gloves, presented a sinister image. Similarly dressed, Eddie lowered the sun visor and gazed in the attached mirror before nodding arrogantly.

Steve gave the thumbs-up and they exited the van. It was a perfect evening for sneaking around; two street lamps nearby were dark, and thick grey clouds blocked out what was forecast to be a full moon.

They moved swiftly across a playground then along a gravel path to the fence at the rear of the third house on the left on Ellen Lane. Eddie's silent gesture took them to a wooden gate.

Standing on tiptoes, he reached over the top, slid the bolt and patiently guided the gate open to make sure the hinges didn't squeak.

Steve moved quickly to the back door where he removed a small metal tool from his holdall and placed it in the keyhole. Eddie studied his father's every move, at the same time keeping an eye on Qasim's house and those around it. Less than a minute later, a barely audible click signalled that Steve was in.

Is there nothing he can't do? Eddie wondered as he followed his father through a small utility room with a washing machine and dryer stacked to his right and a pair of closet doors to his left. In the kitchen they separated: Steve went through to the living room while Eddie checked out the dining area. Both were clear.

At the bottom of the stairs Eddie signalled that Qasim's room was the one on the right, then immediately regretted it. He wanted to be the first to get his hands on the little bastard but his father had taken control and was already heading in that direction. But there was no need for him to fret: the room was empty as was the one across the landing.

After carrying out a thorough search, they returned to the kitchen and looked through the drawers, cupboards and inside the cooker and refrigerator.

'The house is clean,' Eddie said. 'I can't believe there are no phones, passports, weapons, nothing.'

'Could be someone else is keeping them safe.' Steve looked closely at the appliances on the counter.

A few feet away, Eddie pointed the light on his phone into the washing machine and drier, then opened the floor-to-ceiling closet door. 'Speaking of weapons, look what I've found.' He held up a small chainsaw. 'It's Spider's go-to killing machine and it's still got the price tag on it.'

'Not sure the doctor would be too happy to see that. Give it here. Arlo may not like it, but I do.'

Eddie watched as his father sat cross-legged on the floor, the holdall and chainsaw within arm's reach, a small torch clamped between his teeth, before moving to the front of the house to keep an eye on the street through a gap in the curtains.

Twenty minutes later he was summoned back to the kitchen. His father had returned the chainsaw to the cupboard and was wiping the floor with a damp cloth. 'We're done here. Let's go home.'

22

Qasim squinted as the early morning sun streamed through the VW's side window and automatically shaded his eyes with his left arm. He scraped his tongue across his teeth, swirled the tiny amount of saliva around his mouth and swallowed.

Stale air and the sound of a fly buzzing next to his ear pushed him out of the vehicle. Once outside, he arched his back gently and rolled his neck. He filled his lungs with fresh air as he rubbed his face and head before violently scratching his scalp with his nails.

Feeling slightly better, he sat down behind the steering wheel and checked his phone. There was nothing on BBC news about a local shooting. If Steve's wife was dead or even wounded, it would have been all over the press.

Qasim shut the door and started the engine. With both hands on the steering wheel, he stared blankly through the windscreen making no attempt to move the car. His mind was on other things. Was it safe to go back to the house? Why hadn't the mystery caller contacted him? What should he do with the car? Most importantly, what should he do with the gun?

The sound of a child laughing suddenly cut into his thoughts. A young boy dressed in Manchester United football gear was pointing at the VW's dents and scrapes. Another youngster soon joined him, together with two men carrying kit bags. As they moved closer Qasim, aware that the gun was on the rear seat, slammed the gear stick into reverse and quickly drove out of the car park.

A mile down the road he stopped at Tesco's supermarket, climbed over the front seat and picked up the gun, which was in plain sight on the blanket. With shoppers gawking at the beaten-up vehicle as they strolled by, he tucked the weapon inside his jacket, returned to the driver's seat and moved the car forward.

When the phone rang, he stopped. 'Hello?'

'You failed,' the caller announced.

No longer intimidated by the distorted voice, Qasim remained silent.

'He won't be pleased.'

Still no reply.

'Get back to the house and wait for instructions.'

'Stop telling me what to do,' Qasim wanted to say but he didn't. Spider was already pissed off and there was no point in adding fuel to the fire. Instead, he repeated the question he'd asked the first time the mystery person had contacted him: 'Who are you?'

This time there was silence from the other end. When the call ended, Qasim did as he was told.

A solid knock on the bedroom door woke Nick from a sound and much-needed sleep. Wiping his eyes, he shuffled barefoot across the room and opened the door just wide enough to see the stern face of the landlady peering back at him. 'The police are here and want to talk to you,' she said accusingly

He nodded and told her what she wanted to hear. 'It's about

the stolen rental.' He closed the door firmly.

Pat, now wide awake, propped herself against the headboard. 'The police don't usually make house calls when a car is stolen,' she snapped. 'All they do is give you a bloody crime-reference number and tell the DVLA. Are we in trouble?'

Her husband shrugged his shoulders, put on his dressing gown and slippers and went downstairs. Twenty minutes later he was back. 'There's good news and bad news.'

Pat leaned forward, not wanting to miss a single word.

'The police think the van was used to run over some guy in town. When they interviewed him in hospital, he refused to say anything. Since I rented the van, they came to check me out, took one look and thought that an old fart like me couldn't do anything like that. So we're good.'

'And what's the bad news?'

'He's not dead.'

Pat thought for a moment then smiled. 'That's not a problem. It just means that when we've finished breakfast we'll go out and buy *two* bottles of acid.'

✳ ✳ ✳

Arlo had just moved from the couch to the bathroom after a long afternoon nap and was getting ready for the last in a series of night shifts. Looking in the mirror, he spread shaving foam on his face and smiled before picking up his razor.

For the first time in a long time, he hadn't double-checked the locks on the doors or windows. He was no longer carrying a knife, cricket bat or hammer as he moved from room to room. Spider was laid up in hospital unable to walk and, for the moment, unable to kill. Arlo had no idea what the future would hold but, for now at least, he felt safe. And if that changed – well, he still had the scalpel in his pocket.

When Lorraine's name lit up the screen on his phone, he hoped she was about to tell him that there were complications following Spider's operation. The dream scenario would be that he was dead or at least paralysed.

The dream suddenly became a nightmare. 'Spider just discharged himself,' she said.

'What?'

'I'm afraid he's gone. And yes, we tried to talk him out of leaving.'

'Did anyone pick him up?'

'A woman who brought in a wheelchair.'

'Great. At least we can see what she looks like when we check the security cameras.

'That will be a problem.'

'Why?'

'She wore a black one-piece full-length *jilbab* with *niqab*, gloves and sunglasses.'

'I don't understand. What does that mean?'

'She was completely covered from head to toe.'

Expect the unexpected, that's what Qasim had told himself shortly after meeting Spider in Karachi. Spider had been run over and taken to hospital a few hours ago and although Qasim was hoping to return to an empty house, he wasn't holding his breath.

As he approached, a wooden makeshift ramp leading to the front door told him all he needed to know. Spider was home.

Once inside, Qasim crept into the kitchen and sat at the far end of the table. The sound of a toilet flushing and door slamming sent a chill through his body. Spider rolled slowly out of the loo in his wheelchair, turned into the kitchen and parked himself next to Qasim so that their faces were inches apart.

A cocktail of bad breath and hospital odours washed over the youngster, forcing him back on his chair. When he stood up, intending to fetch a glass of water, Spider told him to sit down then tore into him with foul language and accusations of cowardice.

Qasim didn't know where this confrontation was heading but it didn't look good. His mind raced through his options, all of which he'd rejected in the past, but this time the feeling of cold steel pressing against his mid-section filled him with excitement.

I could shoot him now. He's defenceless, an easy kill. But no, there's a third person, the one with the voice. I know nothing about them — but I'm sure they know everything about me and my family.

Chin lowered and hands locked together on the table, he soaked up a flood of verbal abuse. If Qasim's heart had ruled his head, Spider would no longer be alive. He had two bullets left and a target within spitting distance. It was tempting.

When the rant finished, the room fell silent. The boy raised his head and accidentally locked onto cold, dark eyes where not a flicker of humanity was visible.

'You let me down,' Spider spat. 'If you do it again, you're dead.'

Qasim could only nod, his mouth too dry for him to speak.

Grinning unpleasantly, Spider placed a piece of paper on

the table, clamped his fingers on the wheels of the chair and backed away. Qasim's hand trembled as he picked up the paper. The attached photo meant nothing to him but the instructions from Spider took their skewed relationship in a whole new direction.

Nick didn't need to think very hard to come up with Plan B because it was something he'd already considered. He decided to keep it simple, be honest with his wife.

He told her straight: they were too old, too weak and too fat to physically hurt someone. If they messed up while throwing acid, they would get burned; if they tried strangling a man who was forty years their junior, they would fail.

He was a little surprised when his wife agreed without argument. What had changed her mind? Earlier in the day she'd been keen on buying a corrosive substance but now her voice was frail, her eyes tired. 'It was a stupid idea,' she admitted. 'I was too full of anger and hatred to think straight. What should we do now? Go home?'

Wrapping both arms around her, Nick shook his head. 'We may not be able to stop them ourselves, but we still have the camper van,' he whispered

Pat stepped back. 'You mean—'

Her husband interrupted. 'It worked once. Why shouldn't it work again?'

Arlo arrived at the hospital an hour and a half before his shift

286

was about to start. Lorraine watched as he immediately made a beeline for her station. 'You're keen,' she said, looking at the clock on the wall. 'What's up?'

He hesitated and stuttered before finally getting the words out. 'It's not that I don't believe you but—'

'But what?' Lorraine interrupted. 'Oh, I know why you're here early. You don't believe I did enough to stop him. You think I could have done more. Well, you're wrong. Ask Dr Singh or any of the staff at the nurses' station – I tried every trick in the book. You know as well as I do that if a patient wants to leave he can, and there's nothing we can do about it.

'I know. It's just that we had him and now he's gone.'

Lorraine snapped back, 'We didn't "have" him. This is a hospital, not a prison. And besides, what would you do if he was still here? If I recall correctly, when you had your chance you bottled it.'

Arlo winced: Lorraine's comment had hit a nerve. He opened his mouth as if to speak then quickly shut it, turned and walked towards the staff canteen.

Lorraine bit her bottom lip as she watched him go. 'I need a minute,' she said to a colleague before disappearing into the women's washroom. Sitting inside the only vacant cubicle, she placed her head in her hands and wept silently.

Just over an hour later, when her shift finished, she made her way to the car park. There'd been no further conversation with Arlo even though their paths had crossed several times during her final minutes on duty.

Outside, she took in a large gulp of cool evening air. It felt good; a deep inhalation followed by long, slow exhalation slowed the beating of her heart and helped diffuse the anger she still felt following their quarrel. The thought of relaxing on the sofa, kicking off her shoes to relieve her swollen feet and having an extra-large glass of any colour wine also helped to distract her from the day's events.

As she crossed the dimly lit staff car park, she pressed gently on the grey plastic key fob. The headlights on her red Toyota Carolla flashed on and off. She opened the door, tossed her handbag onto the passenger seat and lowered her weary frame into position. She leaned back against the headrest and took another deep breath.

At that moment the passenger door flew open and a young Asian man wearing a baseball cap and a light-blue medical mask jumped in beside her. She screamed, reached for the door handle, then stopped when she saw the barrel of a gun pointed in her direction.

The attacker raised a photo next to her face and studied it. 'Start the car and drive,' he shouted.

'I'm confused,' Eddie admitted. His comment drew no reaction from his father who kept both eyes on the road ahead. 'We know where Qasim lives and we know that Spider is in a hospital not far away. Why don't we do something?'

'What do you suggest?'

Eddie thought for a moment. 'Couldn't we wait for Qasim to come back to the house then kill him?'

'How would we do that?'

'Hack him like he did to Lager. He deserves to die for what he's done, you know that.'

'And what about Spider?' Steve asked.

When Eddie suggested sneaking into Spider's hospital room

and suffocating him with a pillow, his father's silence spoke
volumes. 'Okay, okay, so I don't have the answers. But doing
nothing isn't the answer either.'
'Have you ever known me to do nothing?'
'No.'
'Exactly.'

23

Qasim had one eye on the woman driving the Toyota and the other on the notes Spider had given him. There was a collection of curious, child-like scribbles with details of where, when and how to kidnap Lorraine and a stick drawing of a person with no head on the soiled paper.

He couldn't help wondering if Spider was suffering from the side effects of some drug he was taking for the pain. Was the man's behaviour substance induced, or was the cold-blooded killer playing mind games? He didn't know and he didn't care.

Tiredness had crept in and quashed his enthusiasm. It had been a draining few days and for the second time in a matter of hours he asked himself what the hell he was doing.

Spider's directions took them out of Bracknell and right at a popular waterpark and sports centre. A bend in the road funnelled them through a traffic-calming chicane that led to a country lane shaded by a canopy of trees. Finally, a narrow hedge-lined track appeared on the left.

After about two hundred metres, the dirt road ended. Ahead was a derelict barn with a stone base supporting a wooden structure riddled with huge gaps. Much of the corrugated metal roof was missing. Thinking he'd made a mistake, Qasim ran his finger over the instructions and retraced every turn in is head. There had been no mistake. This was it.

Lorraine's face was filled with terror. 'Why are you doing this?' she cried. 'I don't even know you. Please, if you let me go, I won't say anything.'

Qasim grabbed the keys then gestured with his gun for her to get out of the car. Using the light from his phone, they followed an uneven path to a metal sliding door at the far side of the barn open just wide enough for them to squeeze through,

Lorraine went in first and Qasim followed with his gun pushed firmly in her back. 'Close the door,' came a command from the rear of the barn.

Once he'd stepped inside and pulled the sliding door closed, Qasim gagged as a mixture of stale damp air and old farmyard odours drifted through his nostrils and down his throat. Dodging a cloud of cobwebs dangling from the oak beams, he and Lorraine moved slowly forward until they were told to stop.

Spider was sitting in his wheelchair surrounded by candles, like a king on his throne. Blood-red war paint circled his eyes and formed chevrons on his cheeks; a black ISIS bandana made him look even more frightening, if that were possible. To his left was a zombie knife, identical to the one that Qasim had used on Lager; to his right a chainsaw.

Lorraine screamed and tried to turn back towards the door, but Qasim hooked her arm with his and held her firm.

'On your knees,' Spider hollered pointing his finger at her.

When there was no movement, he repeated the instruction only this time even more venomously. Reluctantly, Qasim placed his hand on Lorraine's shoulder. Her body was shaking as she lowered herself to the dirt floor.

Spider continued. 'Take your phone out of your pocket, call the doctor and then give it to me. I'll tell him what I'm telling you. If he's not here in an hour, you die. If he calls the cops, you die. If he brings the Foleys, you die.'

❋ ❋ ❋

Nick turned out the light, shut the bedroom door and descended the stairs carrying a small suitcase. The landlady was waiting for him at the front door. 'This is a strange time to be checking out,' she said. 'I hope you realise I have to charge you for tonight because I can't get anyone in at this late stage.'

'Money's in the envelope,' he replied.

'Where are you going?'

He opened the door and stepped outside without answering.

'And what about the stolen car? Is there anything more the police should know?' the woman demanded in a shrill voice. 'What if they come looking for you? What do I tell them?'

Nick kept walking and eventually her voice faded as he got closer to Pat, who was already seated in the camper van. 'She's a right pain in the arse,' he remarked as he placed the bag in the back of the vehicle.

'Why? What did she say?'

'She asked me why we're leaving so late, where we're going and if there's anything more the police should know.' He looked back over his shoulder and caught the landlady staring at them from the window.

'Think she suspects something?' Pat asked.

Nick shrugged his shoulders. 'She couldn't have seen anything, but maybe she heard something. Her room was beneath ours and we did a lot of talking up there. Some of it was quite incriminating.'

As the white Ford camper-van engine sputtered, forcing a black cloud of smoke from the exhaust, Nick discreetly glanced again at the window. 'She's still bloody staring at us.'

'Let's go and do what we planned,' said Pat. 'If we feel there's more to do here, we'll come back.'

Nick sniggered. 'And then what? Knock on the door and strangle her?'

'We wouldn't need to knock.' Pat opened her hand. 'I still have our key.'

Fifteen minutes later they were tucked in behind a deep-blue Ford Transit on Ellen Lane. Their view of the third house on the left was unrestricted.

'Get some sleep,' Nick said. 'This could be a long night.'

Arlo's iPhone buzzed and vibrated in the pocket of his white coat as he left Consultation Room 3. When Lorraine's name appeared on the screen, he immediately pressed the red button. A second call followed and once again he rejected it. Finally, a text arrived: *Call me – Spider wants to talk to you.*

She'd got his attention. Arlo ran to the rear of the building, pushed open a fire door and stood between a dumpster and a brick wall. He tapped Lorraine's name in the recents list.

'Good evening, doctor.'

Arlo didn't reply.

'It's funny how quickly things can change, isn't it? Suddenly the shoe is on the other foot, as some would say.'

'What do you want?' the doctor snapped.

'I want you, of course. It's all I've ever wanted since we first spoke in Mosul. You remember Mosul, don't you?'

Arlo gritted his teeth. 'Let her go and I'll do whatever you want.'

'That's not how it works, I'm afraid. I'm sending you

directions. If you're not here within the hour, she dies. If you call the police, she dies. If you bring the Foleys – guess what?' Spider laughed. 'I've got my money on you running away, like you ran away from Jennifer.'

'I didn't run away! I…'

Spider interrupted. 'The clock is ticking.'

A text arrived as the call ended. After studying the route, Arlo phoned the head nurse in A&E and told her he was ill and on his way home.

He checked the time. The short walk to the staff car park seemed to last forever. With legs like jelly, heart beating double time and a stream of sweat dripping from his forehead, he eventually made it to his car. Once inside, he slouched forward and rested his head on the steering wheel, his mind tossing him in all directions.

He was bothered by Spider's comment implying he was a coward, even though he knew it wasn't true. Lorraine would have heard it, too. What would she think? He counted his regrets and there were many: taking Jen to Mosul; teasing Spider to come after him; not killing the bastard when he'd had the chance and involving Lorraine in this fiasco.

He checked the time again. He had to do something. He had to do the right thing.

With ten minutes remaining on the clock, Arlo stopped at the end of the track leading to where Spider was hanging out. He thought about how many people might be waiting for him inside; in his condition, Spider couldn't have kidnapped Lorraine by himself, nor could he have made it across the rough terrain, so there had to be at least one other person helping him. And what about weapons?

Finally he told himself to stop thinking; no matter how much he analysed the situation, the outcome would still be the same. He was going to die. He muttered a quick prayer followed by a final apology to Jen; it was just one of many he'd made since her passing.

Less than a minute later he was outside the barn. Seeing Lorraine's car suddenly made it very real. He swallowed hard, took a couple of deep breaths and tried his best to stop shaking.

As he slid open the barn door, he was welcomed by a loud, derisive cheer. Arlo ignored Spider's attempt to mock him and walked into the cold damp space. He could see Lorraine, kneeling with her hands tied behind her back. She turned as he got closer, her eyes red, her cheeks tear stained. He mouthed, 'I'm sorry.'

The scene brought back horrific memories of his time looking down on the square from the roof in Mosul. It was all too clear: the roar of the chainsaw, the screams of the victims and the lack of emotion from the ISIS killer sitting a few feet away.

'Kneel next to Lorraine and put your hands behind your back,' Spider commanded.

Arlo obeyed. His hands were immediately locked together with a zip tie.

'Meet Qasim, my lovely assistant from Pakistan.' Spider gestured for Qasim to remove Arlo's phone from his pocket. 'When I'm finished, he'll be placing your heads on the spikes beside you. Normally I like to do that myself – it's a nice finishing touch – but with my leg pointing in the wrong direction, I can't stand at the moment.'

Arlo tried desperately to turn things around. 'I'm here. No cops, no Foleys, just as you asked. Now let her go. Please.'

Spider laughed and shook his head. 'Loose ends tell tales.'

Once Arlo's hands were tied, Qasim scurried off into the shadows looking like someone who would rather be somewhere else.

'Let's take a look at the photos you have of me, shall we?' Spider lifted the phone then stared at Arlo and waited.

It took a moment before the doctor realised what he wanted. '2014,' he said.

'How sweet – the year your girlfriend died.'

Scrolling through the photographs, Spider stopped when he came to those taken in Iraq. 'These aren't very good. Poor lighting and I'm covered in hair! My sister Emma is also unrecognisable. Why did you tell me I could be recognised?'

'I was angry. It was stupid. I wanted to get you here so I could kill you.'

'And you had me in the palm of your hand and let me live.'

'I'm not a killer.'

'But you did kill one of my soldiers in a water tank on the roof, didn't you?'

A look of disbelief appeared on Lorraine's face.

'It was either kill or be killed!' Arlo cried defensively.

Spider ignored him. 'So you can take a life like the rest of us when the time comes,' he mocked.

Arlo kept his mouth shut and his eyes on the ground in front of him.

'Look at Qasim over there,' Spider went on. 'Doesn't look like much, but he's a killing machine. Needs must, as they say.' He laughed much longer and louder than necessary.

'Let's get on with it,' he said as if he were about to go into some boring corporate meeting. 'Start the chainsaw, Qasim.'

The boy looked surprised and it was easy to see why. When he picked up the saw, it was obvious he was holding one for the first time because his hands were in all the wrong places. He made a feeble attempt to pull the cord but nothing happened.

'You're useless!' Spider threw Arlo's phone on the ground. 'Give it to me.'

With the chainsaw on his lap, he pressed eight times on the fuel primer, elevated the choke and pushed the chain brake forward. After wrapping his hand around the starter handle, he pulled gently on the cord and the engine fired immediately. He squeezed the trigger with his forefinger and smiled as the roar of the chainsaw echoed off the stone surroundings.

'Music to my ears,' he shouted, holding the machine aloft. 'Push me over there.' He pointed to Lorraine. 'Ladies first.'

Lorraine screamed, 'No! Please don't.'

'Leave her alone,' Arlo cried. 'She hasn't done anything.'

Qasim stood behind the wheelchair and moved it slowly to where Lorraine was kneeling with her head bowed. Holding the front handle of the saw with his left hand, Spider reached forward with his right and pulled the chain brake towards his body. With the brake off, the chain rotated – and suddenly the engine exploded.

A massive spark was followed by a loud bang, and dust, tiny stones and clusters of straw rose like a cloud around the wheelchair. Fingers from both of Spider's hands flew into the air before a full tank of petrol mixed with two-stroke oil saturated his clothing and flames engulfed his body.

The force of the blast blew Qasim to the ground. Arlo and

Lorraine scrambled across the floor on their knees to escape the inferno.

'Do something,' Spider screamed, desperately trying to beat down the flames. 'Help me! Get some water!'

But Qasim just remained on the ground watching. Slowly he started to smile as the fire travelled up Spider's trousers to his shirt. Within seconds Spider's hair was alight, discharging a strong sulphurous odour, while the skin on his face melted. Black smoke billowed from the burning vinyl upholstery that cradled him.

His pitiful cries became muffled groans, and then there was silence.

Arlo was no stranger to death, but this was different. A man had burned alive just a few feet away and he'd done nothing; he'd not even wanted to help. The doctor in him had turned his back, shut down; even if his hands had not been bound, his passion to preserve life had deserted him and he didn't feel the slightest bit ashamed. Instead he felt relief. He was glad it was over, glad Spider was dead.

Curled up in a ball, Lorraine slowly unfolded her left leg and tapped her foot against Arlo's. She was okay; splattered in Spider's blood but alive and smiling. Arlo returned her smile.

His face tightened and his heart sank when he heard footsteps heading in their direction. Qasim was coming towards him holding the Zombie knife, its jagged blade reflecting the glow of the fire burning nearby.

As he moved into position behind Arlo's back, the doctor tried to reason with him, pleading for their lives, but there was no response. Expecting the worst, he hunched his shoulders and closed his eyes but there was no blow and no pain, just the feeling of his zip tie being removed from around his wrists.

'You can cut her free when I'm gone.' Qasim tossed the knife across the room. 'I'm taking your car,' he said to Lorraine. 'I'll leave it at McDonald's.'

'The red light's on. It's almost out of petrol.' Lorraine sounded almost apologetic.

Arlo stayed on his knees until he heard the car engine start. Only then did he stand up and walk around the unrecognisable, charred body in the chair in the middle of the floor.

With the sleeve of his white coat pulled down over his hand to act as a glove, he picked up the knife and cut Lorraine free. An awkward moment followed as they stood apart staring at each other, not knowing what to say.

Finally Lorraine reached out and took his hand. 'So, you killed an ISIS fighter.' She smiled. 'I'm impressed.'

Arlo sidestepped her comment. 'Come on, let's get out of here.' With his phone back in his pocket, he checked the area to see if they'd left anything behind then walked towards the door.

'What about him?' Lorraine looked back at Spider, who was still smouldering.

'Leave him be. He's getting a taste of what it'll be like to spend eternity burning in hell.'

It was almost 1am. Steve and Eddie were completing their check of the doors and windows on the golf-course pro-shop and restaurant when Steve's phone lit up. 'Arlo,' he said.

'Hi. Hope I didn't wake you.'

Steve laughed. 'What's up?'

'Spider's dead.'

The ex-marine smiled and quickly put his phone on speaker. 'What happened?'

The next few minutes were filled with details of the kidnapping, the threat to Lorraine's life and the chaotic scene that had taken place when the chainsaw exploded. 'What are the chances of that machine bursting into flames at that exact moment?' Arlo asked.

'You were very lucky. Sounds like a miracle to me,' Steve remarked. Eddie turned away and sniggered.

'Spider said he'd kill Lorraine if I contacted you or the police, but it looks like I didn't need any help after all.'

'What about Qasim?' Steve asked.

'He's gone. Look, I know he kidnapped Lorraine but he didn't hurt her. And I don't think he wanted to be in that barn with Spider. He could have saved him but instead he watched him burn. He could have killed us but he let us go. Seemed like a fairly decent kid, if you ask me.'

Steve silently counted to ten before replying. 'Do you remember that employee of mine, the one who almost had his head chopped off in your hospital car park?'

'Of course I do!'

'That "fairly decent kid" did that.'

There was silence before Arlo mumbled something inaudible. Eventually he said, 'Sorry.'

'Anything else?' snapped Steve. 'I've got work to do.'

'I think there's a third person, most likely the one who removed Spider from the hospital. It could be Spider's sister, Emma. She's the one in the photo I sent you.'

The call ended. Steve swiped his finger over his screen until he came to Arlo's photo of Spider taken in Mosul. There was a female in the background but it was impossible to see her face clearly.

It was time to move to the next job.

Two minutes down the road, not far from the hospital, they pulled into a derelict old people's home. Eddie jumped out and unlocked the gate as Steve parked on the weed-infested gravel drive in front of the building.

Squatters, illegals and druggies were known to use this place as a base and often resorted to violence if they were told to move on, so he and his son were ready. Eddie was holding the flashlight with the beam that could literally knock you off your feet, while Steve removed his truncheon from the loop beneath his belt. Both men were wearing stab vests.

As they drew closer to the building, Steve was distracted by coughing and giggling coming from the large reception room off to the right. A nod of his head sent Eddie outside and around the building to the back door.

Steve squeezed through the partially open door and crept along the hall until he encountered a familiar sight. Two teenagers were flat out on the floor smoking what looked like a joint. 'What the hell are you kids doing here?' he barked from the reception entrance. 'It's almost 3am.'

Shocked, the boys dumped the smoke, scrambled to their feet and turned as if to head to the back door. Eddie's huge frame was standing in the way.

Steve moved in closer and recognised the taller of the two boys. 'Hey, I know you. You're John, Frank Dillon's son.' The kid nodded. 'Let me guess – he's working nights.' No response. 'Guys, this isn't a good place to hang out. Why do you think we're wearing stab vests? Come on, we'll take you home.'

'Thanks,' John mumbled sarcastically.

The boys sat in the back of the van. Neither of them spoke for a long time until John's friend asked, 'Have you ever been stabbed?' Both Steve and Eddie shook their heads. 'We almost were,' the boy continued.

'Really? When was that?' Eddie sounded almost playful.

'Some Paki pulled a zombie knife on us.'

Steve glared into the rear-view mirror. 'When?'

'The other day. We were in the underpass near the hospital. He said he was going to chop us up but we ran away.'

'What did he look like?'

The boy shrugged his shoulders before adding, 'Skinny, short hair.'

'Age?'

'Nineteen? Twenty? Why? Do you know him?'

Steve shook his head then whispered to Eddie, 'Once we drop these kids off, we're going to Ellen Lane.'

Eddie's smile filled his face.

Qasim never made it home: he ran out of petrol and the red Corolla finally came to rest at a bus stop about a mile away. He'd planned to drive to the house on Ellen Lane, get his passport, take what he could from Spider's belongings and grab a few hours' sleep before leaving the car at McDonalds and making the thirty-minute morning walk to the bus station. From there he'd go to the airport. He'd chosen McDonalds because it was next to Mill Pond, the place where he intended to ditch the gun.

Unfortunately, things had just become more complicated.

A young Pakistani male walking the streets at this hour of the night would be reason enough for the police to employ their stop-and-search powers. He could live with inconvenience and racist jibes, but an illegal caught with a handgun was a different story.

He needed to move away from the bus stop, Lorraine's car and the street lined with terraced houses. Ahead on the left was a play park; it was his only option.

He knew he had to move swiftly but running might look suspicious if he was spotted, so he raced to the park doing an awkward fast walk, both arms pumping and his hips rocking side-to-side. He ducked behind a disused wooden gatehouse and his eyes lit up when he spotted a pair of bottle banks nearby.

'Thank you,' he whispered to no one as he withdrew the gun from inside his belt, wiped it with his T-shirt and pushed it through the circular opening. Metal crashing against glass made him smile.

When he removed his vibrating phone from his pocket, the smile disappeared. No Caller ID highlighted the screen.

The distorted voice came next. 'I've been to the barn?'

'The chainsaw exploded,' Qasim blurted out.

'I could see that. Why didn't you help?'

'I tried but it all happened so fast! I was thrown to the ground, knocked out.' Qasim waited; he could tell the caller was assessing their response.

'Did Spider suffer?'

He grinned, nodded enthusiastically and pretended to pat down flames on his chest before saying in a sombre tone, 'No, I'm sure the explosion killed him instantly.'

'And what happened to Arlo and Lorraine?'

'They got away during the confusion.'

A long period of silence left him feeling nervous. Finally the voice asked, 'Why do think the chainsaw blew up?'

Qasim shrugged his shoulders before answering. 'Don't know – faulty maybe.'

'Do you still have the gun, Qasim?'

'Yes.' He stared at the hole that had just swallowed the weapon.

'Then go to the Foleys tonight and kill Steve Foley.'

This time the pause came from Qasim. 'Sure, I'll go there now.'

'Qasim.'

'Yes?' he replied.

'Spider may be gone but I'm still here.'

As soon as the call ended, Qasim stuck his arm through the hole at the top of the bottle bank but it was pointless and he knew it. He also knew that he had time on his hands. With or without a gun, he wasn't going anywhere near the Foleys' house and it would be several hours before 'The Voice' discovered he hadn't been there.

He checked out the various routes to Ellen Lane on Google maps and took the most direct one.

＊ ＊ ＊

With his left-hand blindly diving deep into a large bag of salt-and-vinegar crisps, Nick glanced at the digital clock illuminated on the dashboard. It was almost 3am. Pat was asleep on the bed in the back of the camper van. He desperately wanted to join her but instead he let her be and kept his eye on the street.

There had been no movement since they'd arrived, and he was beginning to wonder if this stake-out had been a good idea. His right hand raised a can of Coke to his lips and then he gave a silent burp. A moment later he left the van to relieve himself next to a nearby oak tree.

While tucked under a low-hanging branch, he sensed movement close by. On the opposite side of the lane a shadowy figure was crouching by the boot of a Mini.

Nick froze before carefully resting his arm on the branch. *That's got to be him.* A second thought immediately popped into his head as he shifted his gaze to the side window of the camper van. *If Pat stirs, he'll run.*

There was nothing he could do but wait. Five, ten, fifteen minutes passed. He needed to sit down; the branch was a useful crutch, but his knees were burning and sweat was pouring down his face.

Finally, there was movement from the rear of the Mini, and when the slim figure stepped onto the lane beneath one of the few street lamps that was working, his facial features became clear. It was the teenager he and Pat had chauffeured across Europe and into England.

Nick kept watching as the boy approached the third house on the left, peered through the living-room window, stood with one ear pressed against the door then disappeared inside.

When the door closed he lowered himself to the ground, not caring that he was now sitting where he'd just urinated. When the fire in his knees cooled, he returned to the van.

His wife was sitting up, drinking water from a bottle. 'Anything happened?' she asked as she came way through the sliding door to the passenger seat.

'He's just arrived.'

'Is he alone?'

Nick nodded.

'What now?' Pat asked.

'We wait until he leaves, then we kill him.'

With the lights out, Qasim climbed the stairs to his room, collected his passport from under his mattress, threw a few pieces of clothing into a backpack and went down the hall to where Spider had slept.

The light from the quarter moon breaking through a gap in the curtains was all he needed to conduct a thorough search. Not sure what he was looking for, Qasim ran his hands through every pocket and every shoe he could find until he eventually came upon a UK driver's licence in the name of Nigel Brathwaite-Smythe. He sniggered. 'No wonder he called himself Spider.'

Finding nothing more of interest, he descended the stairs until he reached the second step from the bottom. He sat down, pulled out his phone and dialled. 'Dad, it's me,' he said softly.

'Qasim, darling, it's so good to hear from you. Where are you? Are you coming home?'

In the background he heard his mother shouting his name. 'Yes, I'm coming home. Can you arrange a flight from Heathrow for me today? I'm going there now.'

'Of course, I'll do it right away and call you back with the details.' His father paused for a moment. 'You're going now? Isn't it the middle of the night there?'

'Dad.'

'Yes, son.'

'I've done some bad things. I'm sorry.'

'Qasim, I know you and you are not a bad person. Whatever it is, I'm sure there is a reasonable explanation. Let's wait until you are home and we can talk about it then, if you want.'

With the phone back in his pocket, Qasim slung his backpack over his shoulder and left the house.

'He's on the move,' muttered Nick like a cop in a stake-out movie.

As the engine started, Pat reached across and turned the key. 'Move over,' she said sternly. From the look in her eyes he knew that she meant business so he offered no resistance.

As she slid across to the driver's seat, he hurried around the van to the passenger door. The engine turned over again and Pat drove slowly along the lane. The road was lined with parked cars so the camper van remained well behind and out of sight, and she kept the headlights off.

That soon changed when they rounded the corner where the council's double-yellow lines provided an opportunity. There wasn't a parked car in sight. Pat watched as Qasim pulled out his phone and pressed it against to his ear.

She looked at Nick. When he nodded, she increased her speed. At thirty miles an hour she jumped the curb, drove along the pavement and continued to drive faster.

Qasim seemed oblivious as to what was happening.

By the time she hit forty-five, she was a car length away. Her eyes never deviated from the boy and her hands gripped the steering wheel so tightly that her knuckles turned white.

The rattling from the ageing Ford engine acted as an alarm and Qasim turned his head, the phone still snug against his ear. His eyes bulged as he saw the oncoming vehicle but it was too late to react or even scream. Pat smashed into him as she continued to accelerate.

His face kissed the windscreen with an almighty thud before his body was swept under the van. After being dragged along the pavement for what seemed an eternity, his body separated from the underside of the vehicle and rolled onto the street.

Pat stopped, lowered her head and took several breaths. Nick ran his hand gently over her shoulder and said, 'It's done, let's go home.'

Taking another breath, Pat moved the gear stick and revved the engine. Then, without the slightest indication of what she was about to do, she reversed over the body. The camper van flew into the air like they had just hit a massive speed bump and Nick's head brushed the roof fabric. 'What the…?' he cried.

Pat wasn't finished. The engine roared again. She changed gears and released the clutch, thrusting the van once more over the lifeless body. This time there was no speed bump, no stopping and no looking back

'*Now* it's done,' she said. 'We can go home.'

Arlo declined an invitation to 'come in for coffee' when he dropped Lorraine off at her house. He wasn't quite sure what her offer involved but sex and/or caffeine were the last things he wanted. Feeling traumatised, exhausted and nauseous from the cocktail of foul odours carpeting his skin, the only things that mattered were a hot shower and a good night's sleep.

It had been a long and harrowing day. Now it was nice to be home, although that had not always been true. When Spider had been a threat, home had not been a safe place. But that was then, this was now, and home was what it was: warm and welcoming.

Arlo's first stop was the bathroom where he stripped off, turned on the shower and stayed until the hot water began to cool. Once in bed, he placed the scalpel that had been with him since Mosul on the bedside table and propped up his pillow to chat with Jen.

Almost without exception, the recurring one-way conversation started with 'I miss you' and ended with 'I'm sorry'. But things had changed: Spider was dead and it was time to move on. Arlo needed to say more. For several years his friends had been telling him to get a life and he'd done nothing about it. Now it was time.

He struggled to get the words out but he finally said goodbye. Feeling guilty and disloyal, his eyes filled with tears as he turned out the light.

Later that evening, the sound of a creaking floorboard woke him from a deep sleep. He turned his head towards the illuminated digital clock on his bedside table. The screen was black. Instinctively he reached for the lamp switch but nothing happened when he pressed the switch.

His initial thought was that a fuse had blown and it was just a bloody inconvenience until he heard a noise outside his bedroom door. As fear took hold of him, he silently cursed himself for leaving his phone in the pocket of his trousers, which were still in a heap on the bathroom floor.

Lacking ideas, he scanned the room then suddenly

remembered the cricket bat and hammer under the bed. Dropping to his knees, he searched frantically in the dark for the weapons. Nothing.

There was another sound and the door opened. Arlo jumped to his feet and raised both arms as someone wearing a balaclava and carrying what appeared to be a knife raced towards him. He swung his fists wildly, striking the side of the intruder's head; at the same time a burning sensation exploded in his left shoulder. He'd been stabbed.

The force of the blow knocked him onto the bed and the attacker came at him again. Sprawled on his back, Arlo kicked out into the pit of the stomach hovering above him. A loud groan indicated he'd made a direct hit.

Despite the pain in his shoulder, Arlo reached his right hand across his body and, after a couple of misses, grabbed the scalpel from the bedside table. As the intruder made a third attempt to end his life, Arlo slashed the tiny blade from left to right across the attacker's throat.

The full weight of the lifeless body collapsed on top of him and blood from the neck wound gushed freely over his chest. With the scalpel still in hand, Arlo waited for signs of life but there were none. Using his right arm, he pushed the body onto the floor then scrambled off the bed and ran into the bathroom Within seconds he'd retrieved his phone from his trouser pocket and returned.

He removed the balaclava and shone the light on the blood-stained figure lying next to his bed. 'Bloody hell?' he shouted.

He pressed his fingers hard against the laceration on his shoulder and went back to the bathroom to clean his wound and apply a dressing. Once the bleeding was under control, he hurried downstairs and flipped the switch on the fuse box.

With the power restored, he went back upstairs, turned on the bedroom light and rummaged through the victim's pockets. Finally, he called Steve.

'Arlo. Twice in one night.'

'Sorry, Steve. I didn't know who else to call.'

'What's up?'

'I just killed Spider's sister, Emma.'

'*What?*'

'I'm sending you a photo. She broke into my house and tried to kill me. What should I do?' Arlo heard the ping when the photo arrived on Steve's phone.

There was a moment's silence before Eddie screamed in the background, 'Son of a bitch!'

'What?' Arlo shouted. 'What's going on?'

'That's not Emma, it's Carol! I met her on a dating app,' Eddie protested.

'No, it's Emma – I've seen her ID.'

There was another lengthy pause before Eddie spoke again, his voice more restrained. 'Bloody hell. I had coffee with a terrorist and we were about to have our first night out. How lucky am I that she cancelled?'

'Sounds like you dodged a bullet,' Arlo said. Once again he asked Steve what he should do.

'Sorry, I can't get involved,' Steve replied. 'It's a long story. Call the police and tell them what happened. It was self-defence. You'll be fine.'

Shortly after the conversation with Arlo ended, Steve's phone rang again: 'Bloody hell, just what I don't need,' he muttered, before swiping to answer. 'Yes,' he snapped.

'Good evening, Mr Foley.'

Silence.

'I was wondering if you could help me?' Malik said quietly.

Still no response.

'I was talking to Qasim while he was on his way to the airport and suddenly, he wasn't there. I heard a car engine and a lot of noise, and then nothing. I think something terrible has happened to him.'

'Why was he going to the airport in the middle of the night?'

'He was running away from someone. I guess he thought if he got to the airport, he'd be safe. Do you know what has happened?'

Steve's reply intentionally lacked sympathy or tact. 'Yes, I do,' he said abruptly. 'Qasim is dead.'

'*What?*' Malik cried.

'He was run over several times.'

'Are you sure? How do you know?'

'I was on my way to Qasim's place but the road was blocked by an accident. A paramedic at the scene told me what had happened and Qasim's name was mentioned.'

'Why were you going to my son's house?'

Steve thought about keeping his mouth shut then blurted, 'I was going there to kill him.'

'Why?' questioned Malik.

'Because he killed my friend.'

Steve hit the red button then pulled the van over to the side of the road. He opened the door, got out and started pacing back and forth along the pavement. When he returned, his face was no longer red and his breathing had calmed.

A couple of minutes later, Eddie said to him, 'Dad, I think

I screwed up.'

'How's that?'

'I told Carol – or Emma or whoever the hell she was – that Terry Black had quit and Lager would be at the hospital on his own. She had my phone number.'

Steve showed no emotion.

'I also told her we were wearing stab vests. I'm so sorry.'

'Who told you Jesse was a hooker?'

'It was Carol – but what's that got to do with Lager?'

'Jesse had friends in the police force. When she was killed, that information was never released.'

Eddie placed his head in his hands. 'How come I didn't see this coming? Mum was right. Carol knew everything about me and I knew nothing about her. She played me big time.'

Sunrise was still a couple of hours away and the traffic was light. This was Steve's favourite time of day. Cool air drifted through an open window onto his face and slowly washed away the tension in his body. He tried not to think about what Eddie had just said; there was no point. What was done was done. It was time for positive thoughts. The threat was gone and life without drama could resume.

On the way home he stopped at an all-night petrol station and bought a box of chocolates for Victoria. It was a small peace offering for all the bad times he'd put her through over the past few days.

As they crept through the front door, Steve pressed his index finger to his lips. Eddie nodded: Victoria was on the edge and it wouldn't take much to push her over. Waking Victoria or the baby at this crazy hour of the morning was the last thing they wanted to do.

But it was exactly what they did do. As they climbed the

stairs in complete darkness, Eddie dropped one of the boots he'd removed at the door and there were several loud thumps as it tumbled step by step to the floor below. He and Steve froze then looked up as a shadowy figure appeared at the top of the stairs.

A series of gunshots rained down on them.

Eddie was the first to be hit; Steve clutched his throat seconds later and they both tumbled down the stairs to land in a heap near his son's boot.

At the top of the stairs, a trembling hand reached out and turned on the light. Victoria screamed, dropped the gun and raced down the stairs. 'No, no!' she cried as she bent over the lifeless bodies. She pressed hard on her husband's chest. 'Please wake up! Please!'

When Steve didn't respond she turned to Eddie, tears streaming down her face, but her efforts to revive him were also in vain.

For fifteen long minutes she sat on the stairs, her hands covered in the blood of her husband and son. Finally she stood up and walked upstairs as if she were in a trance. Her husband's words were swirling around her head as she collected the gun: '*Carrying an illegal firearm, five to ten years – maybe longer for manslaughter or murder.*'

She moved slowly into her bedroom, where Anne was crying uncontrollably. Cradling her baby with her left arm, she moved to the bed and rested her head on the pillow. Anne's sobs quietened a little, fading to hiccups and gasps as she curled against her mother.

Victoria pressed her phone keypad three times with her thumb: 999.

The operator answered immediately and asked which

314

emergency service she needed. 'Police and ambulance,' she replied calmly.

When she was asked, she gave her name and address then added, 'Please take care of my baby. Her name is Anne. Give her a good home.'

She ended the call then gently put the child back in her cot and gave her one final kiss.

Then she put the gun to her head.

www.ingramcontent.com/pod-product-compliance
Lightning Source LLC
Chambersburg PA
CBHW040216170726
48295CB00014B/696